Learn Magi...

Finally, the dark aura of mystery that surrounds magic is removed! J. H. Brennan's latest work is an accessible introduction to the basics of Western magical philosophy and the most essential exercises and rituals used by practitioners of the Western system of Magic.

The book is divided into two parts: Low Magic and High Magic. In Low Magic you will explore divination, astral and etheric bodies, the chakras, the aura, wood nymphs and leprechauns, chanting, and dowsing.

Low Magic is fun, and serves as an introduction to the more potent system of High Magic. With High Magic you will learn how to correctly prepare your mind before conducting the Great Work—linking yourself to the power and knowledge of the Universal Forces that underlie all reality.

About the Author

J. H. Brennan is an acclaimed author of fifty-two books of fiction and non-fiction, several of which have become international bestsellers. His out-of-body experience book *Astral Doorways* is a classic in its field, and his GrailQuest™ series of adventure gamebooks for young readers is a phenomenal success worldwide.

Brennan started his intellectual journey at an early age, studying psychology virtually from the time he could read, and hypnotizing a school friend at age nine! At twenty-four, he was the youngest newspaper editor in his native Ireland. By his mid-twenties, he had published his first novel.

J. H. Brennan is clearly an active man of ideas. In addition to his work as an author, he maintains a career as a consultant in financial marketing, as well as an active interest in software development, self-improvement techniques, and reincarnational research. He is a frequent lecturer and media guest throughout the United Kingdom and Ireland.

To Write to the Author

If you would like to contact the author or would like more information about this book, please write to him in care of Llewellyn Worldwide. We cannot guarantee that every letter will be answered, but all will be forwarded. Please write to:

J. H. Brennan
c/o Llewellyn Publications
P.O. Box 64383, Dept. K086–8
St. Paul, MN 55164-0383, U.S.A

Please enclose a self-addressed, stamped envelope for reply or $1.00 to cover costs. If ordering from outside the U.S.A., please enclose an international postal reply coupon.

Also by J. H. Brennan

Astral Doorways (Aquarian Press)
Experimental Magic (Aquarian Press)
Reincarnation (Aquarian Press)
Occult Reich (Futura)
The Ultimate Elsewhere (Futura)
An Occult History of the World (Futura)
Nostradamus-Visions of the Future (Harper/Collins)
Ancient Spirit (Little, Brown)
Mindreach (Aquarian Press)
Discover Reincarnation (Harper/Collins)
Discover Astral Projection (Harper/Collins)
A Guide to Megalithic Ireland (Harper/Collins)
Time Travel (Llewellyn Publications)
The Magical I Ching (Llewellyn Publications)
Occult Tibet (Llewellyn Publications)

With Eileen Campbell:
Aquarian Guide to the New Age (Harper/Collins)

With Dolores Ashcroft-Nowicki:
Magical Use of Thought Forms (Llewellyn Publications)

Magick for Beginners

Beginners

The Power to Change Your World

J. H. BRENNAN

2002
Llewellyn Publications
St. Paul, MN 55164-0383 U.S.A.

Magick for Beginners © 1998 by J. H. Brennan. All rights reserved. No part of this book may be used or reproduced in any manner whatsoever, including Internet usage, without written permission from Llewellyn Publications except in the case of brief quotations embodied in critical articles and reviews.

FIRST EDITION
Fifth printing, 2002

Cover design: Lisa Novak
Cover photo: Doug Deutscher
Editing: Rosemary Wallner
Project management: Ken Schubert

Library of Congress Cataloging-in-Publication Data
Brennan, J. H.
   Magick for beginners : the power to change your world / J.
H.   Brennan. -- 1st. ed.
      Includes bibliographical references and index.
      ISBN 1-56718-086-8 (pbk.)
1. Magic. 2. Occultism. I. Title
BF1611.B68   1998
133.4'3--dc21   97-48970
                                                       CIP

Llewellyn Worldwide does not participate in, endorse, or have any authority or responsibility concerning private business transactions between our authors and the public. All mail addressed to the author is forwarded but the publisher cannot, unless specifically instructed by the author, give out an address or phone number.

Llewellyn Publications
A Division of Llewellyn Worldwide, Ltd.
P.O. Box 64383 Dept. K086-8
St. Paul, MN 55164-0383, U.S.A.
www.llewellyn.com

Printed in the United States of America

Dedication

For Anna, Dolores, Jacks and Lyrata—
the most magical women I know.

Contents

Introduction xi

Part One: Low Magic

One: Preparing the Place of Working 3

Two: Contacting Spirits 25

Three: Why Magic Works 43

Four: Occult Anatomy 55

Five: The $100 Bill Trick 85

Six: Occult Eccentricities 103

Seven: Gold and Ghosts 121

Eight: Doorways Inward 135

Nine: Magic and Mind 147

Ten: Ground Plan of the Universe 159

Part Two: High Magic

Eleven: Alien Dimensions 173

Twelve: Preparation for Contact 187

Thirteen: Ritual Workings 211

Fourteen: Searching for Miracles 231

Fifteen: Godforms 255

Sixteen: Conjuration 265

Seventeen: Ceremonial Magic 279

Eighteen: Ritual Invisibility 291

Bibliography 309

Index 311

List of Rituals and Exercises

Banishing Ritual of the Lesser Pentagram 17

Fountain of Light Exercise 83

$100 Bill Trick 93

Depth Meditation Exercise 206

Pore Breathing Exercise 213

Talisman Charging Ritual 220

Invocation of Elemental Energies 222

Rose Cross Ritual 228

City of Bridges Exercise 239

Lady of the Lake Ritual 245

Invisibility Ritual 294

Introduction

Over the years, I've read hundreds of books on magic and the occult. I can't now remember one that didn't leave me with a sense of something missing.

Eventually, I decided the something missing was commitment. Few authors have been rash enough to stress a personal belief that magic works. Fewer still have the guts to spell out in simple language what exactly happens when it does. In this book I've tried to avoid both errors. By doing so, I think I may have learned why they occur so often.

First, claiming magic works in the Computer Age makes you feel like an idiot. It goes against everything you've been taught, everything your friends believe, everything that seems real and practical and worthwhile. So even while you claim it, you keep wondering if you've been hallucinating or taken in by coincidence.

Secondly, once you decide to spell out in simple terms what happens, you're deprived of a wonderful cloak worn by so many magicians—their aura of dark mystery.

As soon as you start to put magic into practice, it loses a lot of its glamour and drama. Much of it is hard slog and repetition, often following months or even years of interminable mental training. Results are often uncertain and appear without theatricals. This can be disappointing, but at least it's a lot less disappointing than no results at all.

In this book I've tried to keep theory to a minimum, but it's not possible to ignore it altogether. Bear with me in the speculative chapters—it's nice to know what you're doing as well as how to do it. This isn't to say that the theories presented should be taken as dogma or divine revelation. The only roads to truth I know are experience and meditation. Meditate on the theories and draw your own conclusions. Try the experiments and learn by your mistakes.

One thing you're going to discover is that suggestion and auto-suggestion play a big part in magical working. I mention this in case you're tempted to dismiss the whole thing for this reason. Before you do, try duplicating magical effects by suggestion alone. You'll find, as I have, that you can't.

Another discovery you'll make is that much magical technique is concerned with manipulating the imagination. That's bad news in an age when the term "imaginary" is often defined as unreal or even worthless. But after more than thirty years' experience in the field, I can assure you that imagination is the most underrated and least understood function of the human mind. Humor me and withhold judgment until you try it.

If you find my approach informal, there are reasons. The first is that I'm tired of the portentous style affected by so many occult authors. The second is that magic can be fun.

It'll stay fun—and safe—just so long as you remember you're working with a very powerful system.

One last thing: I've tended to use the masculine pronoun throughout this book to denote a magician. This is purely a literary convenience to avoid unwieldy constructions like "he/she" and "his or her." What it doesn't do is describe the sex of a typical magician. In my experience, the breakdown by gender of magical practitioners is roughly 50/50.

Part One

Low Magic

One

Preparing the Place of Working

Magic works. But the failure rate is high and success (sometimes) frightening. Magical systems—there are more than one—need careful study and monumental effort. You're the only one who can judge whether the effort is worthwhile, although you're likely to find rewards sometimes come from unexpected directions.

For example, it's possible to produce a hundred dollar bill by magic. It will take you at least four months training and study, plus one month of daily application. A cleaner could make the same money in less than a day just by sweeping floors.

But where the magician differs from the cleaner is in the side benefits. The magician's will power and concentration are vigorously exercised. His ability to visualize is improved. His understanding of the universe becomes a little deeper, as does his understanding of himself. And it's likely that his hundred dollar bill will give him more satisfaction than the cleaner could ever feel.

Magicians are curious people and magic a curious subject. It's large enough to cover, at one end of the spectrum, a sort of pious fakery, and at the other, an advanced knowledge of depth psychology. It is broad enough to take in table tapping, divination, hypnosis, and the Roman Catholic Mass. It is powerful enough to bring you face to face with the gods—or send you plunging into the depths of a nervous breakdown.

When a doctor writes about medicine or a psychiatrist about the human mind, it's usual to present credentials. Unfortunately, there's no equivalent of the M.D. in magic. Certain groups donate high-sounding titles, but without a standard of comparison, their worth is difficult to judge. Like an artist or a poet, a real magician draws whatever authority he may have from what he is, what he does and, to a lesser extent, how he was trained.

My own training consisted of nine years daily study, visualization and meditation, seven days a week, with time off for Christmases and birthdays. This was combined with considerably less intensive experience of ritual. The training was Qabalistically based, but included elements of Neo-Platonist Hermetica and even Oriental occult practice. When the training was over, I specialized in elemental magic, the astral plane, and hypnosis.

But all that came later. My first textbook of magic was Blavatsky's *Secret Doctrine*, six volumes I still find virtually impossible to understand. My first experiments were little better than parlor games. But I was young and it was all very new to me and it led to better things.

I plan to go into some of those "better things" later in this book. For now I'd like to concentrate on those early experiments, childish though they may seem, because they form an accessible and interesting introduction to our subject. Before I do, though, I need to teach you a few safeguards. This is relatively advanced work and in the early days I muddled through without them. But I survived on dumb luck and I'd hate you to have to do the same.

Pause here for a little theory.

Magic is largely concerned with the manipulation of subtle energies. These include the bio-electrical energies of the acupuncture meridians and the chakra energies of Hindu yoga. But they also include an energy almost wholly unrecognized outside of esoteric practice—the energy of the human imagination. Magicians use the term "astral" to describe it.

I'll be going into the whole fascinating question of astral energies and the Astral Plane in some depth later. For now, I only need to tell you that while astral means the same thing as imaginary, magicians view the imagination very differently from other people. For them, the world of the imagination is not a subjective creation but an objective universe. It can be—and is—easily influenced by the human mind, but does not spring from it. In other words, the world of the imagination is as real as the world of physical matter. When we use our imagination, we are not painting inner pictures, whatever we may think. We are using an inner sense to view and manipulate a wholly different dimension of reality.

This second reality—the Astral Plane—has its own energies, entities, and structures, all of which can interact with our more familiar physical world. Astral energies are believed by magicians to be the driving force behind our emotions. They are also the driving force behind many magical effects. Astral entities are what the rest of us call "spirits."

Against this background, let's look at the safeguards you need to learn before beginning your magical practice.

If you were a surgeon preparing for an operation, your first concern would be to make sure the operating theater was clean and sterile. Magical operations should be approached the same way. A clean, uncluttered physical environment is important to safe practice. But even more important is astral cleanliness.

When you cleanse the astral analog of your workplace, you create a sacred space in which you can control the various elements of your magical operation. But this is just the first step. Your second step is to protect that space so that it remains free from contamination and/or outside interference for as long as necessary. Taken together, these two steps are known as "preparing the place of working."

The simplest method to prepare your place of working is smudging. Smudging derives from the Native American shamanic tradition and involves little more than burning sage. The sage is bound into a cigar-like object called a smudge stick. Light the stick and carry the smoke into every corner of your room to ensure the cleansing effect.

Sage is not the only cleansing herb you can use. The sorcerous tradition of Medieval Europe burned copious quantities of asafoetida grass on the premise that the stench was so dreadful even demons couldn't stand it. In the Orient, numerous gums, resins, and other incenses have been developed for cleansing, including the Biblical frankincense and myrrh.

All these materials work in the same way, their effect based on the theory that scent and smoke somehow permeate both the physical and astral levels of reality. Although never subjected to scientific examination (so far as I know), experience shows certain incenses change the inner (astral) feel of a room.

Asafoetida is still quite difficult to come by outside of the most specialist magical providers, but incense isn't and, since urban shamanism has become a fashionable pastime in recent years, smudge sticks are widely available in New Age shops. Even the most thorough smudging only burns a small proportion of the smudge stick, so it can be reused again and again.

Smudging and incense are, if you like, a Level One preparation of the place of working. They represent a minimalist approach, the magical equivalent to a quick wash down with disinfectant. For serious magical work, something more thorough is called for.

One of the most elegant ways to prepare—and maintain—a sacred space is the use of quartz crystals. Because of their beauty, crystals have become even more popular than smudge sticks in the New Age movement. But while they are often used purely for display and ornament, crystal structures are important to serious magical practice. This is particularly true of quartz crystals for an unexpected reason.

Every physical structure, natural or artificial, has its astral counterpart—the "imagination of matter" to use a term coined by the nineteenth century French magus Eliphas Levi. But the astral image seldom looks anything like the physical. You've probably experienced this yourself in dreams. (Dreaming is a direct experience of the Astral Plane.) You meet friends who looks nothing like the way they do in waking life, yet you recognize them instantly. Their dream (astral) bodies are different from their physical counterparts. Alternatively you can find yourself in a dream London that looks nothing like the physical city. Yet here again you recognize it and can find your way around it because something in you is familiar with the astral analog.

But quartz crystals are different. They are rare, perhaps even unique, in the fact that their astral analog is identical to their physical structure. This single property explains why quartz is included in the medicine bag of every knowledgeable shaman on the planet. The crystal functions as a wonderfully reliable doorway to the Astral Plane. It is also a unique conduit and focus for astral energies.

This latter property makes quartz crystals ideal for the creation of a sacred space. Here's how you do it.

First, select your crystals. Quartz is actually a whole family of crystal that includes amethyst and rose quartz. For the preparation of sacred space, you need clear (or white) quartz. The crystal grows naturally in clusters and can be bought in this form, but is also sold as single or double terminated points. What you are looking for is six single terminated clear quartz points. The single termination means that one end of the crystal has grown to a natural point, while the other end is rough where the structure was broken away from the bedrock matrix.

They don't have to be big. A crystal about the size of your thumb is ideal. They don't have to be completely transparent either. You can spend a fortune on perfectly clear quartz, but while it looks pretty, it does the job no better than the more familiar cloudy white specimen.

It is, however, worth taking a little trouble to find crystals compatible with your own personality and temperament. My wife, the crystal therapist and author Jacquie Burgess, who's a specialist in the field, gives the following advice:

Center yourself, slow your breathing and scan the crystals until you find one that especially draws or calls to you. You will know it when you find it. Spend a few moments examining the crystal in the light. Enjoy and marvel at the beautiful facets, rainbows, galaxies, etc., in your crystal. Then close your eyes and form a link with your crystal.

There's a lot of talk about charging and even programming crystals. While both have a place in magical practice, neither is necessary for the creation of sacred space. But cleaning your crystals is *quite* necessary. Most commercial crystals have been handled by large numbers of people, hence influenced (in some cases contaminated) by their astral energies. For effective function they need to be cleaned. Once again I can do no better than quote my wife on the subject:

Crystals like the sun, fresh spring and sea water—keep them on a sunny shelf or window sill and as dust free as possible when not in use.

For general cleaning use two tablespoons sea salt to two pints spring water. Soak the crystal/s in the solution for at least one hour (up to six hours if the crystal is very tired or comes from a shop where its history is unknown). Rinse in clear spring water and pat dry with a soft white cotton cloth. Then place for at least four hours in sunlight, preferably outside. Full moonlight is also good and using both sun and moon light will balance the masculine and feminine energies.

Cleansing should be done as often as needed; at least once a fortnight, or sooner if they look dull and depleted.

There are two simple ways of using your crystals to create a sacred space. The first, using four of your six points, is to place one crystal in each corner of your place of working with their natural terminations facing inward. This gives an energy grid roughly equivalent to that shown in figure 1 where the crossed lines represent the main tracks of astral energy. The cleansing effect on your place of working is almost instantaneous and more or less permanent, although the crystals should be physically cleaned after each magical operation.

For a preparation of your place of working that involves protection as well as cleansing, use all six of your crystals as shown in figure 2.

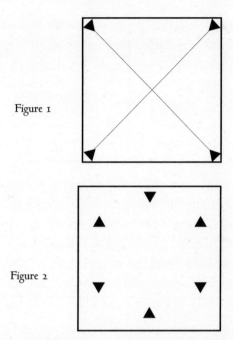

Figure 1

Figure 2

Once again, the termination points should face inward. The energy lines generated by the layout in figure 2 form a pattern that will become very familiar to you as you continue with your magical practice. This pattern is known as the *Megan David* (Shield of David) or Seal of Solomon as it is more usually called in magical practice (see figure 3 on the next page). The protected sacred space lies inside it.

Of course, you may not always have crystals handy, so you need to know how to prepare a sacred space without them. Perhaps the most powerful of all the methods—and one that teaches you a great many magical elements—is the Banishing Ritual of the Lesser Pentagram.

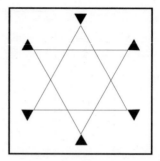

Figure 3

This ritual is a short piece of magical ceremonial popularized by the Hermetic Order of the Golden Dawn, a Victorian organization that is one of the wellsprings of modern magical practice. Like all magical ritual, it has an inner (astral) and an outer (physical) aspect. It contains a great deal of symbolism and much of this symbolism works in two ways. At one level, it has a mythic impact—an archetypal resonance, as the depth psychologists might say. At another, it has a literal astral reality and structure. As such it generates astral energies and effects.

Since I believe it's always worthwhile knowing what you're doing, I'd like to first give you some information about the various symbols in the ritual. They include the circle, the cross, the pentagram, the hexagram, the element Fire, and four telesmatic figures. Virtually all these elements have strong mythic roots, which is another way of saying they have predictable influences on the unconscious mind. Please take time to read through the information before you try out the ritual.

The **circle,** which is the most efficient definition of an enclosed space, is linked with Omphale of Lydia whose cosmic spinning wheel permitted her to weave the destinies of humanity. The root form of the word identifies with Circe, the Homeric enchantress able to transform men. The fact that (at least in the case of the Argonauts) she transformed them into swine is not as bad as it sounds. Pigs were the favored animal of the Great Goddess of ancient times, reflected in the enduring folk tradition that the pig is the only animal that can see the wind; a specific gift of the Goddess. There was also a tradition of pig sacrifice in the Hellenic period, so that the transformation might be seen as a preparation for sacrifice, making the human fit to meet the gods.

Unlike Homer, Pliny considered Circe a goddess rather than a witch and believed she commanded the stars themselves. These various mythic associations underline the concept of the circle as marking the bounds of the cosmos—or more correctly, since we are dealing with multiple realities, of a cosmos.

The religious usage of the **cross,** now thought of as exclusively Christian, actually predated Christianity in Europe and western Asia, even in its so-called Latin form. It did not actually appear in Christian art until the seventh century. The ancient usage was protective: Crosses were set up in fields to safeguard and fertilize the crops. A crucified figure was often shown on such crosses, representing the divine king whose blood gave new life to the earth.

Associations with the **pentagram** are more complex and possibly even more ancient. It was the symbol of the Goddess Kore, the innermost soul of the Earth

Mother, who was worshiped in Neolithic times and perhaps even earlier. It was known as the Star of Ishtar and later as the Star of Isis. Pythagorean mystics associated it with life and health. The protective properties of the pentagram were so profound to the ancient mind that the Babylonians often drew it on storage jars to protect their contents from decay. Pre-Christian Celts honored the pentagram as the sign of the Goddess Morgan; the hero Gawain inscribed a pentagram on his shield in her honor.

Despite these ancient feminine associations, Hermetic practice has tended toward a more masculine linkage. The naked figure of a man was placed inside a circle (representing the cosmos) with hands, feet, and head marking the points of the inscribed pentagram. In this figure, the genitals marked the exact center. As Firmicus Maternus remarked, man was shown as a microcosm ruled by the five stars. But whatever the masculine/feminine overlay, the pentagram has long had the primary association of protection, particularly from spirits.

The **hexagram,** which we've already met in connection with a crystal layout, is clearly associated with Judaism in modern minds. It appears on the flag of Israel and is known in Jewish communities as the *Magen David,* or Shield of David, often translated as the "Star of David." In magical tradition it is usually known as the Seal of Solomon. In point of fact, there seems little reason to accept a connection with either Solomon or David and even the close association with Judaism is relatively recent. The figure is not mentioned at all in Jewish literature prior to the twelfth century and was certainly not adopted as an emblem until the seventeenth century. The real roots of the symbol lie in the Far East where it is known as the Great Yantra of Tantric Hinduism. The downward pointing triangle represented the Primordial Female who existed before the universe itself began. She created within herself a seed that grew into the Manifest Masculine, represented by an upward-pointing triangle. The hexagram symbolizes the union of these two forces to form the Primal Androgyne.

Jewish Qabalism, on which much modern magical practice is based, took over the symbol in full realization of its sexual nature when Tantric practice was introduced (secretly) into Moorish Spain by returning Crusaders. There is a rabbinical tradition that the Ark of the Covenant should contain not simply the Tablets of Law, but a representation of a man and a woman in sexual embrace in the form of a hexagram.

Modern Qabalists, many of whom hold Christian or other non-Jewish beliefs, have forgotten, or tend to ignore, the sexual associations. One contemporary mystery school teaches that the symbol represents the union of evolutionary and incarnatory personalities, linking it with the basic structure of the human soul and the doctrine of reincarnation.

In its original form, however, the Qabalistic hexagram, like its Tantric counterpart, showed the union of the masculine Godhead with its essential feminine essence, the Shekina. Sexual intercourse between men and women thus became a sacramental act. At the spiritual level, the hexagram is the supreme symbol of balanced divinity.

The Banishing Ritual of the Lesser Pentagram combines these elements to produce a sacred space that's the astral equivalent of a completely sterile area: The environment is cleaned completely. It also establishes protections that are strong enough to throw out and keep out just about any troublesome entity you are likely to meet. The effect lasts until what's called the "turning of the tattva tides"—that is, until the next rising or setting of the Sun.

This is a particularly important ritual for a number of reasons. It's designed as a solitary ceremonial, so you practice it without having to find others to help you. It has a refining effect on the personality if practiced over a period of time and as such is an excellent preparation for more varied magical practice. As well as establishing a sacred space, it can be used as an exorcism. Many practitioners claim it helps reduce distractions in meditation.

You should practice the ritual once a day until you are so familiar with it that you can perform it entirely from memory and your visualizations are strong, vivid, and automatic. This usually takes between one and two weeks, although you're obviously free to take as much time as you need.

The term "vibrate" as used in the ritual needs explanation. Magicians believe that sound has a specific influence on the Astral Plane (and even the physical world, come to that). Consequently, some ritual words and phrases are sounded in a particular way: They are pronounced back in the throat to create a vibrato quality that can be felt as much as heard. This process is known as vibrating the word or phrase and is a knack that can be developed with practice. Ideally, a magician aims to combine vibration with a sort of ventriloquism, so that the vibrated phrase appears to sound in a relevant part of the room.

Here now is the full form of the ritual.

Banishing Ritual of the Lesser Pentagram

1. Walk to the eastern quarter of the room and face east.

2. Perform the Qabalistic Cross. This is a sub-ritual that you can practice separately if you like. It goes as follows:

   a. Raise your right hand to a point about three inches above your head. Visualize a glowing sphere of pure white light hovering there.

   b. Visualize drawing down a shaft of pure white light as you bring your hand down to touch your forehead.

   c. As you touch your forehead, vibrate the word *Ateh* (Ah-Teh).

   d. Bring the hand down to touch your breastbone. Imagine that the shaft of white light penetrates the center of your body and extends downward all the way to the ground.

   e. Vibrate *Malkuth* (Mal-Kuth).

   f. Touch your right shoulder. Visualize a second sphere of white light in this location.

   g. Vibrate *Ve Geburah* (Veh-Geb-Your-Ah).

h. Bring the hand across to touch your left shoulder. A third white sphere should be visualized at the left shoulder. Imagine yourself drawing a second shaft of light from the second (right hand) sphere to join with the left hand sphere.

i. Vibrate *Ve Gedulah* (Veh-Ged-You-Lah).

j. Clasp your hands together in the form of a cup at a level with your chest. Visualize a small flame, like a candle flame, between your cupped hands.

k. Vibrate *Le Olam* (Lay-Oh-Lah-Eem).

l. Vibrate *Amen.* (Ah-Men).

3. Trace a pentagram (five-pointed star). Visualize the lines appearing in blue fire, exactly like the flame produced by burning methylated spirit. This should be done in the air directly in front of you using your index and middle fingers pointing together. You should draw each pentagram in the sequence A, B, C, D, E, and back to A again, as in Figure 4. Point A should be roughly on a level with your left hip. Point B should mark the comfortable limit of an upward sweep of your extended right arm. Since the remaining points are in proportion, the figure you draw will be large.

4. Stab pentagram with your outstretched fingers.

5. Vibrate *YHVH* (Yod-Heh-Vav-Heh), imagining the sound rushing away from you into infinity.

6. Move clockwise to south with your arm still extended. Imagine that your outstretched fingers

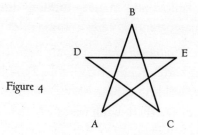

Figure 4

continue to draw a line in blue fire, forming a quarter segment of a circle as you reach south.

7. Trace second pentagram as above, stab it, and vibrate *Adonai* (Ah-Doh-Nay).

8. Move clockwise to the west. Imagine that you continue to draw the circle of fire so that it is half complete by the time you reach the west.

9. Trace third pentagram, stab it, and vibrate *Eheieh* (Eh-Heh-Yeh).

10. Move clockwise to the north, visualizing a continuation of the circle as before.

11. Trace fourth pentagram, stab it, and vibrate *AGLA* (Aye-Geh-Lah).

12. Return to the east and complete the imaginary circle as you bring your outstretched fingers to the center of the first pentagram.

13. Stretch your arms out sideways to stand facing east in the form of a cross.

14. Vibrate *Before me Raphael* (Rah-Fi-El). Visualize a tall archangelic figure in shimmering robes of shot

silk in yellow and mauve standing directly before you. Imagine cool breezes coming from this quarter.

15. Vibrate *Behind me Gabriel* (Gah-Brah-El). Visualize a second archangelic figure robed in blue offset by orange, holding a blue chalice and standing in a stream of swiftly flowing water which pours into the room behind you.

16. Vibrate *At my right hand Michael* (Me-Kah-El). Visualize a third archangelic figure robed in flame red flecked with emerald standing on scorched earth with small flickering flames at his feet and carrying a steel sword. Intense heat emanates from this quarter to your right.

17. Vibrate *At my left hand Auriel* (Or-Eye-El). Visualize a fourth archangelic figure whose robes are a mixture of olive, citrine, russet, and black. He holds sheaves of corn in outstretched hands and stands within a very fertile landscape to your left.

18. Vibrate *Around me flame the pentagrams; above me shines the six-rayed star.* Visualize the hexagram shown in figure 5. The ascending triangle (point upward) is red in color, the descending triangle is blue.

19. Repeat the Qabalistic Cross Ritual (step 2) to end the Banishing Ritual of the Lesser Pentagram.

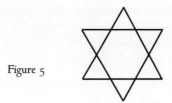

Figure 5

The main astral structures of this ritual are as follows:

Circle: Defines an area of protection and acts as a barrier against external influences.

Pentagram: Destroys or repels antagonistic entities in the astral world.

Flame: Disinfectant. Fire is the one element in which nothing can live.

Archangelic figures: Protective. These images are believed in occult theory to provide linkage with the actual entities they represent. The entities themselves, however, are thought to inhabit more subtle spiritual universes beyond that used in magical practice.

Hexagram: Conduit of divine power, via the psyche of the operator.

The spheres of light visualized in the Qabalistic Cross sub-ritual are related, but not identical, to the chakras of Oriental yoga. The words used while stabbing the pentagrams are all Hebrew God-names and hence provide emotional and psychological linkage with the supreme divinity in Judeo-Christian tradition. Magical practice further suggests the sonic attributes of the names have an energizing effect.

Putting all the bits together, the ritual works this way:

- The Qabalistic Cross draws energy into the operator's body to "fuel" the ritual.

- The visualization of the pentagrams rids the immediate area of unwanted influences.

- The circle defines the area to be protected and halts any incursion.

- The telesmatic figures of the archangels act as security officers.

- The visualization of the hexagram draws divine energy into the confines of the circle.

Thus, by means of a combined physical and astral operation, the banishing ritual cleanses the immediate environment, then defines an area of working, protects it, and finally converts it into sacred space on a temporary basis.

Experience shows the ritual is remarkably effective when applied to purely subjective ends. The refining action referred to earlier has the effect of gradually eliminating phobias and producing a foundation of increased self-confidence. Specific phobias can be tackled by first giving them an astral shape (that is, imagining a form most suited to the particular fear) then using the ritual to banish and/or destroy it. This involves a slight variation in the ritual itself. The outer form remains the same, but the inner changes.

First, imagine the form of your fear, then "project" it out of your mind into the room with you so it stands three or four feet away from you. Next, perform the ritual and imagine the form of your fear disintegrating beyond the guardian ring of flame.

As an alternative, when dealing with a particularly stubborn phobia or obsession, imagine the pentagram shape emerging from your heart during the ritual as you draw the pentagram figure at each cardinal point. The heart pentagram should strike the form of your fear and either carry it outward to infinity or shatter it into fragments that are carried outward into infinity.

The heart pentagram expands as it emerges. It should be the size of the pentagram you are drawing when it reaches that astral structure. The heart pentagram enlivens the astral pentagram on contact, then continues outward, leaving the drawn pentagram behind.

You should repeat the process (imagining the form of your fear and banishing it with the heart pentagram) at each of the cardinal points as you continue with the ritual. When the ritual is complete, the fear is not only banished, but the establishment of the complete astral structure—pentagrams, archangelic figures, circle, etc.—ensures that it can't come back.

The ritual works in direct relation to your ability to visualize your fear in the first place. If the visualization is appropriate and complete, the ritual will banish your fear completely. In practice, however, it is difficult to make a complete and wholly appropriate visualization first time around—for most of us our fears are nebulous and little understood—so it may be necessary to repeat the process on a daily or weekly basis until satisfactory results are obtained.

A further use of the ritual is that of exorcism. In this respect it is best used to exorcise places rather than people and will deal very effectively with "atmospheres" elemental intrusions and, indeed, just about anything you are likely to come across in your magical work. If exorcising buildings, you will, however, have to work on a room by room basis, repeating the ritual in each one.

While the ritual may theoretically be used to exorcise people (you place the subject supine in the middle and work around him or her), this is a tricky operation best left alone until you have considerable magical experience. One difficulty is that you need to determine clearly whether the possession is by an external force/entity or an aspect of the individual's own subjective psyche. The ritual can be used very effectively by the individual himself for removing either type of possession—the approach is identical to that for banishing phobias—but when imposed from the outside, unfortunate side-effects can sometimes occur.

When you've become really familiar with the ritual, it's interesting to experience it at a wholly astral level. While you are physically seated, eyes closed, imagine yourself standing robed in the east. Project your consciousness into this figure and try to get the feel of actually standing there. Perform the ritual; then, when finished, withdraw the projected image of yourself back into your psyche.

By the time you've practiced for a week or two, you'll start to feel (rightly) like a real magician. Now let's find out the sort of thing real magicians do.

Two

Contacting Spirits

I n the days before Belfast was set alight by petrol bombs, I traveled to an old Victorian house off University Road to court Helen, the woman who eventually had the misfortune to become my first wife, and discuss the Summerland with her landlady, Miss Johanna Kerr.

Helen found Johanna fascinating. So did I. She was very pale, very blonde, a vaguely neurotic spinster approaching forty with a feeling of unease. She was the first medium I'd ever met, a natural psychic improved by Spiritualist training who specialized in healing.

She entertained us to tea in a cold drawing room heavy with archaic furniture and—once she'd satisfied herself our interest wasn't frivolous—agreed to contact spirits with an inverted whiskey glass.

The unique appeal of this little magical operation lies in the fact that it needs neither preparation, training, nor elaborate equipment. What it does need is a glass, a polished tabletop, the letters of the alphabet, and a minimum of three people. With a few years more experience, I might have started looking for a Ouija board, which performs much the same function, but a glass was what we had so a glass was what we used.

Probably the trickiest part of the experiment is the alphabet. Index cards are ideal, but if you don't happen to have any, the simplest approach is to write the letters on squares of paper. It's a good idea to add "Yes" and "No" squares as well. The figures one to nine, plus zero, can also be helpful.

Arrange the letters in order in a circle round the tabletop. Leave as much space as possible between each one. If you're using "Yes" and "No" cards, place them in the east and west. Now invert the glass in the center of the table. Almost any glass will do as long as it moves freely over the polished surface and doesn't have a stem.

To start the séance, establish the protection of your sacred space, then have everybody sit in a circle round the table and place one finger of either hand lightly on the bottom of the glass, preferably near the edge. After that, the only other thing you need is patience.

On our first attempt all those years ago, it took twenty minutes before the glass moved. But move it did. Johanna, who was well used to these things, showed no embarrassment in asking the traditional question, "Is anybody there?" The glass shuddered slightly, then with growing speed began to circle the letters. Eventually it returned to the center and waited.

We asked our questions—most of them pretty stupid—and the glass spelled out answers. Afterward,

Johanna confessed she never felt entirely happy about glass moving. In her opinion, such physical phenomena blocked out the spiritual truths of her religion. Since that evening, I've used this crude form of Ouija—and Ouija itself—more times than I can count. Today I don't feel entirely happy about it either, although for different reasons than Johanna.

The first question is why the glass moves. The skeptic's answer is obvious—because it's pushed. Obvious or not, it's often a difficult objection to overcome. A subtle joker is almost impossible to detect, so it's as well to sit with people you trust. But even if you're sure nobody's pushing the glass, this doesn't rule out unconscious influence. At least that was the explanation that most appealed to me until I talked it over with a psychiatrist.

"How many people attend these séances?" the psychiatrist asked

"Five or six," I answered.

"Then you'd have five or six unconscious minds influencing the direction of the glass. The result would be garble. Was it garble?" he asked.

It wasn't. Unfortunately, it isn't always the most inspiring communication either. My own experience has been that the glass reacts to the mood of the gathering. I've watched glass moving played as a party game—under the curious name of "hookie"—and it produced lighthearted party answers. A more sober experiment, conducted by a group that may have read too much Stephen King, contacted an entity claiming to be Satan, with vaguely comic opera results.

Between extremes described above are a hundred and one variations. And among the variations are a few surprises. Regular sitters will find that as their series of experiments progresses, there's much less variation in the type of contact made. A single entity will come through again and again until, as often happens, a very clear personality picture of the spirit is built up.

But is the spirit really a spirit?

A few years ago, a group of investigators from the Toronto Society for Psychical Research, under the leadership of Dr. George and Mrs. Iris Owen, decided to attempt an experiment. They set out to make a ghost.

First they created a fictional character, then invented a background and life to go with him. The group's character, Philip, would have done justice to a historical romance. He lived at the time of Cromwell, in a house called Diddington Manor, fell in love with a beautiful Gypsy woman named Margo and subsequently had an affair with her. His wife, Dorothea, found out about the relationship and took her revenge by accusing Margo of witchcraft. Margo was tried, convicted, and burned at the stake. Philip, mad with grief, committed suicide by throwing himself off the battlements of his home.

All of this was fiction, except for one thing. There actually was a Diddington Manor, pictures of which were obtained by the group. But no one named Philip had ever lived there; nor did Margo or the jealous Dorothea ever exist.

Having dreamed up this story, the group then tried to bring Philip to life (so to speak) by means of a series of séances. Photographs of the manor were placed around the séance room and the group met regularly to concentrate on the fictional Philip.

For several months nothing happened. It seemed as if the experiment was a failure. Then the group decided on a different approach. Intensive concentration was abandoned in favor of a much more informal atmosphere. The group chatted about Philip and their experiment. At one point they even sang a few songs.

Surprisingly, this approach proved productive. At one séance, a rap was heard. The group set up a code and communication was established. Sure enough, the "spirit" was Philip, claiming the life history they had invented for him.

This was an extraordinary development, given the circumstances of the experiment. As the séances continued, the fictional Philip continued to behave exactly as séance room spirits have always behaved. He caused raps and brought through such a richly detailed description of the Cromwellian period that the experimenters actually double checked to make sure they hadn't somehow based Philip on a real life character. But they hadn't. He was fiction through and through.

The Toronto experiment has been successfully duplicated by other groups. One of them dispelled any lingering doubts about the fictional nature of the spirit by communicating with a talking dolphin named Silk. I was personally involved in the evocation of a fictional character by means of a magical ritual. The entity, a wholly fabricated "early British priestess" named

Coventina, temporarily possessed one of the participants and answered questions.

The original Philip went even further. There is a videotape of his bouncing a heavy table up a flight of steps and onto a platform during a public appearance.

Poltergeist activity is by no means confined to Philip. I began to take glass moving really seriously the first time I watched a glass slide toward three sitters while there were no fingers on the other side to push it. I've seen the glass tilt, fly off the table, even shatter in circumstances that rule out a natural explanation.

It's best to admit most communications that come through the glass are rubbish, even where the experiments are undertaken seriously. And yet there are exceptions that are well worth searching out. Two drawn from personal experience may be of interest.

☆☆☆☆

We were sitting around Johanna's heavy polished table determined to discover if our glass-moving spirit could forecast the future. Paul, who suggested the experiment, was careful to sit distant from us in another corner of the room. He wanted to make sure he didn't influence the glass. He proposed only to ask questions and take notes.

"Will I change my job?" asked Paul.

"Yes," spelled out the glass.

"What will I do?"

"Study."

"What will I study?"

"Art."

"Where will I study art?"

"London."

Every answer in this short sequence proved to be inaccurate. Paul failed to change his job and never became an art student in London or anywhere else. Yet the experiment wasn't a complete failure. Paul had concealed some facts from us. In recent months he'd become dissatisfied with his job and had decided to make a change. He thought he had the makings of a professional painter and decided to study art. For personal reasons he wanted to avoid the Belfast College of Art and applied for a scholarship that would take him to London.

I suppose when someone asks if he's about to change his job, it's fairly obvious he must be considering a switch. But if the rest was coincidence, it's a long one. Apart from me, none of the sitters knew Paul before the sitting—and he carefully kept his plans from me.

Telepathy seems a much more likely explanation, even though no one round the table had displayed much telepathic talent before. There is support for the theory in Helen's report that she used the glass very successfully for telepathic experiments between her brother and herself.

This is an area worth investigating. Experiments are very easy to set up. You need a sender with a short, simple message to transmit (which should be written down in a sealed envelope and given to a third party for safekeeping). You need a receiver—a small group if you're using the glass, or a single individual if you have a Ouija board. Arrange for the sender to concentrate on the message at the same time you're conducting your séance. If the message comes through, you've got a telepathic link on your hands.

There are even more interesting variations on this basic theme. You might, for example, ask the sender to concentrate not on a message but a particular personality and see if the personality manifests.

☆☆☆☆

Occasionally the glass will bring gratuitous information. In the middle of an evening's séance, it suddenly spelled out, "Contact Sheila."

"Who is the message for?" I asked.

"You."

"Why should I contact Sheila?"

"She needs help."

"Why does she need help?"

"Ill."

I hadn't seen Sheila for months, but at least I had no qualms about getting in touch with her. She was a psychic and a witch who believed people should act on occult communications. I phoned her home. There was no reply.

After three days of frequent phone calls there was still no reply and I was growing very uneasy. Although Sheila's husband didn't altogether share her views on esoteric matters, I decided to risk phoning him at work. He wasn't there. His secretary told me he and Sheila had gone off on vacation.

This eased my mind. Nobody goes off on vacation if they're ill. I assumed the message from the glass had been just plain wrong and forgot all about it.

Weeks later I met Sheila in the street and told her the story. She then told me she'd gone on vacation to prepare herself for a surgical operation. At the time of our séance, she had indeed been ill.

Stories like these are even odder than they sound. There's obviously something peculiar going on, but nothing is quite what it seems. The glass fed back to Paul what he was thinking, but in the form of a prediction that didn't come true. My urgent message to contact Sheila sounded almost like a call from her Guardian Angel. But it would have made no difference if I'd managed to reach her right away. What Sheila needed—and got—was a competent surgeon.

Over the years I've seen many other examples of this sort of strangeness. The glass told one sitter he'd been a sailor in a previous incarnation. Perhaps he had. Or perhaps the glass was picking up a periodic emotional obsession about running away to sea—something only he knew at the time of the séance.

On another occasion, we had a sitter who asked for a reply in Spanish and got it without garble, despite the fact that no one who was touching the glass spoke the language. Then, just as our belief in spirit entities was strengthening, somebody suggested blindfolding the sitters. We agreed—and the result was garble.

It may be disconcerting to find so much space devoted to a parlor game in a book on magic. But there are reasons.

First, almost anybody can play this game. Once you do, you'll soon discover you get out no more than you put in. Try it in a frivolous frame of mind and you'll get an evening's entertainment. Take it seriously and you'll get serious (though not necessarily accurate) answers. Keep at it and something strange will more than likely happen.

But to reach the strangeness takes time, as if glass moving generates strangeness as slowly as an oyster generates a pearl. If you can persevere, this little operation may become worthwhile, if only for its lesson in patience. Every magical operation needs patience. Big ones require most patience of all. Preparations can go on for days, months, or even years. Even then, the final result may be failure. Magicians require the resilience to accept this and try again.

And glass moving teaches another important lesson: discrimination. Because when you move into the world of magic, not everything is as it seems.

☆☆☆☆

At about the time I was starting to experiment with the moving glass, a British psychologist named Kenneth Batcheldor was leafing through the early records of the Society for Psychical Research when a curious thought struck him.

Back in Victorian times, a fad for Spiritualism swept Europe like a raging fever. Physical phenomena were commonplace—and none more commonplace than table turning. Yet despite its spectacular nature and obvious importance to psychical research, almost no work had been done on it for more than half a century. Batcheldor decided to step into the breach.

The result was spelled out in an article in the September 1966 issue of *Journal of the Society for Psychical Research*, which opened with these words: "As the writer has had the good fortune to witness and experiment on total levitation of tables and allied phenomena, he offers here an account of his experiences."

His experiences were a lot more spectacular than the dry opening would lead you to suppose. By the time his report appeared, he had run more than 200 table-turning séances. 120 of them produced no worthwhile results, but then Batcheldor got the hang of it. After that, in no less than eighty sittings, the table moved.

Not only that, it moved before the eye of a video camera under the most stringent test conditions. It moved strongly, violently, sometimes with people touching it, sometimes on its own. It produced raps and pistol-like reports. It floated in the air and hung there with no one near it.

But perhaps even more important was the fact that Batcheldor discovered how almost anybody could duplicate results like this to order. I once put his ideas into practice with a group of thirty people and five hefty tables. Three of the tables refused to move. The remaining two moved so violently that one of them pinned me against a wall.

How did this happen?

In a table-turning session, a group of five or six people sits around a table with their hands resting lightly on the surface and waits. If they get lucky, the table will eventually start to move. The first movement is usually a slight tilt, but later the table may dance about the floor like a mad thing. In a few cases it will levitate. In a very few cases it will levitate without anybody touching it.

The whole thing is so simple, yet so sensational, that you can see why it was popular with the Victorians. The only real problem with it is that very often it just doesn't work. You can sit for hours without so much as a twitch from the table. Unless, that is, you use Batcheldor's approach.

Batcheldor's approach is based on the theory that most of us are capable of producing magical effects like levitating tables, but we block our abilities with our own disbelief. So the first step toward producing miracles is to convince yourself they're possible.

This is harder than it sounds. It's no use just *telling* yourself something can happen. You've got years of personal and social conditioning to overcome. What you need is proof. What you need is *Show me*.

Batcheldor discovered that the way to get tables to move was to start out his sessions with no controls whatsoever. The séance room would be in complete darkness. There would be no cameras, no pressure pads under the feet of the table, no precautions against cheating. This meant that if anything odd did happen, the sitters wouldn't get defensive or upset. They could tell themselves there was lots of room for a rational explanation. In other words, they stayed relaxed.

At the same time, in conditions like these, odd things were very likely to happen. Very few of us are used to sitting with our hands on a table in pitch darkness for hours on end in the company of a bunch of strangers waiting for a ghost. The experience produces a great sense of anticipation so that when something happens—say a twitch of the table brought about by an involuntary muscle movement—it seems so strange the sitters will often start to believe something supernatural has happened.

Batcheldor called these oddities "artifacts"—natural but unusual occurrences that people tricked themselves into believing were examples of psychic phenomena. He discovered that by starting out with little or no rigid controls and permitting artifacts to occur he could create an atmosphere in which genuine, significant manifestations resulted. (For a much fuller look at Batcheldor's work, see my book *Mindreach*, Aquarian Press, Wellingborough, 1985.) These manifestations weren't confined to table moving. They included breezes, intense cold, lights, touchings, pulling back of sitters' chairs, movement of objects (rattle, trumpet), "gluing" of the table to the floor so that it could not be budged and "apports"—the appearance of small objects out of nowhere.

If you're familiar with Spiritualist literature, you'll recognize almost all of these phenomena. Most Spiritualists take them as proof of contact with entities from the Other Side. But despite the similarities, Batcheldor was never happy that spirits were involved, although for some time he did consider the possibility that one of his sitters was a natural medium. Later he concluded that the important factor was mindset. He noticed that when sitters trained themselves to inhibit discursive thinking, the levitated table or tube remained suspended in the air for a much longer period, whereas any intrusive thought caused it to come crashing down.

So is it spirits or some unknown ability of the human mind that makes a table move? The same question arises out of another form of "spirit contact": automatic writing. This is something else worth your attention and, perhaps, a little experimentation. Like the other techniques described in this chapter, it needs no unusual equipment and has the added benefit of being something you can do on your own.

Find yourself a pad of paper, a pencil or ball-point pen and a good novel. Make yourself comfortable, pencil in hand with its point resting lightly on the pad of paper. Relax as deeply as you can and read your novel. If all goes well, your hand will eventually start to write interesting messages of its own accord. Variations on this theme include sinking into trance with pencil poised and holding the pencil in your "wrong" hand: the left hand if you're right handed, the right hand is you're left handed. The bottom line seems to be that automatic writing is a knack rather than a technique. You either have the talent or you don't. But it's not a talent that will necessarily manifest the first time you try it, so a few sessions are recommended.

Despite the simplicity of the approach, automatic writing can produce some very interesting results. I was introduced to the art by Sheila—the same Sheila the glass told me to contact—who had trained herself to produce automatic script to order. She sat down with her pen and pad and started to chat to me about the local amateur dramatic group. Suddenly the pen began to move rapidly across the paper (in China, automatic writing is known as the art of the flying pencil). Sheila's chat about drama never faltered as she filled several pages of her note pad.

The message that came through had nothing to do with amateur dramatics. It was a description of conditions in the Spirit World purporting to come from one of Sheila's guides, a masculine entity whose name escapes me at the moment. The handwriting looked nothing like her own.

At the time I found it difficult to believe Sheila had really been in touch with a spirit. The whole operation was too quick, too easy. Even the handwriting failed to convince me. Anyone can disguise the way they write and I'm no expert so I would have been easy to fool. At the same time, Sheila managed to talk fluently about one subject while writing fluently about another. That's not easy. In fact it's so difficult it suggests split in the psyche if you rule out spirit intervention. In all the years I've known her, Sheila has shown no sign of mental instability.

And automatic writing has produced some of the clearest evidence ever that spirits actually exist. In the early years of the twentieth century, some 2,000 messages—writings and drawings—came through a variety of mediums sitting in different countries at different times, all quite unknown to one another. These messages made little or no sense on their own, but formed a sort of psychic jigsaw which, when fitted together, gave rational, intelligent information.

★★★★

Are there dangers in this sort of experimentation? The honest answer seems to be yes. My wife developed a talent for automatic writing as a child, but abandoned it in horror when the messages she brought through became increasingly threatening and obscene. A student group at the University of Aston in Birmingham, England, set up a table-turning group on the Batcheldor model and generated such violent poltergeist activity that they had to disband after only a few months. Even simple glass moving can be tricky. I can still recall the tears of a young girl who broke off a romantic relationship on the basis of lies told to her about her boyfriend by a moving glass.

Beyond this, there is a distinct tendency for mediums and other regular psychic practitioners to develop ill health. Obesity and diabetes are rather more common among them than in the general population. Inexperienced psychic healers will often "take on" the conditions of their patients. Thirty-five years ago when I first began my study of psychical phenomena, it was almost a cliché for spiritual healers to die of cancer.

Biblical references to "unclean spirits" are not, in my experience, simple superstition. Nor, so long as you don't take it too literally, is the myth of the vampire. Some entities drain vitality. Some make you feel uncomfortable and even ill. So even though such experiences are not exactly commonplace, you do need the discrimination I mentioned earlier.

You also need a healthy dose of skepticism. Not everything that presents itself as a spirit is necessarily a spirit—although some probably are. Not everything you are told by a spirit is necessarily true—although much of it may be.

You can minimize the dangers. I'll show you how, using magical techniques, in Chapter Four. But before I do, it may be useful for you to learn why magic works.

Three

Why Magic Works

When you learn arithmetic, geometry, or algebra, certain things are held to be self-evident. Two plus two will always equal four, no matter what the circumstances. If a = b and b = c, then a = c.

Magic is also based on a couple of vital axioms. Every magical cause works from the inside out, and in magic, there are no such things as miracles.

The common idea of magic is conditioned by fairy tales. You expect a thunderclap to follow the waving of a wand—and a shower of gold to follow the thunderclap. Even the most sophisticated of us is a little disappointed when nothing like this happens. If you tell a friend you're studying magic, he'll ask you for proof in a conjuring trick without the mirrors. No wonder certain magical and occult Lodges count discretion as a prime virtue. Sometimes it's easier to keep your mouth shut.

One of the problems is the difficulty in defining magic. Aleister Crowley used to talk about it as "the art of causing change in accordance with will," a definition that could just as easily describe the brewing and drinking of a cup of tea. Another high-grade initiate, Violet Penry-Evans (née Firth)—better known by her pen-name Dion Fortune—put a much more interesting twist on the definition. She said magic was "the science and art of creating changes of consciousness in accordance with will." This is a lot better. Many magical operations involve a change of consciousness—mediumistic trance, heightened perception, or whatever—by somebody. But it's still not a perfect definition unless you believe dropping acid, smoking pot, or drinking beer are magical acts.

My own definition—for what it's worth—is that magic is a collection of techniques, dating back at least 70,000 years, aimed at manipulating the human imagination in order to produce physical, psychological, or spiritual results. It's long-winded, but it covers the subject. My experience is that effects, even physical plane effects, really do follow manipulations of the imagination. But they do so in their own good time, through natural channels.

To understand how this works requires a grasp of magical theory, which isn't the easiest thing in the world, even when the theory is as simplified as I propose to present it here. But hang in there. You'll find the effort worthwhile.

Virtually everybody subscribes to the idea that mind and matter are two different things. This seems so self-evident it's seldom questioned. Sometimes these familiar aspects of our life are seen as direct opposites, like black and white, sometimes as complementaries, like yin and yang—but always as separate and different.

Which is the one thing a magician denies.

To the magician, mind and matter are a continuity. At one level he agrees with the Buddhist sages that the world is *maya* or illusion. At another, he simply assumes certain mental gymnastics can produce specific physical effects because ultimately there's no real difference between the two.

How the magician arrives at this extraordinary conclusion is not important. He may perhaps accept it as an article of faith—a sort of working hypothesis that lets him get on with the job. You might even make the case his theories are untrue, that magic works for some other reason altogether. It won't worry the magician. He enjoys his work and gets reasonable results.

Let's assume you're still agog at my throwaway reference in chapter one to the magical production of a $100 bill. It's a mundane example, but not as frivolous as it sounds. Most of us devote a lot of work, time, and energy to the production of $100 bills, not always as successfully as we would like. Learning how to do it by magic vividly illustrates the differences in approach and basic thinking.

If you analyze the normal ways of getting a $100 bill you'll find they break down into this sequence:

Desire…Belief…Action…Reaction.

First comes your desire for the money. If that's lacking, you'll obviously take no steps to get it.

Next comes belief in your ability to earn the money. If you don't have that, you'll freeze into helplessness.

Next comes action. You may decide to buy a coat and sell it at a profit. You might set a $100 fee on some service you're able to provide.

Finally comes reaction. The coat is sold, the service accepted. The result is that you've earned the money. You have your hundred dollars.

In this sequence, almost all the emphasis is placed on action. The remaining factors obviously have to be there, but they operate almost as a reflex and nobody pays much attention to them.

The magician follows the same sequence, but places the emphasis differently.

Back in the old Medieval grimoires, the magician was advised to "Inflame thyself with Prayer." This refers to the first step of the sequence outlined above. In your magical operation, desire has to be stoked to white heat. Remember I mentioned astral energy was the driving force of the emotions? Magicians believe astral energy and emotion are more or less the same thing, or at least aspects of the same thing. So if you stoke up the emotion of desire, you stoke up the astral energy. It's desire that provides the fuel for your operation and the higher the octane, the better the results.

It is no mean feat to maintain a single burning desire for days or weeks on end, but the magician, to have the best chance of success in his work, must achieve it. This single factor is the reason few advanced magicians bother with such trivia as $100 bills. There are bigger fish to catch in a net that strong—and certainly far easier ways of making money.

Belief, too, is important to the magician. A feeble, take-it-for-granted self-confidence is not enough. Nor is an open-minded scientific approach. The magician strains for inner certainty, the gut conviction that he cannot fail. This is the ancient secret Kenneth Batcheldor stumbled on when his groups started table turning (see chapter two). Belief is the factor that most often limits a magical operation. In theory there's no real magical difference between producing a hundred dollars and a million dollars but very few magicians have the conviction necessary to achieve the latter figure.

By contrast, the action taken receives much less emphasis. It's routine—and an inward one at that. When the routine is finished, the magician waits—and lets go. To paraphrase that great contemporary American occultist Shakmah Winddrum, having asked the universe, the magician gets out of the way. He knows results are seldom quick and never miraculous. The money will come eventually. When it does, it may arrive by mail as the return of a long-forgotten loan. Or it may arrive by hand as a spontaneous gift from an admirer. It may be a bonus from the boss or a chance find in the street. In other words, the money will arrive through perfectly natural channels.

So what's the curious routine the magician follows to conjure up his $100 bill? Oddly enough, it varies. Even more oddly, the variations never seem to matter.

We have it on the authority of Sir James Frazer that the shaman accepts certain correspondences in the universe. He has grown up with the belief so the correspondences are as natural to him as his walk. His system of magic is based on the equation Like = Like.

Just what does that mean? Well, water sprinkled from a pan looks like falling rain. So to make rain, you have to sprinkle water from a pan. Whistling imitates the sound of the wind. So it should be possible to whistle up a storm. It looks silly when you write it down in black and white, but this is sympathetic magic and its roots run deep. Sailors won't whistle on board ship. It's considered unlucky because it brings on storms. If you're not convinced, you only have to wash the car to start a downpour; I bet your neighbor is.

When Frazer wrote his *Golden Bough*, it was customary to devalue shamanic practice as "primitive" or downright superstitious. Today there's a new appreciation of shamanism: urban shamans shake their rattles in Washington and London. But while much shamanic practice transplants effectively into an urban setting, I'm not at all sure this holds good for sympathetic magic. The problem is sympathetic magic depends on a profoundly held belief that Like = Like, and in the West, most of us are taught that's nonsense. We may notice the downpour that follows washing the car, but we mention it as a joke. We don't take it seriously. We'd think twice about betting our shirt on it.

There are few people in the developed world innocent enough or wise enough to embrace the Like = Like equation wholeheartedly. The rest of us find our cultural conditioning just too difficult to break. For this reason even high-grade occultists often find themselves unable to perform an operation that would give no trouble to their brothers in the bush. But this doesn't matter. Magic hasn't died; it's just increased in complexity.

Today's student of the Arts is taught a new set of correspondences. What they are depends largely on his school. Probably the most widespread are drawn from the Qabalah, often with additional material drawn from Greek, Egyptian, Celtic, and even Asian sources.

If the magician has been trained in this system he will have built into his mind a series of associations with hard cash (before any attempt at the $100 bill experiment). He will, for instance, associate it with a planet and a color and a particular sphere of the Tree of Life (a Qabalistic model of the emanation of the universe from the Godhead; see chapter ten.)

Then, at the simplest level of practical working, he will flood his aura with the associated color through an act of imagination and visualize strongly the $100 bill coming to him. If he wishes to go further, he may surround himself with further associations He may even perform ritual actions of symbolic value. All have exactly the same purpose to turn his mind in the right direction and keep it there. For the $100 bill trick, the basic chain of associations for a Qabalist would be:

Sephirah: Tiphareth
Color: Gold
Planet: Sun

All this seems too easy. But simply knowing the links won't necessarily attach the chain to anything. The magician is a worker if nothing else. He'll spend weeks, months, maybe even years in daily meditation on the spheres of the Tree of Life, building their associations into the deepest levels of his being, making them a part of him, slowly realizing why the associations hold good and what they mean. Only after that will he feel truly confident about his $100 bill. And by that time, as you'll discover, he'll have bigger fish to fry than dollars.

How does this fascinating conjuration work? Many magicians don't have the slightest idea. They learned the method (as you can learn it more fully in chapter five), did their preparatory homework, and found, eventually, the cash came home to roost. The power of magic was proved by experiment.

But magic isn't a power. It's a collection of techniques. When a television set works, it doesn't prove there is a power of electronics. It merely demonstrates the practical application of certain principles. These principles may be a mystery even to the person who repairs or even manufactures the set. All he needs to know is which wire to solder onto what, or where the plug-in module goes.

It's probably true to say that the most penetrating insights into why the $100 bill trick works didn't come from a magician. They came from one of the founding fathers of modern psychology, Carl Gustav Jung.

Like most clinical psychiatrists, Jung came across some very odd occurrences while treating patients. But unlike too many of his colleagues, he did not ignore them. His investigations of their curious experiences led him to the theory of synchronicity. An actual case history will make the theory clear.

At one stage of his career, Jung was treating a patient, Mr. X, for an emotional disorder. Apart from this disorder, Mr. X seemed fit and well.

After one of his treatment sessions, Mr. X happened to complain about a sore throat. This isn't the sort of symptom that disturbs a layman, but Jung's medical experience led him to suspect there might be more behind it than a chest cold. He felt there was a possibility of heart disease and advised the man to see his doctor. Mr. X agreed. En route to the surgery—and unknown to Jung at the time—he had a heart attack and died.

Meanwhile Mrs. X entered the story. She called Jung in a panic to ask if there was something seriously wrong with her husband.

Pause now to consider, as Jung did. Mr. X was being treated for a psychiatric illness, a category that rarely proves fatal. While Mrs. X may well have known about her husband's throat, she was unlikely to have been too worried by it—certainly she wouldn't have made the same diagnosis Jung did. Indeed, Jung himself didn't know at the time that his suspicions had been proven only too well founded. He reassured her as best he could and asked her what had prompted her question.

The woman's answer was very odd. She said a flock of birds had arrived at her husband's bedroom window.

To make sense of this, you have to know about Mrs. X's family background. Years before, as her grandfather lay dying, a flock of birds came to his bedroom window. The same thing happened at the death of her father. Because of this, Mrs. X had learned to associate the arrival of birds with death. The flock at the window became a sort of personal omen.

When Jung learned of the husband's death—which meant the omen had proven correct three times running—Jung began to wonder about the mechanics of its operation. He started from the basis of two premises, both logically undeniable:

- Flocks of birds arriving at windows don't cause death. If they did, half the human race would have been wiped out years ago.
- Human death doesn't attract birds. If it did, our hospitals would be faced with a huge problem.

In other words, no cause-and-effect relationship exists between flocks of birds and death. But self-evidently there was a relationship of some sort. It was plain enough to prompt Mrs. X to call Jung.

Jung concluded a relationship did indeed exist. But it had to lie outside of cause-and-effect. He felt there was something else at work in the world, largely hidden from immediate attention. He saw the link between the two factors in the X case was meaning.

Meaning is, of course, a function of the human mind. The link between Mr. X's death and the flock of birds was, almost incredibly, the mind (and/or belief) of

Mrs. X. Jung considered he had discovered an acausal connecting principle, which he labeled "meaningful coincidence" or "synchronicity."

Synchronicity is a fairy-tale conclusion; an open invitation to conclude that wishing will make it so. Even coming from Jung, it might have remained no more than an interesting idea if he hadn't chosen to test his conclusions by experiment.

Jung's experiment was both unusual and delightful. He looked around for a suitable tool to test synchronicity and hit on the idea of using astrology. Astrologers accept that certain planetary configurations give clues to the likelihood of certain terrestrial occurrences. Belief in astrological relationships goes back millennia. Yet it's quite obvious the actions of humanity can't influence the planets in their courses. And if some mysterious planetary rays influence the actions of individuals, astrology would be an exact science, which even astrologers admit it's not. In these circumstances, astrology seemed like the perfect test tool.

With this tool, Jung set up his experiment. He searched the horoscopes of selected married couples for traditional marriage conjunctions. He made note of the cases in which the conjunctions did indeed occur. Then he analyzed his findings statistically and found the percentage was significantly above what would be expected by chance occurance..

Astrologers rejoiced that a distinguished psychiatrist had proved the truth of astrology—but in fact he hadn't. Rather, he had proved there was a certain truth in astrology. But he concluded, with reason, that he had proved the existence of synchronicity.

The discovery of an acausal connecting principle in nature was as important in its own way as Einstein's $e = mc^2$. But since the practical application was less obvious than the A-bomb, synchronicity has been largely ignored. Only the lunatic fringe, of which magicians find themselves uncomfortable members, paid much attention to the weirdness Jung had discovered. The skeptic, who couldn't be bothered to investigate, met their claims with knowing smiles.

In recent years, however, those smiles are beginning to fade. Even in Jung's day, there was some interest in synchronicity among physicists. The original scientific paper on the subject was actually co-authored by the Nobel prize winner Wolfgang Pauli. Since Jung's death, however, modern physics has moved on to a point where it may provide a theoretical basis not merely for magic, but for synchronicity itself.

That's something we'll examine in our next chapter.

Four

Occult Anatomy

A Victorian scientist once distinguished himself by announcing the imminent death of physics. It was only a matter of a few years—ten at most, he claimed—before everything would be weighed, measured, categorized, and explained. When that happened, we would know all there was to know about everything and the need for science itself would simply disappear.

This prediction was possible because Victorian scientists believed themselves to be living in a clockwork universe, wound up some time ago by the Great Clock-maker and gradually running down ever since. It was a common-sense universe of energy and matter. It had a beginning and it would one day have an end. There was no difficulty in defining its two main components. Matter was the stuff that hurt if you dropped it on your foot. Energy was what you needed to push matter around.

Today, a great many people still cling to these superstitions. We continue to say seeing is believing. We continue to hold the ultimate test of reality is to see, touch, taste, hear, or smell it. If it lies outside the range of our senses—or the range of our senses as extended by mechanical and electronic instruments—we have trouble accepting it's really there.

But several interesting discoveries have forced scientists to move on. The first thing they discovered was that the solid world around us wasn't solid after all. Atoms, once thought of as the very building blocks of reality, turned out to be capable of splitting. Inside them was mostly space and a few sub-atomic particles.

At first particles were thought of much the same way atoms had once been thought of—as tiny cannonballs. But it soon became clear this definition wouldn't do. Particles behaved like waveforms just as often as they behaved like little lumps of matter. Physicists talked for awhile about a wave-particle duality (which described their problem but didn't explain it), then threw in the towel and reluctantly concluded that particles were simply the traces of probabilities.

Most of these discoveries are categorized within quantum physics; and quantum physics is not easy to understand. But its conclusions are, even though they remain difficult to accept. Quantum physics tells us that when you dig deep enough into the universe, there's nothing there. Its structures are information structures. If it's like anything at all, it's like a dream.

This is a mystical perception, of course, and as such has been difficult for both the scientists and the general public to swallow. But there's worse to come.

You and I live in this unreal universe, equipped from the moment of our birth with what appears to be a solid body. But the solidity of the body is in the same category as the solidity of the world. It's a perception of the senses. If you could see your body as it really is, most of it consists of empty space. And even the atoms in it are constantly changing.

You renew your liver (completely) every few weeks. You shed skin constantly in the form of flakes, while building new layers. You expel and acquire part of your substance with every breath. In fact, over the course of no more than six months to a year, every molecule and fiber of your entire body has been replaced.

Scientists estimate that at the moment, as you sit reading this book, you contain about a million atoms that once occupied the body of Jesus Christ. Unfortunately, you also contain a million atoms donated by Adolph Hitler and a million more that belonged to Genghis Khan. They jostle (literally) with atoms from distant stars, from the depths of the sea, ejected by volcanoes, excreted by octupi, and handed on by bugs.

The body you occupied when you started this chapter is a different body to the one you're using now to read these words. If you were capable of experiencing reality as it actually is, instead of reality as interpreted by your fallible senses, you would know that your body swirls around you like an ever-changing whirlwind round a central core. This is not science fiction, nor is it religious speculation. It is the inescapable conclusion of hard-nosed scientific investigation.

The really interesting question, of course, is the nature of your central core.

Clearly, the behaviorist idea that "you" are somehow the product of your body no longer holds water. For your body to change constantly, yet retain the same shape (give or take a few pounds) presupposes the existence of some sort of guiding pattern, some sort of energy matrix or container for the new atoms to occupy as the old ones leave.

And since your physical body is subject to exactly the same laws as the rest of matter, we know that beyond this matrix, beyond the clouds of sub-atomic particles within your atomic structure lies ... nothing. You are, at your most fundamental, an information pattern used by the Great Unmanifest to generate a space/time event. From this perspective, you are one with everything. It is this unity which is the enabling factor of magic. For while these ideas have reappeared in quantum physics, they are the same ideas, expressed in different language, that have been taught by mystics and magicians for millennia.

You are One with the All. You are not only part of the universe, hence subject to its laws, but part of the unmanifest foundation of the universe, hence beyond all natural law. The trouble is you have largely forgotten this birthright. You act, most of the time, as if you were helpless and powerless when, clearly, you are neither. You act as if the physical world was all there is, when it is, in fact, no more than your current perception—in one sense no more than your current dream.

When you learn the secrets of occult anatomy, you learn some of the structures by which the Unmanifest created you and your current dream of reality. It's a doctrine that not only defines you as a spiritual entity involved in an experiential space/time event, but as an entity that can be persuaded to remember how to manipulate your world to a far greater degree than you ever believed possible.

If this is getting obscure, think of dreaming. Most of the time when you dream, the world around you seems solid and real, the events you experience are pleasurable or frightening. It is only when you awaken that you realize the dream has been a self-created illusion.

But suppose it were possible to wake up while you were dreaming…and yet remained dreaming? Suppose during a dream, you suddenly realized you were dreaming, yet remained in the dream state?

It is, in fact, perfectly possible to do so—the process is known as lucid dreaming. When it happens, you can take control of your dream and do anything you want. You can fly, create gold, visit strange lands, talk to gods, call friends to keep you company, make love to an angel.

All this sounds like a fairy-tale description of a magician's abilities and in many ways that's exactly what it is. If a magician can truly awaken in the physical world, he has the same potential as the lucid dreamer. Nothing is beyond him. The trouble is, as Gurdjieff or any Hindu mystic will confirm, waking up in the physical world is difficult and staying awake nearly impossible. So the magician remains limited by his degree of wakefulness. In practical terms, this means he's limited by his awareness and experience of occult anatomy.

This is a difficult point. Awareness and experience are quite different from simple knowledge. For example, you are currently aware you have a body. You don't have to be taught this or work it out logically. You experience it directly. You just *know* it.

But you probably don't experience your *second* body in this way.

If you've been paying attention, you'll certainly realize you must *have* a second body. The energy matrix that holds in place all those new atoms you absorb from the universe must be the image of your physical body—otherwise you'd change your appearance visibly every moment of the day. By any reasonable definition, this makes it a second body—an energy body that exactly mirrors the physical.

It's entirely possible you've heard about this second body before. Occultists, especially Spiritualists, call it your etheric body or sometimes (wrongly) your astral body. But however much you've learned about it in theory, the chances are you don't actually *experience* it the way you experience your physical body. For that to happen, you need training. But before we start, it could be useful for you to see what it is you'll actually be training.

When Western scientists first investigated Eastern notions of the chakras, they noted the coincidence between chakras placement and certain nerve plexi and glandular centers in the physical body. This led to the theory that the chakras were really no more than the plexi and glands themselves.

Yoga practitioners have vigorously denied it, insisting that, while certainly linked, the chakras are an energy system that, so to speak, "stands behind" the endocrine and nervous systems of the physical body. They act as contact points and "transformers" for universal energy. So in yoga the body has three systems: nervous, endocrine, and chakra.

In magic, there's a fourth system known as the *astro-mental* system. The centers of the astro mental system are often confused with the chakras, just as the chakras have often been confused with the endocrine system.

Careful study of the astro-mental centers suggests they represent a system one further step removed, which stands behind the chakras, as the chakras stand behind the glands. More to the point today, this system appears to exist not in the physical world at all, but in the astral (imaginal) realm we have been discussing. Because of this, the centers can be manipulated by magical—which is to say astral, which is to say imaginative—means.

Occult anatomy is not an easy subject. But you'll need to grasp its rudiments before you can successfully undertake any serious magical operation.

The Magus is at one with the Mystic, who teaches that we are at One with the All. What this means, in rather more banal terms, is that you are part of the universe and subject to its laws. Because of this, everything that happens in the universe influences you, if only to an infinitesimal degree. And, conversely, everything you do has an effect (to the same minute degree) on the entire universe.

This disturbing thought is probably easy enough to grasp on the physical level, but there are, of course, the other levels to consider, each with its own set of laws. In order to keep the picture as simple as possible, I shall limit the discussion to just two of them—the mental and the spiritual.

The magician believes that these two levels, along with the physical, form part of a super-embracing All, grade into one another and have certain distinct points of contact. Further, on the evidence of mystics and clairvoyants, he feels he has a fair idea of what the inner levels are like .

He sees himself surrounded, as it were, by a vast, inexhaustible sea of spiritual energy. The extent of the power available is literally beyond imagination. But at least part of the power is fortunately not beyond control. The problems are really contact and transformation. Your electric light won't work until the wires make contact with the power source; and since few of your household gadgets will work on direct current, a transformer is needed somewhere along the line.

Making contact with the spiritual power source should, in theory, be an easy, natural thing. You are part of the One, so this aspect of the One should flow through you without hindrance. But it is hindered, quite unconsciously, by one of humanity's most prevalent habits: stress.

Stress is much more insidious than people imagine. When I worked in a therapy clinic, I watched patients claim to be perfectly relaxed—from the edge of their seats. Stress creeps in undetected and establishes itself as a habit pattern. Sometimes the habit is a tricky one to break, but you can manage it with time and practice.

This is how to break the stress habit.

Leave aside a time each day to practice relaxation. Ten or fifteen minutes is enough in the early stages, although you can increase this later if you like. Early morning is the best time, since there are less distractions and far fewer temptations to do something else.

Next, get firmly into your mind that you are going to practice relaxation every day. It is, in fact, worth doing every day for the rest of your life; as worthwhile as your daily ritual of cleaning your teeth and combing your hair. A continuing sequence is important. Even two minutes daily practice is worth several hours at irregular intervals.

With this in mind, you are ready to begin. Make your first attempts on your bed, lying flat on your back with your hands by your sides. Your unconscious mind, which has a lot to do with habit formation, associates bed with sleep and hence, relaxation. So by performing your first exercises on a bed, you are automatically taking a step toward the desired result.

In theory, relaxation is the easiest thing in the world, simply a matter of "letting go." In actuality, it is usually a learned response nowadays, built up by conscious practice and much repetition.

In order to be sure of complete relaxation, it is first necessary to be aware of tension. This may sound very obvious, but the fact remains that very few people are genuinely aware of tension in a particular set of muscles. At best (or worst) they experience the general effect in terms of discomfort.

So your first job is to stimulate awareness. Begin with your feet. Curl the toes downward and inward, as if you were trying to pick up a handkerchief. When you have done so, hold that position…and keep holding it until the toes are uncomfortable to the point of cramping. This discomfort will make you fully aware of the deliberate tension in the toe muscles. Once you are fully aware, let go.

Now go further. Point your feet forward like a ballet dancer and hold them so until the discomfort occurs. Then let go.

Now move on to the calf muscles, tensing them to the point of discomfort…then letting go.

Continue with the sequence, moving slowly and deliberately up your body. Take your time so that no set of muscles is left out. When you reach your face, grit your teeth and grimace. Then let go.

Finally, remember that the scalp has muscles too. Frown to bring the scalp forward, hold it…then let go.

By the time you have finished the sequence, it is likely enough that some tension will have crept back into the muscles you treated earlier, so do a mental roll call and if tension is discovered anywhere, increase it to the point of conscious discomfort…then let go.

Now put the whole lot together. Strain every ten-
don and fiber of your body. Then let go…and relax. if
you have been accustomed to tension, you will find the
experience of complete conscious relaxation a very
pleasant one. Practice it daily.

After you have the hang of the conscious relaxation
sequence; after, that is, you can do it easily and fluently
as a matter of routine, the time has come to improve
the level of your performance. In doing so, you will
learn a trick that will be of very considerable benefit to
you in everyday life.

At this stage it is wise to dispense with the bed.
Continue your morning exercises in a chair. There's a
good reason for this. As your depth of relaxation
increases, so does the danger of falling asleep. Since you
have better things to do, this should be avoided. If you
practice relaxation in a chair and fall asleep, you will
also fall off. It is a rude awakening, but a sure one.

Make yourself comfortable in your chair. You are
about to add a breathing exercise to basic relaxation.

Breathing exercises, particularly those of the Yoga
system, can cause Westerners a lot of trouble. Even the
one given here, simple though it is, should not be overdone, especially in the early stages. Do not use it for
more than three minutes on your first attempt and build
it up slowly, minute by minute, over a period of weeks.
Should any trouble arise, stop the exercise immediately.

Avoid also breathing too deeply in the early stages.
Here again, depth of breathing should be built up very
gradually over the weeks.

One final word of warning. This exercise involves retaining breath. This should be done by holding out the diaphragm, *not* by closing the throat. If you feel any strain during the exercise, you're doing it wrong.

Now the exercise itself. First, empty your lungs. There's no need to empty them completely in the early stages and certainly no need to force. Now breathe in to the mental count of four. If you find you have taken a full breath before finishing the count, regulate your speed of counting. Don't attempt to force more air in. The object of this exercise is to establish a rhythm, not to increase lung capacity.

Next, hold your breath to the mental count of two. Remember this should be done by means of the abdominal muscles, not by closing the throat.

Now, breathe out to the count of four. It may not be easy at first, but you are aiming to establish a situation where you are counting at a steady pace throughout the entire sequence.

Finally, hold your breath out for a count of two.

The sequence again in brief: *In* to the count of four; *hold* to the count of two; *out* to the count of four; *hold* out to the count of two. Repeat this sequence, increasing your practice time gradually each day, until it becomes fluid and trouble-free. Eventually, once begun, it will become quite automatic—your unconscious, given time to learn the sequence, will take it over and do the work for you.

During this exercise, you will find you take in more air than when breathing normally. This holds good even without straining, since most people tend to breathe in a very shallow manner. Increased oxygen in your lungs means an increase of oxygen in your blood. You have begun a minor biochemical reaction. The end result is improved relaxation.

The benefit does not end there. You are practicing this exercise in conjunction with conscious relaxation. Combine the two often enough and regularly enough and a curious psychological mechanism comes into play. It is a mechanism mentioned earlier in a different context—the mechanism of association.

Eventually (Pavlov's basic research suggests fifty to seventy consecutive sessions should do the trick) your mind will firmly associate 2/4 breathing with relaxation. Afterward, you have only to embark on the breathing sequence to produce relaxation via a conditioned reflex.

It is a particularly useful talent to develop, apart altogether from its occult benefits. When a crisis arises, you can fight panic with a breath, regain poise through a spontaneous 2/4 sequence. For the body and the mind are closely interlinked and when the first becomes relaxed, the second relaxes too.

Once you have achieved the art of relaxation, you have broken down the barrier between that vast sea of spiritual energy and yourself. Your next job is to provide the necessary channels for its flow.

Here we hit on a difficult concept. The channels are already there. They exist as inborn organs of the mind. But to bring them into conscious function requires time and effort. There is no real parallel on the physical plane. Your heart either beats or it doesn't. Your liver will work or it won't. And, surgical transplants aside, there is very little you can do about this; indeed, very little you need to do.

The nearest physical analogy I can think of is that of muscles. You were born with a full set, but they needed exercise to grow and still need it to function efficiently. The analogy is not perfect, but the psychic channels are at least a little like that.

If you are at all familiar with the Asian systems, you may have come across the idea of chakras. You will also have met the notion that Man is equipped with more than one body—exactly the same idea we saw arise out of Quantum Physics earlier in this chapter. The doctrine of subtle bodies is a complex study in itself, but for the moment it's possible to limit consideration to two bodies other than the physical. These are the etheric and the astral (or astro-mental).

Your etheric body is your invisible double. It interpenetrates your physical body and some schools of thought believe with the physicists it is essentially a pattern of forces on which your physical body is built. It is closer to matter than to mind. That is to say it belongs to the material plane in the way that electricity and magnetism do. It seems to function as a link between your physical body and your mind.

Your astral body is a step beyond the etheric. And this step takes you into the realms of the psyche proper. The astral body is composed of mind-stuff: or, more accurately, imagination stuff.

The chakras are "nerve points" in the etheric body. They are closely linked on one hand to the spiritual channels of the higher bodies; and on the other to the glands and nerve plexi of the physical.

Many of the Hatha Yoga exercises are designed to stimulate the chakras, thus producing beneficial effects on the physical body. The Western occultist will usually do well to avoid this method. Without a guru on the spot to keep the chela out of trouble, it can be dangerous. So the Occidental magician turns his attention to the astral body. By working on it, he gets the same results eventually. The process is slower, but safer. However, for those interested in pursuing Hatha Yoga further, a good source of information is *A Chakra and Kundalini Workbook* by Dr. Jonn Mumford. Dr. Mumford is trained in both Western chiropractic and psychotherapy, but is also a yoga initiate.

In a moment, I'll teach you a basic Western magical technique for training your astral body. But before I do, I'd like to make sure you take it seriously. These days, with electrical measurement of acupuncture meridians and Kirlian photography, it's not too difficult to accept the reality of the etheric body. The astral body is much more of an act of faith. Since I have difficulty with acts of faith myself, I worry that the same may be true for you. In these circumstances, I would very much like to present you with hard scientific proof that the astral body actually exists. Since I can't, I propose to do the next best thing and show you how you can experience the astral body for yourself.

The technique that allows you to do this comes not from the files of a working magician (at least I don't think she's a working magician) but from the spiritual development seminars of America's remarkable Jean Houston. In its original context, the exercise that follows is designed to let you contact the image of your physical body that's encoded in the motor cortex of your brain. But you can't fool an old magician with fancy terminology. Take it from me, Ms. Houston's "kinaesthetic body exercise" is just about the best way you'll find of developing an awareness of your astral body.

Get a friend to talk you through the following, or record the instructions and follow them:

First find space, indoors or out, where you have lots of room to move about. Then stand quite still, arms hanging at your sides, feet comfortably apart and sense your body at rest. Actually concentrate on your body, trying to become as aware as possible of yourself just standing there.

(This is more tricky than you'd think. We spend so much time looking outward at interesting people and things that we seldom really consider our own bodies until something like injury or illness draws our attention to them. Fortunately in this exercise you don't have to focus on your body for long.)

After a moment, raise your right arm. As you do so, become aware of the physical sensations—what muscles you use, the movement of your clothing across the skin, and so on.

Now lower the arm, again paying close attention to what you're feeling. Repeat this—raising and lowering—several times.

When you're ready, use your memory of what you've been doing to imagine you're raising your right arm. Let your physical arm hang relaxed by your side, but raise an imaginary right arm as vividly and realistically as you can. Try to call up all the sensations you experiences when you lifted the physical arm.

Okay, now lower that imaginary (astral) arm.

Next, alternate raising your physical right arm and your astral right arm. Use the immediate memory of what happens in the physical, to increase the depth of your experience of the astral.

When you've done that a few times, repeat the whole process with your left arm. First, raise it in the physical several times, then imagine raising your astral left arm. Again alternate between the astral and the physical.

(This may sound a little complicated when it's written down, but if you actually follow the instructions, you'll very quickly get the hang of the process.)

When you've finished raising and lowering your physical and astral arms, continue the exercise with the following sequence. In each case, repeat the movements, both physical and astral, several times.

Roll your physical shoulders forward. Repeat this motion several times.

Roll your astral shoulders forward. Repeat several times.

Alternate several times between the two.

Roll your physical shoulders backward. Repeat.

Roll your astral shoulders backward. Repeat.

Alternate between the two.

When you have finished this sequence, stand centered, perfectly still and at ease, arms dangling by your sides.

Now make a sword-fencing lunge to your right. Return to your center, then repeat.

Follow this with an astral lunge right. Return your astral body to your center then alternate between the astral and the physical for several movements.

Next, make a fencing lunge left, return to center and repeat once. Then make an astral lunge left and return to center.

   Now you come to the kernel of the exercise. Follow this sequence exactly and smoothly:

Lunge physical left, return to center, and lunge physical right.

Lunge astral left and back.

Lunge physical left and back.

Lunge physical right and back.

Lunge physical right and back.

Lunge physical left and back.

Now lunge right with your astral body and simultaneously lunge left with your physical body. (This is the moment most people become fully aware of the reality of their astral body. The result is usually a burst of delighted laughter.)

Bring both bodies back to center.

Lunge with your astral body left while sending your physical body to the right.

Again, bring both bodies back to center.

Alternate left and right several times, simultaneously sending physical and astral bodies in opposite directions each time.

When you have developed a real awareness of your astral body using this exercise, please examine figure 6. This figure shows the locations of the seven major chakras of the human body. These centers exist, like the acupuncture meridians, in the etheric body. They are, in numbered order:

1. BASE (Muladhara chakra). Centered on base of the spine/public bone or, according to some systems, the perineum between genitals and anus.

2. SACRUM (Svadhisthana chakra). Centered on the body's midline, about four finger widths below the navel.

3. SOLAR PLEXUS (Manipura chakra). Centered on the solar plexus.

4. HEART (Anahata chakra). Centered on the midline at a level with the heart.

5. THROAT (Visuddha chakra). Centered on the midline at a level with the throat.

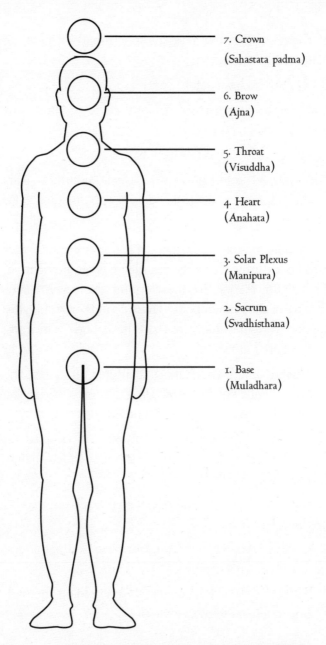

Figure 6: Seven Major Chakras of the Human Body

7. Crown
(Sahastata padma)

6. Brow
(Ajna)

5. Throat
(Visuddha)

4. Heart
(Anahata)

3. Solar Plexus
(Manipura)

2. Sacrum
(Svadhisthana)

1. Base
(Muladhara)

6. BROW (Ajna chakra). Centered between the eyebrows.

7. CROWN. (Sahasrara-padma chakra). Centered on the crown of the head.

You'll notice they're listed from the base chakra upward. This is because the Eastern Esoteric Tradition considers that the major spiritual energy circuit of the human body, the kundalini, runs from the base of the spine upward to illuminate the brain, and that the Great Work is to move matter upward into the realm of spirit.

Now look at figure 7, which shows five important centers in the astral body. Each is linked with one or more chakras. Each is also linked with the Tree of Life as it is finally established in the aura of a Qabalist (see figure 8).

Because of this, the centers are known collectively as The Middle Pillar. It is these Middle Pillar centers that you will have to bring from latent to actual functioning. This is how you can do so. (A variation of this exercise formed part of my own basic magical training, which is where I learned it, but the original seems to be drawn from Israel Regardie's *The Middle Pillar*)

Assume your relaxation posture and go into the 2/4 breathing sequence. When the breathing is going smoothly, visualize a sphere of brilliant white light hanging in space above the crown of your head. If you have ever watched the early morning sun breaking through mist or light cloud, you will have a perfect reference for the brilliant whiteness of the sphere. As you visualize, vibrate the sounds *Eh-heh-yeh*.

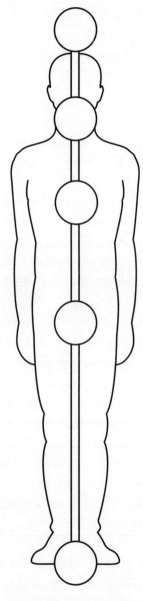

Figure 7: The Middle Pillar Astro-Mental Centers

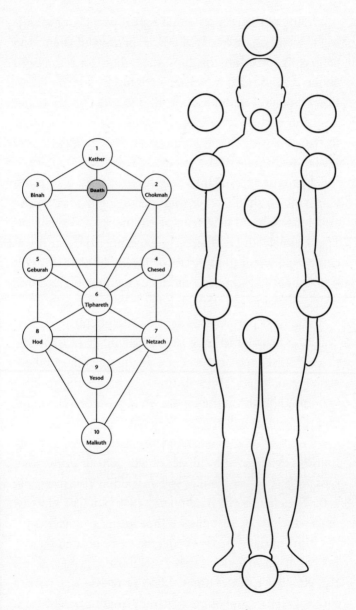

Figure 8: The Tree of Life and its Correspondence in the Qabalist's Aura

Many of the grimoires make great play about vibrating the barbarous words of power, but few of them stop to give instructions on how the vibration is brought about. This has led to needless confusion, for the vibration of a sound is simple enough. It is also a practice that has been with us for a very long time. Russian shamans to this day use "throat singing" in their work—a very similar technique to the one we're investigating here.

The best approach to magical vibration is to pitch your voice a shade lower than you would normally use and let the word originate at the back of the throat. Speak slowly and deliberately, experimenting until you can actually feel the vibration. This is neither difficult nor dramatic. All sound produces a vibration and it is only a question of intensifying it.

The next part sounds a lot more difficult, but isn't. You must attempt to have the sound vibrate in a specific place, in this case at the center of the imaginary sphere above your head. You will find you have only to keep your mind firmly on the sphere while repeating the name and the sounds will trigger there of their own accord.

This sparkling sphere of energy, experienced as imagination, established by an act of will, is your prime contact with the vast store of spiritual energy surrounding you. The sounds given, phonetics of an ancient Hebrew name of God, also establish a link with the storehouse.

Nor is any of this mere dogma to be accepted as an act of faith. Once the sphere is established, you will feel the effects of the contact. Usually the sensation is a surge of energy and often a distinct tingling sensation is experienced. Like everything else, your contact is improved as it is more firmly established with practice.

Patience is a prerequisite of magical training, which tends to build at a stately pace. Take your time in establishing this sphere firmly. Keep up the exercise until you can visualize the energy source clearly. It will occur to you eventually that you are engaged in an exercise of auto-suggestion; and so you are. But it should become clear later that auto-suggestion is not the total answer. The results are too far-reaching.

When the first sphere is established to your satisfaction, move on to the next. Visualize a shaft of brilliant white light moving downward from the sphere through the center of your skull and blossoming into a second sphere of white light at your throat. As this sphere is established, vibrate the sounds *Yeh-ho-vo El-hoh-eem*.

With two spheres properly established, the shaft of light continues down to the solar plexus region and produces a third sphere. Here you should vibrate *Yeh-ho-vo-El-hoh-ah-vey-daas*.

Next, you should extend the shaft to your genitals where a fourth sphere is established to the sounds *Shad-ay-El-chay*.

Finally comes the fifth sphere at your feet, built up by an act of imagination and reinforced by vibration of the sounds *Ah-do-nay-ha-Are-etz*.

Here's that sequence again, step by step. Practice this exercise twice a day, morning and evening, for at least a month. You can continue to practice it thereafter whenever you wish.

1. Memorize the positions of the centers as shown in figure 8.

2. Sit upright with your spine straight, or lie flat on your back.

3. Begin 2/4 breathing. Breathe in to a count of four, hold your breath to a count of two, breathe out to a count of four, hold your breath out for a count of two. Practice the sequence until you are comfortable with it.

4. Visualize a brilliant sphere of white light above the crown of your head. Vibrate *Eh-heh-yeh*. Imagine the sound vibrating within the sphere. Concentrate on this sphere, noting sensations, for about five minutes. This Name and all others may be vibrated several times in establishing the sphere.

5. Visualize a shaft of light emanating from the sphere to penetrate your skull. See it flower into a second shining white sphere at your throat. Vibrate *Yeh-ho-voh Eh-loh-eem*. Again imagine the sound vibrating within the sphere. Contemplate for about five minutes.

6. Visualize the shaft of light continuing to descend to flower into a third shining white sphere at the Tiphareth center. Vibrate *Yeh-hoh-voh Eh-loha ve-Dah-ahs*. Imagine sound vibrating within the sphere. Contemplate for about five minutes.

7. Visualize the shaft of light continuing to descend to flower into a fourth shining white sphere at the Yesod center. Vibrate *Shah-di El Chay*. Imagine sound vibrating within the sphere. Contemplate for about five minutes.

8. Visualize the shaft of light continuing to descend to flower into a fifth shining white sphere at the Malkuth center. Vibrate *Ah-doh-nay hah-Ah-retz.* Imagine sound vibrating within the sphere. Contemplate for about five minutes.

9. Contemplate the entire shaft of silvery light and the sparkling centers for a few moments, sensing the inflow of energy.

Once you have achieved the full sequence, you will look, in your imagination, something like figure 7. The difference, if you have been visualizing properly, is that no illustration can convey the dynamic quality of those sparkling spheres.

Build the spheres in white light during the early stages of your training, a period of weeks. When you have gained proficiency, build the spheres in color. What colors you use depends on the books you've read; or rather, the books you've read and believed.

This is not so cynical as it sounds. Even the best sources vary. In *The Art of True Healing,* for instance, the late Dr. Israel Regardie, who was one of the greatest twentieth-century authorities on magic, ascribed the following colors to the spheres.

Crown—White
Throat—Lavender
Stomach—Red
Genitals—Blue
Feet—Russet

Those in the know are hard put to disagree with Regardie, whose prestige was enormous. At the same time, any Qabalistic magician past the apprentice stage tends to make a considered choice from the four color scales of the Qabalah. Any conflict is more apparent than actual. A tube is not a transistor, but you can build a perfectly good radio set with either.

The same thing goes for the curious sounds you vibrated to open the psychic centers. They are Qabalistic God-names only because I happened to take Qabalistic training and am more familiar with that system than any other. The association of the Names with the spheres was taught in the original Golden Dawn and contemporary Western Tradition Mystery Schools, like the Society of the Inner Light and the Servants of the Light. And long before any of these schools were established, you'll find the Names (somewhat differently pronounced) in the scriptures of the Jewish religion.

But you don't have to use these particular names at all. Other traditions have discovered sounds with the power to awaken the psychic centers and several of them, like the ancient Hebrews, have put them to work as names of God. If you consult *Magical Philosophy* by Aurum Solis, you'll find Greek counterparts. Latin power words also exist, as do Native American, Australian Aborigine, Siberian, and many, many more.

When you have used the color version of the Middle Pillar for several weeks and are comfortable with it, you can give yourself a dramatic energy boost by using the exercise that follows, known as the Fountain of Light.

Fountain of Light Exercise

1. Perform the Middle Pillar.

2. Focus your attention on Malkuth.

3. On the inbreath (four-count) imagine drawing a shaft of energy up the Middle Pillar from Malkuth.

4. This energy should reach Kether at the end of the inbreath.

5. Hold the energy in Kether for a count of two.

6. On the outbreath, imagine light fountaining out of Kether in all directions to shower around the aura. (Count of four)

7. On hold breath (count of two) imagine the energy being absorbed into Malkuth.

8. Repeat seven times.

This exercise has a cleansing and energizing effect and can go a long way toward keeping you fit and healthy in conjunction with more orthodox attention to your physical body.

Now you've increased your health through magic. Let's see how you might go about increasing your wealth as well.

Five

The $100 Bill Trick

S tand up and stretch your arms as far as they will go. Now congratulate yourself on having discovered the practical working limits of your aura. It varies in size in relation to your moods and several other factors, but when you're at peace and at rest, off drugs and unhassled, neither sexually stimulated nor angrily threatened, that's about where it will be.

In the stately days of Queen Victoria, men of science thought the aura was a myth. Today they generally accept there is a weak electrical field surrounding the human body, one that can be reliably detected by electronic instruments. But they still have a long way to go before agreement is reached with the occultists.

The magician, who enjoys structuring, divides this weak force field into two—the inner and the outer auras. Together they envelop the body like an egg and are usually invisible—although in the case of the inner aura that's often because people don't actually bother to look for it.

If you want to see the inner aura, rub your hands briskly together, then hold the tips of your fingers about a quarter to half an inch apart and look between them. A dark background is usually best, but this varies from person to person, so it's worthwhile trying the experiment against a variety of surfaces. Move the fingers slowly together, then apart again. Take your time, look carefully, and you should be able to catch a glimpse of the inner aura. It extends about an inch from the surface of the skin and looks for all the world like grey-blue cigarette smoke. It behaves like molten plastic. Frankly, the inner aura isn't very interesting and after more than thirty years of occult study, I'm still not quite sure what it's there for. But the outer aura is something else again.

In the first edition of this book, published back in 1972, I noted that the only person I knew who could see the outer aura turned out to be a liar. Since then I married a woman trained to see auras at the College of Psychic Studies in London, England, and have been forced to revise what was once a fairly cynical opinion.

Clairvoyants claim they can see colors in the outer aura. Some go so far as to say they can judge moods or diagnose ailments from them. If you have been doing the exercises outlined in Chapter Four with diligence, clairvoyant examination of your aura will reveal the Middle Pillar spheres strongly established.

With those spheres glowing brightly, you're almost ready to try the $100 bill trick. All you lack is a little extra knowledge. Again, it is knowledge of associations that have been accepted for so long they've embedded themselves into the collective psyche of our race.

The question of embedding has always been important to occult practice, and now science has started to pay attention. The name they use is *morphic resonance*, a term coined by Britain's Dr. Rupert Sheldrake.

Dr. Sheldrake became interested in the way information spreads through the animal kingdom. Sometimes the route is obvious. Cats teach kittens how to hunt and the kittens pass the information on when they grow up to have kittens of their own. But sometimes animals pick up tricks that spread through their population in ways that can't be explained by direct teaching or observation.

What first attracted Dr. Sheldrake's attention was something very odd that happened to the British milk bottle. Throughout Britain until relatively recently, milk was delivered to household customers every morning. Typically, the delivery man would leave one or two pints in glass bottles on the customer's doorstep before anybody in the house was awake.

After World War II and throughout the 1950s, these bottles were sealed with sturdy cardboard discs, but as production methods became more streamlined, the discs were eventually replaced by foil caps.

One day, in a suburb of London, a little bird called a tit—the European equivalent of a chickadee—discovered that if it pecked through the foil, it could drink the cream that had collected on the top of the milk. Some of this tit's pals must have noticed what she was doing, because after a while more and more householders in the London suburb came down in the morning to opened milk.

At this point, what was happening was far from mysterious. Nor was it at all mysterious that the irritating theft of cream began to spread slowly through the whole of London. But then something very strange did happen. Suddenly, almost overnight it seemed, the tit population throughout the country learned the trick. Tits in the Outer Hebrides—islands off the north of Scotland—were pecking through foil. The ability to steal cream promptly jumped to tits on the neighboring island of Ireland, then to tits on mainland Europe. Pretty soon, nobody's milk was safe.

But the tit is not a migratory bird. So the question was, how did the Irish and European tits learn how to do the trick?

It was this little unimportant mystery that stimulated Dr. Sheldrake to embark on a study of enormous importance to magicians. From his observations of a number of animal species, Sheldrake found that when a new talent or technique was developed, it spread very slowly to others of the species. But once enough members of the species learned the trick, it suddenly became available to all. It was as if there was a sort of critical mass to knowledge. Once reached, the knowledge exploded instantaneously throughout the entire population. Sheldrake referred to this phenomenon as *morphic resonance*.

The next question was whether our species, humanity, is subject to morphic resonance. Sheldrake mounted an elegant experiment to find out. He took groups of young British schoolchildren and asked them to learn by heart two pieces of text. One piece of text was composed of nonsense syllables. The other, of exactly equal length and complexity, was a poem that had been a favorite of Japanese children for centuries.

Although none of the British children knew a word of Japanese, they learned the Japanese poem far more easily than the nonsense text. Sheldrake concluded that the efforts of Japanese children over the years had embedded it firmly in the collective psyche of humanity by morphic resonance.

The channels of power used by generations of magicians have been embedded in the collective psyche. They lie today in the depths of your unconscious mind ready to be reawakened by a little study and attention to energize your magical experiments.

Should you train in Qabalah, you will eventually revive magical associations so complex and far-reaching that they could literally fill a book—as they have more or less filled Aleister Crowley's master reference work, *Liber 777*. (See *777 and Other Qabalistic Writings of Aleister Crowley*, Samuel Weiser, 1987.) But for now, I propose to stick to a more simplified approach.

The Middle Pillar color scheme given in chapter four was based on associations between the astro-mental centers and the ancient Elements of Spirit, Earth, Air, Fire, and Water. For your working of the $100 bill trick, you'll use a second set of associations just as ancient—the planetary powers of astrology.

We know for certain that astrology was practiced in Mesopotamia in the third millennium B.C. and it may have originated long before that. Today, astronomers have detected nine planets in the solar system including Earth, but astrology, which developed without the aid of telescopes, was concerned in its earliest times with only five—Mercury, Venus, Mars, Jupiter, and Saturn, all of which could be seen with the naked eye. To this list was added the Sun and the Moon, giving a mystical total of seven heavenly bodies with magical associations. Those associations (already burned into the depths of your soul through morphic resonance, remember) are as follows:

Sun: The life force, growth of all kinds. Health. Political, commercial, or personal power. Success. Money. Imagination and the efficient working of the mind. Spiritual illumination. Employers, kings, presidents, rulers, and other superiors.

Positive color: orange

Negative color: gold or yellow

Mercury: Information exchange of all types, including writing, Internet, and broadcasting. Business, contracts, buying, and selling. The abstract quality of judgment. Neighbors, intellectual friends. Short journeys. Books, papers, literary talents, and endeavors.

Positive color: yellow

Negative color: orange

Venus: Emotion, love, and affection. Social life. Femininity. Young people. Pleasure, particularly sensual.

Luxury and extravagance. The graphic and performance arts. Self indulgence. Beauty.

    Positive color: emerald green

    Negative color: emerald green

Moon: Creativity, women's matters and health, particularly menstruation, pregnancy, and childbirth. Change. Your personality. The unconscious. The senses. Hallucinations and the imagination. Channeling, psychism, and the occult.

    Positive color: blue

    Negative color: puce

Mars: Energy, vitality, will power, and personal magnetism. Destruction (but often as the preparation for rebuilding). Danger, haste, anger. Conflict up to and including war. Dominance and strength.

    Positive color: bright red

    Negative color: bright red

Jupiter: Abundance, prosperity, good luck, expansion, growth, generosity. Banking and finance. Gambling. Debtors and creditors. Religion, spirituality, dreams, and visions. Long journeys, particularly international travel.

    Positive color: purple

    Negative color: blue

Saturn: Debt and repayment. Old age, old people, old plans. Coldness, inertia, death, wills, and funerals. Infertility. Stability, unchanging situations, stagnation. Agriculture and real estate.

    Positive color: indigo

    Negative color: black

The first thing you'll notice from this list is that there are overlaps. The Sun is associated with money, as is Jupiter and Saturn, while Mercury is associated with our civilization's favorite way of making money—i.e., business. This is where you start to realize that magic is far more of an art than a science—and requires powers of analysis to boot. You're going to have to decide between the various financial options when you undertake your $100 bill trick…but since it's your first time, I'll give you a little help when we get there.

The next thing you'll notice is that there are two color associations with each planet: positive and negative. It's important that you don't start to think of these terms as meaning good and bad. They don't. They're like the old Chinese classification of *yang* and *yin,* which carry no moral or utilitarian judgments. In the present context, you would use the positive color when you want to send something out from you, the negative when you want to draw it toward you. The associations themselves come from the Golden Dawn's color scales—the positive color from what's called the King Scale, the negative color from the Queen Scale. These scales are in turn related to planetary attributions on the Tree of Life.

The third thing you'll notice is that some of the planets have the same color in both the positive and the negative classifications. Don't let it worry you. That's just the way the (magical) world is.

The final thing you'll notice is that some of the celestial bodies share the same color associations. The

Sun and Mercury are both associated with orange and yellow. The Moon and Jupiter both carry associations with blue and purple. In each of these cases, however, the associations are differently classified according to planet. Blue is positive when associated with the Moon, for example, but negative when associated with Jupiter.

Furthermore, there's a difference in hue that the magician normally learns by experience. I was able to differentiate between the negative purple of the Moon and the positive purple of Jupiter by using the term "puce" for the former, since puce is a distinctive shade of purple. Moon blue tends toward grey and silver, while the blue of Jupiter is far more definite and rich. The negative color of the Sun and the positive color of Mercury are both yellow, but the Sun's yellow leans more toward gold. The orange associated with the Sun tends more toward the yellow end of the spectrum while the orange associated with Mercury is more reddish.

All of which brings you to the moment you've been waiting for—the full, detailed instructions for the $100 bill trick. Here's how to proceed.

The $100 Bill Trick

Start on the first day of the month. Leave aside fifteen minutes to half an hour each morning and each evening. Determine not to miss a single day or night for the next four weeks—unless, that is, results come quicker than you thought.

Sit, or lie down, whichever you find most comfortable. Begin the 2/4 breathing sequence as described in

Chapter Four. If you've been practicing as instructed, 2/4 breathing will trigger off the relaxation response. Should you notice any tension, get rid of it by the conscious relaxation process. A good clue to complete relaxation is that your body and limbs tend to feel heavy, so that any movement is an effort.

Now activate the Middle Pillar centers by visualization and vibration of the words of power (again, see Chapter Four).

Having broken down the barriers by relaxation and set up the channels via the Middle Pillar spheres, your next job is to circulate the power obtained throughout your aura. One easy and effective method for doing this goes as follows.

Throw your mind to the topmost sphere. On an outbreath, which, you recall, is being done to the count of four, visualize a sheet of light emanating from the sphere and traveling down the left side of your body. Try to feel the sensation as this light passes down the side of your head and on down your body, moving just beneath the skin and glowing through it. Imagine too that as the main sheet passes, it leaves a strong afterglow. The whole thing in some respects is like the sweep of the light arm on a radar screen.

As the light reaches your feet, it will, of course, become absorbed into the shining bottom sphere. In terms of your 2/4 breathing, the downward sweep took place to the count of four on an outbreath and the absorption into the lowest sphere lasts for a two count with the breath held outside the body.

On your next inbreath, again to the count of four, visualize the light traveling upward, following a similar path along the right-hand side of your body until it reunites once more with the uppermost sphere for a count of two with breath retained.

(Spelled out, the sequence seems complicated, but in practice it is easy enough and will soon become a fluid, semi-automatic movement or visualized light.)

Repeat the process until you can feel the effects of the flow, which probably will not be in less than half a dozen circuits.

Once this is achieved, set up a second circuit. This time the light should travel downward over your face and the front of your body, returning upward along your back. You will obviously have to visualize a broader beam, but otherwise the breathing sequence remains identical. Again, continue for at least half a dozen circuits.

Recapitulating briefly, you have at this stage broken the barriers between yourself and the spiritual sea by relaxation. You have formed the channels for and transformers of the power flow by activating the Middle Pillar. And you have circulated the power through your aura by rhythmical descent and ascent of light. You have, in short, charged your being with an unusual type of energy. It remains only to direct it.

Since your heart burns with desire for a $100 bill, it is necessary to attune yourself to its astrological association. But which association? Do you go for Jupiter, associated with prosperity and finance, Mercury for a little help in business, Saturn in the hope somebody might repay a long-forgotten $100 debt, or the Sun with its bright associations with gold and money?

The reality is you could use any one of them and achieve results—after a fashion. Quite obviously you won't get repayment of a debt if you've never loaned a penny in your life. Equally obviously, activating your business interests just won't hack it if you're unemployed. Jupiter looks a much better bet, except that the influence here is broadly based, a general betterment of your finances and well-being. If you want to hit the target with precision; that is, you want a clear-cut return of $100 (perhaps to prove to yourself the system really works beyond all question of coincidence), then select the simple hard currency association of the Sun.

The positive color association of the Sun is orange. Avoid it like the plague. You'd only use that one if you wanted to create a situation in which you could send one of your own $100 bills outward, perhaps as a gift to a friend. Instead, in this operation, you will use the negative color association.

Consult the chart and you'll find the negative colors for the Sun are yellow or gold. You can strengthen the association in strictly common-sense terms by working with the latter. Visualize the color gold strongly. Feel it permeate your being until you reach the stage where, in your mind's eye, your entire aura glows with golden light.

Next, picture the $100 bill clearly. Picture it in your possession. The exact circumstances of its arrival do not matter so long as you visualize with confidence, the sort of utter confidence you would experience if the money was actually in your pocket.

At this stage, only one more step is needed. That final step is one of the most neglected magical secrets of them all—the Opening of the Channels.

There are times when even practicing magicians forget how magic actually works. At some half-conscious level we expect miracles. There's an important difference between magic and miracle. Magic works itself out through perfectly natural, normal circumstances. A miracle breaks the laws of nature. Miracles do happen, of course, but magicians aren't in the business of creating them—we leave that to the saints. So when you want results, don't expect miracles—just coincidences that arise in the normal, everyday course of events.

All of which means that if you don't want your work to be wasted, you must take care to open the channels. This is probably the most important and least appreciated aspect of magical work. When you've performed your ritual, empowered your talisman, contacted your spirits, or saturated your aura with the Sun-associated color of a $100 bill, you've completed the preliminaries. To finish the job, you must open the channels that will allow the desired result to manifest.

What does that mean? It means living and acting in a way that permits your results to occur naturally. Let's suppose you're a freelance designer. You work a ritual to increase your business over the next month. Then you go on vacation for four weeks. It doesn't matter how well you worked the ritual, you won't get results because you closed the channels. There was no way you could do more design work, no way your business could increase, if you went on vacation. If you come back and suddenly find your bank balance has doubled, it's a miracle, not magic.

That's a pretty crude example to illustrate the point. What I'm really saying is that whatever it is you're wishing for, you must continue to work toward it, or at the very least make sure you're in a position to receive it. It's no use undertaking magic to attract a $100 bill if you lock yourself in your room all day and refuse to answer the phone.

In theory, it's perfectly possible to produce the required effect at a single attempt. In practice—especially at first—it will usually be necessary to repeat the process. Some authorities suggest repeating it twice a day, night and morning. Give yourself a month. If the trick hasn't worked by then, revise your technique.

After working with this method for a while, it becomes possible to simplify. An example will show you what I mean.

Years ago, in some occultist publication, I read an article about the magical use of visualization. The author, whose name escapes me, suggested it was only necessary to visualize a situation clearly with intent and it came about. When he was late for an appointment, he had only to visualize a parking space at his destination and, lo!, one was always there waiting for him.

The theory seemed a bit far-fetched, but I tried it. Probably his parking-space example swayed me since it was certainly a minor but recurring irritation in my life. I visualized furiously…and turned a minor irritation into a major problem. Every time I visualized a space, I arrived to find no spaces open. When I forgot, I had at least an even-money chance of parking.

At the time, I had no knowledge of synchronicity and only a superficial knowledge of magic. Had it been otherwise, I might have spotted a clue—the recurrence of a negative effect.

As you perform the Middle Pillar exercises and their associated visualizations, you set up a synchronistic situation. The ritual has a meaning for you. And since there is confidence and belief behind it, whatever strange forces make synchronicity tick are directed in a positive manner.

But as I visualized for parking, I was setting up exactly the reverse situation. I did not believe it was going to work. The theory was ridiculous and the method lacked any element of drama. So synchronicity went into operation in the direction of my belief and made damn sure I could not park the car.

The point is worth remembering: Magic works in the direction of your belief, not necessarily in the direction of your intent. After I learned to use the Middle Pillar, I tried the simpler parking trick again and found it worked. My inner attitude had been reversed.

Once you've achieved the $100 bill trick (and parked your car a few times without too much sweat) you might consider varying the technique you've just learned to achieve an even more worthwhile purpose—cleaning out your aura.

All of us are subject to astral influences from time to time and magicians are more subject than most due to their habit of meeting astral influences halfway. Not all of those influences are pleasant.

Having said that, they're not nearly so unpleasant as the latest crop of horror movies (or, indeed, the dire warnings in some esoteric books) would lead you to believe. I suppose it is possible to meet up with a demon or some other personification of ultimate evil, but in a lifetime of occult work, I've never managed it…nor do I know anybody who has.

I have come across obsessive, sometimes malevolent entities, but their malevolence (and power) is more like the malevolence of a nasty little boy than of Satan. I have also come up against entities that were dangerous in the way a wolf or bear is dangerous—no evil involved—and required knowledgeable, careful handling.

It's quite difficult (although not actually impossible) to overreach yourself in magic. When you're a young, brash, rash beginner—I remember it well—you lack the training and experience to generate the sort of situations likely to cause real problems. And by the time you develop the power, you've usually learned enough techniques and common sense to deal with them.

But if your dramatic astral conflicts are some distance down the road, it's never too early to learn the basic elements of occult hygiene. My experience has been that virtually everyone engaged in esoteric work, particularly healing and magic, picks up astral leeches the way dog-handlers pick up fleas.

Astral leeches are little mindless entities that attach themselves to the aura and absorb energy. Most of the time you're unaware of them, but if your aura is weakened by illness or emotional upset, they can become quite troublesome. Circulating clear light through your aura as you did in preparation for the $100 bill trick, encourages them to drop away. As you practice this circulation in conjunction with the Fountain Exercise (see the end of Chapter Four) regularly over a period of time, your aura takes on a polished "mirror" surface that prevents the little critters fastening on in the first place.

(For those of you who can't wait, it's also possible to get rid of astral leeches by "combing." Paracelsus invented a delightful magical trident for this purpose, terrifyingly fortified with words of power—see his *Archidoxes of Magic*, published in facsimile by Samuel Weiser, New York—but you don't actually need it. Having a friend simply run their fingers through your aura will usually do the trick— but make sure they're in good health, otherwise they run the risk of picking up your castoffs.)

This cleansing of the aura should become your habitual conclusion to all esoteric work, but particularly that which involves contact with elementals or spirits. It's exactly like brushing your teeth after a meal to cut down on the bacteria that cause plaque, or washing your hands after you've picked up something dead.

As your aura takes on a polish, it generates an interesting additional benefit. But I almost hesitate to mention it, because beginners often try to use magical protections to achieve physical plane results—and this is almost always a mistake. An astral fortress will protect your astral valuables, but if you want to keep the burglars off your jewels, call a security company and have them install an alarm system.

Having said that, astral magic can influence the physical world in various subtle ways. Not so very long ago, psychologists in the United States carried out a fascinating survey in which they showed convicted muggers movies of urban street scenes and asked them who in the milling crowds they would select to attack.

The muggers were surprisingly consistent, both in their choice of victims and in identifying those passersby whom they would avoid attacking. When obvious factors like physical size and signs of prosperity were eliminated, it became obvious that certain people "broadcast" subtle signals inviting attack while others broadcast equally subtle warnings that effectively keep muggers at bay.

The one-to-one impact of a skilled, high-grade magician can sometimes be considerable. In most cases, this is due to the amount of energy running in the magician's aura, exercised, polished, and stimulated by years of inner practice. I won't guarantee that keeping your aura exercised will protect you from physical harm.

But it can't hurt.

Six

Occult Eccentricities

Returning from a stroll one summer afternoon, Mrs. Hilda Morgan, a guest of my then-landlord, walked through a thicket and came upon a wood nymph.

Mrs. Morgan was elderly, but there was nothing wrong with her eyesight. The entity, in the shape of a beautiful young girl with long brown legs and long blonde hair, dipped its toes in a pool beneath the trees.

I was very familiar with the spot. The pool was artificial, some centuries old, arid, and disused. It was fed, via a sluice, from a little stream. The mechanism of the sluice was rusted and it is doubtful if it had been opened within living memory. Besides, an outlet in the bottom of the pool remained free: rainwater failed to collect, even in the sharpest downpour.

Mrs. Morgan knew all this as well as I. Yet the pool, she said, was brimful of crystal water when she saw it.

Did she, I asked, say anything to the creature? Mrs. M. looked shocked. "Good heavens no! It certainly

wasn't my place to speak to such an ethereal being."
She paused, then added, "She had such a lovely aura."

I had never seen a wood nymph and the thought of
talking to someone who had met one such a short time
before excited me enormously. I tried to guess what my
own reactions would have been under the circumstances. "If you didn't speak to her, what did you do?" I
asked. Mrs. Morgan's calm eyes focused on my own and
a faint expression of surprise crossed her features. "I was
rather late for tea," she said, "so I walked on down to
the house."

In fiction, people suddenly faced with the occult
behave in all sorts of dramatic ways. In life—it least so far
as my experience goes—their behavior is simply eccentric. Who, faced with a wood nymph, would worry about
being late for tea? Only, one might imagine, such a civi-
lized and genteel lady as Mrs. Morgan. But one would be
wrong. Swept up in the experience of the preternatural,
the varieties of human reaction seem endless.

On Easter Sunday, a friend arrived to say he'd seen
a leprechaun in the late afternoon or early evening of
Good Friday. Curiously enough, the apparition had
appeared quite close to the spot where Mrs. Morgan
came across her wood nymph.

Hollywood and the toy industry have made leprechauns silly nowadays, but they have always been a
serious enough part of Irish folklore. But for some reason, it remains easier to believe in wood nymphs and I
was immediately convinced my friend was joking. But it
soon became obvious that he was not.

He was planting trees in the little wood when a sound caused him to look up. Sitting on a stump, watching him with interest, was a leprechaun—or, at least, something very strange.

It may be as well to explain at this stage that the wood in question is on private property in Ireland, considerably distant from the road. It is not a spot where one might expect to find casual callers.

The creature on the stump was small, masculine, and old. In telling me about it, my friend mentioned that at first glance, he assumed it was a child of four or five years old. But it was quite close and the features were those of a little old man. The clothing was all wrong too. Modern children tend to wear light colors. This soul had clothed himself in dark, rough homespun.

To those who have never seen one, leprechauns are fiction, foolishness, or lunacy. But such convictions are difficult to maintain when faced by a creature who looks like a leprechaun in all Irish wood. All the ancient folklore about the Little People comes flooding back. A suspicion creeps in: Could so many generations of the Irish have believed in leprechauns if there wasn't something behind it? Perhaps some subtle vibrations in the air of Ireland open the eyes to an Otherworld where fantasies become reality.

My friend was no fool (he held an M.A. from Oxford). Although neither a psychic nor a mystic, he had enough self-confidence to believe the evidence with his own eyes. He concluded that, unlikely though the situation might be, he was looking at a leprechaun.

He also concluded that any searching analysis of the experience would have to wait. Just then, the important thing was to establish contact.

With some vague notion that the Little People must speak Gaelic, he searched his limited vocabulary of that language and came up with the only phrase he knew that seemed even vaguely appropriate. My friend greeted the leprechaun with the words, "Erin go bra!"

At this point, the account becomes less than clear. It may be that the leprechaun replied—for it made some sound—but the words were indistinct or the language strange. In any case, my friend was unable to communicate. He became excited, so that, later, he was unable to recall exactly what he said. But he said something, and waved his arms.

There were two frisky terriers in the vicinity. They belonged to my friend and, bored by his tree-planting activities, had wandered off in search of rats or rabbits. Now, however, they began to race back, barking, attracted by the noise.

My friend heard them and turned to shout, "Keep back! Keep back!" He wanted no dogs worrying his leprechaun. The dogs stopped obediently, but when my friend turned again, the leprechaun had vanished.

Had my friend studied folklore, he might have remembered the tradition that, to catch a leprechaun, you must never, never take your eyes off him…

How much credibility can we attach to such stories? I knew Mrs. Morgan only a short time, but she struck me as a scrupulously honest woman. She was perceptive and

serious-minded; interested in the occult, but hardly credulous. None of these qualities guarantees immunity from
hallucination, but the essence of hallucination for the
insane is its fascination. You do not simply leave your
hallucination behind because you are a little late for tea.

My friend is a slightly different case, for he was not
above playing an occasional practical joke. Was he joking in this case? I doubt it. The trouble with reporting
you have seen a leprechaun or wood nymph is that the
joke's on you. People assume, almost as a matter of
course, that you are being silly, or perhaps mad.

Since these curious manifestations took place, I
have discovered that at least two pieces of alleged physical evidence for leprechauns exist in Ireland. One is a
little shoe, hand-stitched and beautifully made to fit a
mature (but tiny) foot. The other is a pair of gloves, discovered packed into a walnut shell and walled into the
mortar of an old house. Examination of these artifacts
soon shows they were not designed for children: the
proportions are all wrong. If we leave the Little People
out of our considerations for a moment, we fall back on
two possibilities—they were made for midgets or as
curios. Midgets are rare, curios less so. People do still
engrave the Lord's Prayer on the head of a pin.

But what makes these little curios so very unlikely
is the material of which they are made. The shoe has
some of the properties of leather, but is not leather. The
gloves are stranger still, having the feel of silk and the
strength of nylon, but being, in fact, neither. If we were
talking of the modern age, we might speculate that the

material was a synthetic. The shoe was, however, discovered prior to the development of modern synthetics. The gloves, while a much more recent discovery, were walled up for more than half a century.

I have other, less tangible reasons for a suspicion that leprechauns may really exist. Many years after the sighting in the wood, I was showing an overseas visitor around a stone circle in County Cork when she fell spontaneously into trance. Her blank eyes swept around the circle, then looked beyond it as she started to describe what she was seeing.

The circle, she said, was the physical aspect of a mystic gateway to other worlds, a sort of inter-dimensional crossroads where creatures from the beyond could pass into realms other than their own. On the inner levels, the site was bustling with activity. Beyond the circle in the trees, we were being watched by tall, slender, featureless creatures with silver skins. Closer to hand, cheerful little people rode furiously around us on tiny horses.

It was, of course, a subjective vision and may have been nothing more than the product of the visitor's unconscious. But all the same, I wondered. She had little detailed knowledge of Irish mythology, yet the tall, slender watchers sounded suspiciously like descriptions of the ancient *Sidhe* (pronounced *She*) race believed to share Ireland with humanity. I was also interested not so much in the Little People, who are well known outside Ireland, but in their little horses—and for a very personal reason.

Jim Henry is a rally driver who runs his own motor mechanic business in Ireland. In the early 1970s, he and his wife were visiting some friends who had recently moved into a remote country estate. The night of their visit was Halloween, a time when, by tradition, ghosts and spirits walk abroad.

Over the course of the evening, influenced both by the fact it was Halloween and, quite possibly, by the quantities of home-brewed beer being drunk, the conversation turned to matters weird and mysterious.

The hosts—a journalist and his wife—mentioned that on the estate, some distance from the house, was a prehistoric standing stone with a circular embankment of earth around it. This site, known as a *rath,* was believed locally to be the focus of all sorts of mysterious happenings. Years before, for example, an old woman out gathering firewood had broken some branches off a "fairy thorn" near its entrance and was found lying dead on the spot the next morning. Furthermore, cattle that grazed in the field sur-rounding the rath never entered the rath itself. Some strange force seemed to keep them out.

Henry was intrigued and asked his host if he might visit this rath. The host agreed, but there was a problem. It was raining heavily that night and very dark. The rath lay more than a mile away, through a wood, over fields and across a stream. It would be difficult, if not impossible, to reach it unless the weather cleared.

At this point, the little party decided to try something peculiar. They had read that certain primitive tribes were able to make rain by means of magical ceremonies. They decided to see if they could work the magic in reverse and make the rain stop.

Not altogether seriously, they burned quantities of incense and called on the rain to go away. At first, nothing happened. Then, about 11:20 P.M., the weather suddenly cleared to bright moonlight with no more than a few scudding clouds, and the host said a visit to the rath was now possible.

Both the hostess and Judy Henry, Jim Henry's wife, decided to forego the trip. Henry and his journalist friend dressed warm, pulled on Wellington boots, and set off at approximately 11:40 P.M. They reached the rath only a moment or two short of midnight.

The rath was set on high ground. Jim Henry and his host entered the earthwork ring through a gap in the structure near the fairy thorn that (according to legend) had killed the old woman.

Inside the ring, the ground sloped upward like an inverted saucer, with the massive standing stone in the exact center. Around the stone, about six feet distant from it, was a low metal fence put up when the site was excavated by archaeologists in the 1930s.

Henry's host remarked that there was an open cyst grave immediately below the standing stone. The archaeologists had found ancient bones in it—of a woman and a wolfhound.

Together Jim Henry and his friend walked over to the fence and stood looking up at the stone. After a moment, Henry began to feel distinctly uneasy. It seemed as if hidden eyes were watching him. The hair on the back of his neck began to prickle. It was, he knew, now midnight on Halloween.

"I don't think this place likes me," he told his host.

"Do you want to leave?" asked the journalist.

Jim Henry nodded. The two turned away from the standing stone and started to walk back toward the entrance. As they did so, a herd of about twenty-five tiny, pure-white horses, none larger than a spaniel dog, appeared at the top of the earthwork, galloped a distance of about twenty yards, then disappeared down the slope at the far side.

Henry and his host looked at one another, then broke into a run. They emerged from the earth-work only seconds later, but there was no sign of the tiny horses anywhere. They then climbed to the top of the earthwork and examined the soft ground with the aid of an electric torch. There were no hoofprints or marks of any sort.

The following day, the host made inquiries. He found there were neither horses, cattle, nor sheep grazing in the vicinity of the rath at that time. But he also discovered there were persistent legends of "fairy" or "ghost" horses associated with certain prehistoric sites. The legends insisted the beasts were white, much smaller than ordinary horses, and that they left no traces on the ground.

It would be comforting to decide Jim Henry was a little the worse for drink and making up the tale, but that conclusion has never been open to me. The journalist who accompanied him was myself. I saw the horses with my own eyes.

Fascinating though such evidence may be, I tend to believe Mrs. Morgan and my friend for less tangible reasons. They behaved in an eccentric manner. One went home for tea, the other waved his arms and shouted, *"Erin go bra!"* Such odd reactions in the face of the unknown have, to me, an absolutely genuine ring about them. They are not exactly what I would do in similar circumstances, but they are the type of thing that I would do.

I am very much aware how easily eccentricity manifests in circumstances like these, for once I found myself trying to defeat a lie-detector with a nursery rhyme. And there is nothing more eccentric than that!

✯✯✯✯

Yoga, to the West, means Hatha Yoga. But there are other branches of this great Oriental system. One of them is Mantra Yoga and it is probably the least understood Way of Union with the One.

A mantra is a sound, or series of sounds, used as an aid to meditation. It is often thought of as the Oriental counterpart of the Western words of power, but this is not altogether true. The immediate mechanics of the two are different. As explained earlier, words of power are vibrated in the West to open psychic channels. They can also be used to bring semi-autonomous complexes (the new name for spirits) to the surface of consciousness. At their most spectacular level, they can evoke the archetypes (gods) themselves.

A mantra does something very different. Properly used, it sets up a closed circuit in the mind, forcing the attention in a specific direction, opening the way to ecstatic experience..

There are many examples of a mantra. The simplest and most widely known is *Om*. Om is a written symbol of the basic background vibration of the universe. This is a lot less esoteric than it may appear. If you find a quiet spot, still your mind, and listen, you can hear the vibration for yourself. Although perhaps "hear" is the wrong word. You will experience the vibration largely as sound, but part of it will be felt rather than heard: and a further part will be largely psychic in origin.

The vibration is worth listening for. It gives you the key to the mystery of pronouncing Om, which is hummed rather than spoken. The best approach is to break the word into three syllables: *aw-uh-mmmm*.

Om is frequently expanded into a sonorous phrase that is also widely used as a mantra—*Om mane padme hum*. If you take the subjective viewpoint, the words are translated "Hail to the jewel in the lotus." As such they salute the essence of the uppermost sphere in our diagram of the psychic channels. In the West, this sphere is referred to Kether on the Tree of Life. In the East, it is associated with The Thousand-Petaled Lotus, the sahasrara-padma chakra located at the crown of the head. Should you prefer an objective (i.e., cosmic) viewpoint, a better translation of the manta might be "Hail to Thee the Ever-Becoming One."

On its own, Om is repeated with a rise-and-fall rhythm, like a sine graph. The full phrase, however, will give you a better example of the essentially circular nature of a mantra. In visual terms, a mantra is a ring of elephants or a snake swallowing its own tail.

Try repeating *Om mani padme hum* a few times. Pace the words evenly, half humming the natural rhythm of the phrase. You will soon find that the final *hummmm* blends into the initial *aummmmm* to form an integrated circular sequence.

This is a natural sequence in a mantra and the key to its effect. If you have ever been plagued by a tune that you can't get out of your head, you will know what the effect is like. With a mantra, however, you remain in control of the situation.

To establish the closed circuit, repeat the mantra aloud, slowly and evenly. Make sure there is a distinct pause between each repetition. Now speed up. Close the pause down gradually until you are repeating a single circular phrase. The next step is to let your voice die away, taking up the mantra mentally, so that it seems the mantra, which began as a spoken phrase, is gradually absorbed into the mind.

Continue to speed up until you have reached the stage where the mantra is spinning mentally. At this stage, you will find it continues, as it were, of its own accord. In fact, the spin has been taken up by your unconscious mind.

As with most magical techniques, it is inadvisable to overdo the practice in the early stages. Build up your efficiency at a slow and steady rate, gradually increasing the length of time you keep the mantra spinning.

The Yoga adept trains his concentration to the point where he can fix his attention on a single thing for incredibly long periods of time. He forces all other considerations, all other thoughts, from his mind. He holds to one thing and waits.

What he waits for is absorption. As he forces out all distractions, he moves toward a simple, basic duality—the observer and the observed. But when he reaches the duality and holds the awareness of it, a strange thing happens: he ceases to differentiate between his self and the observed. The Yogi becomes his thought, and since his thought is single, he becomes single too. He has merged with the focus of attention. He has become One.

The mantra is a powerful technique for forcing the mind in the required direction. Its spin throws off intruding thoughts until the person becomes the mantra—but it is seldom wise to start something you can't stop. Stopping a spinning mantra requires a reversal of the process that began it in the first place. Slow the spin gradually, then externalize the mantra by speaking it aloud. Slow further until the circle is broken by ever-lengthening pauses, then stop.

Om mani padme hum is Indian in origin, forming part of Buddhist practice. So many excellent mantras have come out of India that Westerners tend to conclude that great continent has a monopoly on the product. But this is not so. Many cults in many countries have coined phrases that act as mantras. A useful example from the Middle East is *Hua allahu alazi lailaha illa Hua* (He is the One God and there is no other God but He). For many others, consult the useful sourcebook *Words of Power* by Brian and Esther Crowley.

A lie-detector is a machine designed to measure certain subtle changes in the human body. It works because mind and body are closely interlinked. We can maintain a poker face while we tell a brazen lie, but we cannot control a host of tiny physical symptoms of the untruth. We cannot, for instance, halt the slight rise in blood pressure, the minute tension of the muscles, the faint stimulation of the sweat glands that result from our attempted deception.

These changes pass unnoticed in the average person unless quite delicate measuring instruments are used. One of the simplest devices meters the rate at which the skin conducts electricity. This rate varies with our emotional state. An instrument measuring the variations is an efficient enough lie-detector, although perhaps "emotion detector" would be a better term.

In a room used for the meetings of an esoteric organization that interested me, I sat having my emotions measured. After a while, the success of the machine began to annoy me. Finally it became a challenge. I decided to apply the mantra principle in the hope of deadening my reactions. I succeeded completely.

The "mantra" used was more familiar than those quoted from India and the Middle East. It ran:

Twinkle, twinkle, little star,
How I wonder what you are,
Up above the world so high,
Like a diamond in the sky.

Eccentric reactions...eccentric techniques. I sometimes wonder if eccentricity may not be the trademark

of the magical and the occult. But you have to be careful. Witness the following fascinating account.

Alfred Sutro was being driven along a country road
by his chauffeur when he heard a sound. Although not
absolutely certain, he thought it might be a child crying
and asked his chauffeur to stop.

The car pulled to the side of the road and Sutro
asked the driver if he could hear anything. The chauffeur
listened, then shook his head. He could hear nothing.
But Sutro could. In fact he could hear a child crying so
clearly now that he was able to follow the sound behind
some trees and down a slope to the bank of a river.

There he found a pretty little girl of three or four,
sobbing bitterly and soaking wet. Sutro realized she
must have fallen into the river. He gathered her up and
carried her back to the car, but could not get her to stop
crying long enough to tell him what had happened.

When he asked where she lived she would not tell
him, but then Sutro pointed ahead and she nodded. He
instructed the chauffeur to drive on. Only a short distance away they came to a gate. The child became
excited and pointed toward it. Sutro instructed his
chauffeur to drive in.

They traveled up the driveway to the front door of a
largeish house. As Sutro got out and headed for the door,
a man and woman rushed out, both very obviously upset.

"Have you any news of the child?" the woman asked.

"She's in my car," Sutro told her, greatly relieved.

But when they went back to the car, it was empty
except for the chauffeur.

"Where's the little girl?" Sutro asked.

The chauffeur looked at him blankly. "What little girl?"

"The child I brought in the car," Sutro said.

"You didn't bring any child in the car," his puzzled chauffeur replied.

Accompanied by the parents of the missing child, they drove back to the riverbank. There was the body of the little girl, drowned in a few feet of water. Sutro had carried back her ghost!

Alfred Sutro is an actual person. He was a well-known, successful, and respected playwright. He told the tale of the ghostly child in an autobiography, *Celebrities and Simple Souls*, published in 1933. It was, he said, the only psychic experience he ever had.

The dramatic details of the story are oddly convincing. The little lost girl...the worried parents racing from the house in case their visitor had news...just the sort of thing you would expect to happen if their daughter had gone missing.

What's more, it ties in quite well with the sort of ghost reports you hear elsewhere. There is, for example, a ghost called Resurrection Mary in Chicago. This young girl is frequently reported to accept lifts from cars passing the Resurrection Cemetery where she was buried following her death in 1939.

But Alfred Sutro's story is untrue. We know this because Sutro himself admitted it. He made up the whole thing to show how easy it was to fool people who believed in the supernatural. He told the story to lots of people and listened smugly as they put forward theories about what happened. Nobody, he said, ever gave him the real explanation…which was that he was lying.

Even without the admission, simple logic casts doubt on the tale of the ghost girl. Sutro claimed he was traveling in a chauffeur-driven car. Nothing unlikely about that: He was a highly successful playwright who could easily afford to employ a driver. But then, while being driven, he heard what he thought was a child crying. He called on the chauffeur to stop and followed the sound through some trees to a riverbank.

This, of course, is nonsense. Driving in a car, you would not be able to hear a child crying who was standing by the side of the road, let alone some distance from it through a clump of trees. You might, of course, object that Sutro only thought he heard the sound—that, in other words, he was psychic. But why then did he not find it strange? He does, after all, say that this ghost story was "his only psychical experience," yet he mentions the crying as if it was the most ordinary thing in the world.

This is not the only weak spot in the story. Sutro claimed that when he found the little girl, he picked her up and carried her back to the car. Later, however, the chauffeur was supposed to have said there was no child in the car at any time. If both these statements were correct, then Sutro must have looked very odd carrying an invisible child. Why didn't his driver ask him what he was doing?

Worse still, Sutro was trying to persuade the girl to stop crying and tell him where she lived. Didn't the driver wonder why his boss had started talking to himself?

Arriving at the house, Sutro got out of the car and was met by the parents—leaving the child behind. Bear in mind that at this time he was supposed to believe the child was a living, breathing, not to say dripping wet, youngster. Surely, if he thought he had found her home, he would have carried her to the door. Or, if he really did decide to leave her in the car, wouldn't he have handed the sobbing bundle to his driver, or at very least asked the man to keep an eye on her?

These are small enough details in themselves, but they add up. And what they add up to is the clear conclusion that Sutro was making up his story.

It may seem a strange thing to say, but I believe every magician owes a debt of gratitude to the late Alfred Sutro. Should you ever be accepted for training in any of the more traditional Lodges of the Western Esoteric Tradition, your very first lesson will be concerned with two qualities vital to the practice of magic.

The first of these is discretion. A magician must learn to keep his mouth shut—to preserve power, avoid ridicule, and protect the uninitiated.

But the second is, if anything, even more important: Discrimination. You will be told many weird and wonderful things in your pursuit of magical truth. Remember Alfred Sutro and don't believe everything you hear. An interest in magic gives no one the right to leave their common sense behind.

Seven

Gold and Ghosts

Virtually anything can be put to a magical use. I learned this lesson not from a magician, but from a BBC news reader. Aware of my interest in oddities, he dragged me away from the main body of a spirited party and whispered, "I can tell you what to do with your coat hangers…"

It is not, unfortunately, a case of any old coat hanger. What you need are the wire ones laundries use for your dry cleaning. If you look in a closet, chances are you'll find half a dozen you've saved up for emergencies. Take two and accept the fact that you are about to ruin them for hanging clothes. You are, however, about to build a very versatile magical implement.

First, untwist one of the coat hangers. You will find it is comprised of a single piece of wire that is twisted together at the hook. Straighten the whole thing out as best you can. You will find it straightens reasonably well, except for the hook part, which you can safely ignore for the moment.

Trim the difficult ends off with wire cutters and bend the remainder into an L shape. The shorter leg of the L should be quite short, about six to eight inches. Exact size is not critical, but since you'll be using this end as a hand grip, make sure it's comfortable.

Step One

Start with your basic wire coat-hanger.

Step Two
Untwist, so it begins to open out.

Step Three
Bend into a rough L-shape.

Step Four
Use wire cutters to trim the ends.

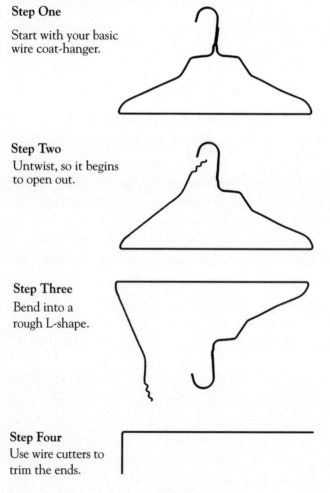

Figure 9

When you have completed the L, untwist the second coat hanger and make a duplicate of the first. Together they form an instrument that will detect water, gold, or ghosts.

Don, my friend from the BBC, discovered the magical use of coat hangers from an unlikely source. A Major in the Royal Engineers had developed them as an implement for water divining. Unlike the common hazel twig, he claimed the coat hangers could detect metals and ceramics as well as water.

At the time, Don was something of a skeptic. But he followed the Major's instructions and found, to his surprise, he had charted the location of an Army underground water tank. Subsequent experiments convinced him his talent with the coat hangers was not unique. Most people could work them once they knew how.

I quickly discovered they could detect just about any metal you cared to name. Steve Peek, a U.S. veteran of the Vietnam War, told me American troops had used them to find land mines in preference to the sophisticated electronic detectors issued by the Army.

The *modus operandi* is simplicity itself. To use your dowsing rods, hold each one loosely by the short leg (see figure 10).

Figure 10

That word "loosely" is important. The rods should be able to swing easily, left and right, so a light grip is what you want.

Becoming a dowser takes a little practice. The best place to start is on any piece of land where you know there is an underground stream or water main. Ideally, you should know the exact location of the watercourse.

It is important that the water is running water, which is one of the easiest things to detect. Start out some distance from where you know the watercourse to run and hold your two rods parallel (see figure 11).

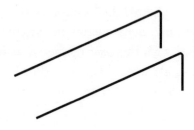

Figure 11

Grip them loosely, exactly as shown in figure 10. (I haven't drawn in the hands in figure 11 so you could see exactly how the rods should be held.)

Now, tucking your elbows into your sides and moving slowly, walk in a line that will take you across the underground watercourse, roughly at right angles.

As you cross the stream or pipe, you will find that the two long arms of the rods swing slowly inward and cross (see figure 12).

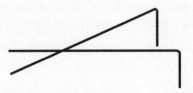

Figure 12

Absolutely no effort on your part is needed. Hold the rods loosely, walk slowly, and they will swing and cross entirely of their own accord.

If you're too impatient to make coat hanger rods, you can rig up workable substitutes using paper clips and the tops from two ball-point pens. Straighten out the clips, then form them into the same L shape as you would the coat hangers. Drop the short leg of each L into a pen top so the longer end swings freely. You'll look as if you've stolen dowsing rods from a leprechaun, but they still work perfectly.

Like so much magical activity, there is an enormous amount of suggestion involved in operating dowsing rods. Your first experiment will be the "detection" of a bowl of water on the kitchen floor. As you pass over the bowl, the wires will cross simply because you have suggested to your unconscious that they should.

The next most common form of experiment, detecting underground drains or waste pipes, is only a little more sophisticated. Here again, the wires will cross easily enough—but most people are perfectly well aware of where the drains are located. Even if you have never thought of it consciously, logic could still provide you with the most likely path of an outlet and the unconscious mind is far from stupid.

When I became reasonably proficient, I taught the system to three unquestioning novices. To determine how far suggestion went, I gave them a list of purely arbitrary rules. I told them initially that if a penny was held in the hand, the wires would cross when held above a penny on the floor. And so they did.

I then suggested that if the penny in the hand was changed for a sixpence, the wires would cross over another sixpence, but swing outward if held above a penny since copper and silver were "antagonistic" metals. Again the coat hangers behaved as predicted.

Finally, I stretched credibility to the limit. I would imagine a bowl of water on a certain (well-defined) spot on the floor. The wires would cross as they picked up this "thought-form." In two cases they did. In the third, nothing happened. The girl who held the wires that didn't cross told me she believed the whole business of "thought-forms" was nonsense.

In face of this, there would seem to be little doubt that the it is the unconscious mind that operates the wires, and not subtle emanations from water, silver, copper, or dubious thought-forms. But despite the element of suggestion, the coat hangers cannot be dismissed as merely an example of a psychological novelty. Nor can the pendulum, which is a slightly more complicated way of achieving the same results.

You can make a pendulum quite easily. All you really need is a small weight and a length of thread.

Metal beads work well for the weight since they already have a hole for the thread to pass through. Wood works well too and looks good if you polish it up.

You may even find a small weight like the one in figure 13, with a loop to which you can attach the thread. Don't look for anything particularly heavy: if you are trying to use something that weighs more than an ounce, then the whole thing is getting out of control. Half an ounce is usually ample.

The only warning I should give you is to avoid synthetic materials like nylon or plastic for your weight since these do not seem to work as well as metal, stone, or wood.

Try to avoid using thread with a twist, unless you are absolutely desperate. This rules out most of the cotton threads you will find in the average family sewing box, which, if you look closely, are all made up of even finer strands wrapped around each other.

Nylon thread, which is stronger, is often a single filament without any twist at all. In order to get some, you should go to a sporting goods store or

Figure 13

bait shop and ask for monofilament fishing line. You will be able to get your weight there, too.

When you first make up your pendulum, use at least a yard of thread—two yards if you have it. This is far more than you will need in practice, but it allows you to "tune" the pendulum accurately. But before embarking on experiments, it is necessary to determine for yourself the "wavelength" of various items.

A divining pendulum will make one of two movements—backward and forward, or in a circle. Traditionally, a pendulum of the correct length will swing backward and forward if held over the hand of a man, and describe a circular movement if held over the hand of a woman. This association is so strongly established that you will often find the pendulum used to determine the sex of an unborn child. How successful this is in practice I have no idea. But I know it works for other things.

Before you can start using the pendulum, you need to decide what you want to use it for. Let's suppose that, like the Faustian adepts, you want to find gold. Take the handiest piece—such as a wedding ring or similar piece of jewelry—and hold the pendulum over it. Chances are that absolutely nothing will happen. Now slowly adjust the length of the thread, pausing frequently. Sooner or later you will find a length at which the pendulum describes a circle over the gold. With a permanent felt-tip pen, mark this length on the thread.

If you can resist the urge to go prospecting right away, you can make a multi-purpose pendulum. Simply repeat the process with, say, tin, copper, and silver, marking the length each time.

The one danger in the process is self-deception. Make no attempt to move the pendulum yourself: just let things happen. Like the coat hangers, the pendulum is a tap to your unconscious mind. Prepare it properly. The results are well worth the effort.

Where the pendulum scores in practice is that it does not need to be held over an object to determine its presence. Try the following trick and, as the ads say, astound your friends.

Have someone hide a gold object somewhere in a room. You are not engaged in conjuring, so don't try to listen or work out where the item might be. Once it's safely stowed away, come in with your pendulum. (It goes without saying that the pendulum should be adjusted to the gold "wavelength.")

Take up a position near the door. Hold the pendulum in your left hand and set it swinging to and fro. Now hold out your right hand and sight along it as if you were pointing. Move your right hand slowly and systematically, so that eventually it will have pointed to all parts of the room. At some stage in this maneuver, you will find the pendulum changes its swing from a back-and-forth motion to a circle. When this happens, you are pointing at the object.

I had better admit that while almost everyone can work the coat hangers, the trick with the pendulum seems to call for a special talent—but even here the talent is far from rare. From my own experiments, I would conclude that the number of people able to find hidden objects in this way is well over fifty percent.

You can take all of this into very occult realms as first demonstrated during 1994 by a small psychical research group in Sweden. In a report published by the prestigious Society for Psychical Research in London, they described their basic experiment as follows.

First you dowse around outdoors until you find an area where water lines are either very scarce or don't exist. In other words, an area where you don't get many dowsing reactions.

Next, a "sender" goes out into that area and mentally selects a target. The target can be anything the sender wants—a spire on the horizon, a nearby bush, or anything else. The sender then concentrates on the target for a moment, marks the spot where he was standing, then leaves the area. If you want to be really scientific, you can have the sender write down the target and hand it to a third party for verification afterward.

A dowser goes out into the area after the sender leaves and walks slowly around the spot where the sender stood (don't forget this was marked by the sender). When he gets a dowsing reaction, he marks the place. He then moves out and walks around the spot in a wider circle. Once again, he marks any dowsing reaction he might get and does the whole thing again in a wider circle still.

If all goes well, the spots where you get a dowsing reaction will form a straight line that points toward the target. The line formed is known as a psi track—an invisible pathway that is somehow laid down by the mind of the sender.

The Swedes found this doesn't work every time, but if you're prepared to try it a few times over an afternoon, you'll start to get results. They also claim that when you get the knack, you can actually establish the width of the psi track and its height from the ground.

You can use psi tracking to find objects that are purposely hidden. It works even if the target is under water (say in a pond or lake) but the effect can be blocked by certain materials, notably plastic, which acts as a screen.

The researchers in Sweden discovered something else about psi tracking that almost boggles the imagination—the sender does not have to know where the target is. You can get a third party to hide a target, and so long as the sender knows what it is and can visualize it, he will automatically send out a psi track to where it has been hidden.

The implications of these experiments—which you can easily duplicate with the help of a few friends—are profound, especially to anyone interested in magic.

Once you've had a few practice runs, a variety of uses for your rods and pendulum will suggest themselves. One that may not occur to you is ghost hunting.

✮✮✮✮

We had finished dinner in one of Ireland's most delightful stately homes. It was snowing heavily outside, but a huge log fire in the library kept the chill at bay. Our hostess, who was interested in such things, had just told us that the house was haunted.

The information could not have fallen on more delighted ears. My companions included my dear friend Desmond Leslie, a Theosophist and authority on flying saucers, and Kevin, whose past experiences included involuntary etheric projection.

The ghost was a "Grey Lady," an unhappy shade who flitted through the corridors without doing a great deal of harm to anyone. According to Sibyl Leek, a well-known witch and psychic who investigated the phenomenon, she was strongly associated with a particular room.

Had our hostess actually seen the ghost herself? She stared into the fire and nodded. The Grey Lady might be a ghost, but she was certainly not a myth.

We retired from the library to pace the carpeted corridors. None of us was particularly sensitive that night, for no ghost appeared. We asked our hostess if we could see the haunted room. At that stage she suggested an experiment. None of us had been to the house before. None of us knew which of the many rooms was associated with the ghost. Why not test our sensitivity to atmosphere and find it for ourselves?

We tried without success. When inspiration had almost run its course, Desmond suggested using a pendulum. The butler appeared bearing thread and a weight on a silver tray. We constructed our pendulum. No one knew if ghosts had a specific wavelength, but we set it to react when brought close to a woman and hoped the Grey Lady had not lost her femininity along with her life.

It took twenty minutes before Helen found a room in which the pendulum reacted madly.

"Is this it?" she asked.

Our hostess nodded.

The coat hanger dowsing rods will also pick up ghosts—at least those ghosts that stand still long enough to be picked up. My own home developed a cold spot that a clairvoyant diagnosed as "an elemental trapped in a cone of force."

One evening when some friends were amusing themselves with the coat hangers, we suggested trying them out in the corner where out house elemental lived. They did so and an odd thing happened. Instead of crossing, the wires went into reverse, swinging outward. It seemed our elemental involved some form of negative energy.

With pendulum and coat hangers, we have come full circle to the moving glass mentioned in Chapter Two. A discussion of theory is the next step and then, hopefully, on to more important things.

But before we leave Low Magic, it is interesting to take notice of a device which, although bordering on High Magic because of its use, is nonetheless in the same category as the instruments described in this chapter. I discovered the device when introduced to Roy Ogden, a healer who had, in his lifetime, a practice that was the envy of many Dublin doctors. He used, he said, a black box to diagnose illness in his patients.

The "black box," as it happened, turned out not to be a box at all, although it was certainly black. It was, in fact, a solid block of wood with a rubber membrane stretched on top. The whole thing was small enough to slip comfortably into the pocket, not very much larger than a packet of cigarettes.

When diagnosing, Roy had the patient stand in front of him. He would then hold the block aimed, so to speak, at the patient's head and begin to stroke the membrane lightly. As he did so, he would lower the device slowly, covering the whole of the body. As soon as he had reached the seat of the illness, he found that he could no longer stroke the membrane smoothly. It crinkled beneath his fingers.

This is a very specialized use for a tap to the unconscious. Although Roy could see no reason why anyone should fail to be able to use his black box, the fact remained that very few could do so.

Whether your unconscious has a gift for diagnosis is something you can only discover by experiment. A "black box" is easy enough to make. But be extra careful not to take your experiments too far. A lot of patients have died from an acute attack of self-appointed healers.

Eight

Doorways Inward

Walk into any New Age shop and you'll find an embarrassment of Tarot decks. What you won't find very often is information on the magical way to use them.

Occult tradition has it that in the distant depths of prehistory, the world faced a cataclysm—perhaps the destruction of Atlantis—that would wipe out the whole of civilization. Faced with this disaster, Initiates of the Great White Brotherhood (the esoteric Lodge charged with the spiritual welfare of humanity) met to decide how the sacred wisdom could be best preserved.

Many possible solutions were put forward and rejected. Books were too vulnerable, oral traditions too prone to distortion. But eventually it was decided that while civilization might collapse and customs be abandoned, human nature itself would never change. Men and women would always be drawn to gambling.

In face of this insight, the leaders of the Brotherhood decreed that their deepest secrets be expressed in

135

symbolic form and collected together in a deck of cards that could be used for gaming. That way even though the world might sink into chaos, even though humanity might forget the meaning of the symbols, the great secrets would still be preserved, awaiting the day when the light of occult knowledge burned sufficiently bright to rediscover them.

The deck of cards created by the Great White Brotherhood was the Tarot.

How much, if any, truth is vested in this myth I have not the slightest notion. But I do know the Great White Brotherhood is no longer right about the gambling. There was a game of Tarot popular during the Renaissance and in parts of Europe up to the eighteenth century, but you'd be hard put to find anybody who could play it now. Today the Tarot is used, almost universally, for divination or its kissing cousin fortune-telling.

There are seventy-eight cards in a Tarot deck. Fifty-six of them are suits, equivalent, but not identical, to the suits in an ordinary deck of playing cards with one face card (the knight) added. This group is known as the Minor Arcana. The remaining cards are the Tarot Trumps or Major Arcana, twenty-two examples of complex pictorial symbolism that bear no relation whatsoever to anything you'll find in an ordinary deck.

Every card in the Tarot deck has an assigned meaning. The seven of wands, for example, stands for good communication while the ace of swords speaks of authority and stress. I don't propose to list the remaining meanings here, since they've already been published in a thou-

sand modern books about the Tarot—and besides, I'm
going to teach you how to read Tarot a much better way.

But before I do, I'd like to mention another system
of divination that's well worth your attention. This system is the *I Ching*, an oracle that originated in the
depths of Chinese prehistory and is still in widespread
use throughout Asia today.

The term I Ching translates as the Book of Changes
and is among the very oldest published works in the
world. It is based on a series of geometrical figures, sixty-
four in all, each made up of six broken and unbroken
lines. The figures are called hexagrams and, like the
cards of a Tarot deck, each is assigned a traditional
meaning. Since Western interest in the I Ching has not
yet matched interest in the Tarot, I will give both the
hexagrams and their basic meanings here (see figure 14).

Should you buy a copy of the I Ching (as worthwhile an investment for a magician as a Tarot deck),
you'll find the meanings listed here are no more than
the titles of the hexagrams. Far fuller meanings are
assigned to each one in the form of a vividly descriptive
Image and extensive commentaries known as the Judgment. Even the individual lines have meaning.

In consulting the I Ching, hexagrams are generated
in a variety of ways. Perhaps the simplest and least
respected is the use of I Ching wands: sets of bone, ivory,
or wooden sticks drawn at random by the querant and
more often used for fortune telling than serious divination. A rather more profound approach is the Yarrow
Oracle, which involves the ritualistic counting of fifty

Figure 14: The I Ching Hexagrams

dried yarrow stalks, an activity that can generate a degree of trance. But the most popular means of consulting the I Ching is the Coin Oracle, which combines depth with convenience. It is the technique of the Coin Oracle I would like to teach you now.

To use this technique, you'll need three identical coins, a pencil, and paper. Purists insist on ancient Chinese coins, but frankly, any common small coin will work just as well.

First, you must decide which is the front side of the coin and which is the reverse. If the coins you're using have a head stamped on one side, you can take it that's the front. In any case, I propose to call the front of the coin the head side and the reverse the tail side.

Think of the question you want to ask the oracle and write it down at the top of your paper; then toss all three coins together and note how they fall.

The front (heads) side of each coin has the value of two, while the reverse (tails) side has a value of three. This means that if all three coins come down heads, your throw has a value of six. If they're all tails, the value is nine. Two heads and one tail makes seven. Two tails and one head makes eight.

Since you're going to build your hexagram from the bottom upward, start about a third of the way down your paper and draw the first line as follows:

If you throw a six, draw this line: — x —
If you throw a nine, draw this line: — o —
If you throw a seven, draw this line: ———
If you throw an eight, draw this line: — —

Now throw the coins five more times, drawing each new line above the last. When you've finished, you'll have completed a six-line figure that looks something like one of those listed in table 14 except for any —x— or —o— lines you may have generated.

Here's what you need to know about those peculiar-looking lines. A line drawn as ——— is known as a *yang* line. A line drawn as — — is a *yin* line. But when the line appears as —o— it's known as an *old yang*, while —x— is an *old yin*.

The Chinese have always venerated antiquity—an attitude I have come increasingly to appreciate the older I get—so it comes as no surprise to learn that old yangs and old yins have more power than ordinary yangs and yins. So much so, in fact, that they exist on the point of changing into their opposites. An old yang is about to become an ordinary yin. An old yin is on the point of becoming an ordinary yang.

So when you draw a hexagram that contains old yangs (—o—) or old yins (—x—) you have, in fact, generated not one hexagram but two.

Redraw your first hexagram showing any old yangs as ordinary yangs (—o— = ———) and any old yins as ordinary yins (—x— = — —) since this is the way they appear at first. Then draw a second hexagram beside your first, changing the old yangs of your original hexagram into ordinary yins (—o— = — —) and the old yins into ordinary yangs (—x— = ———).

The first of your redrawn hexagrams refers to the situation as it is at present. The second reflects the situation as it can potentially become if you follow the advice of the oracle.

At this point, any orthodox book on the I Ching would refer you to the traditional Images, Judgments, and Commentaries to interpret the hexagrams you've just drawn. But as with the Tarot, I propose instead to teach you the magical method of consulting the I Ching.

In order to do so—at the risk of confusing you completely—I need to tell you something about my personal magical specialty: the tattva doorways to the Astral Plane.

The tattvas are a series of symbols, developed in the Orient but imported into the Western Magical Tradition via the Golden Dawn, which permit access to specific aspects of the Astral. The basic tattva symbols are found in figure 15.

To make use of these doorways, you need first to prepare tattva cards by painting each of the symbols shown in figure 15, in the colors noted, on an individual white card. Each card should be about two and a half to three inches square with a plain white back.

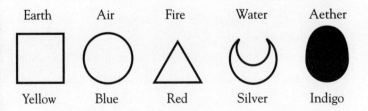

Earth	Air	Fire	Water	Aether
Yellow	Blue	Red	Silver	Indigo

Figure 15

Make the colors as strong and clear as possible—the silver crescent will need metallic silver paint. If you find painting difficult, or do not have access to suitable colors, cut the shapes from colored papers and glue them down.

The cards can be used in one of two ways. The first, safest, and easiest is to relax, close your eyes, enter a meditative state, then place a symbol against your forehead and note what images arise in your mind. Meditate on each of the first four symbols in turn, devoting about fifteen minutes per day to a meditation session and using only one symbol each day. In this way you get a subjective "feel" of each element.

The second method is to select a symbol and sit quietly staring at it until a halo effect develops around it. Then transfer your gaze to any plain white surface like a ceiling, wall, or simply the back of the card. When you do so, you will see a complementary color image of the symbol. (This arises through an optical reflex.) Close your eyes and draw this complementary image into your mind so that you can see it in your imagination. Imagine it existing directly in front of you and enlarge it until it is about six feet high. Then step through the symbol.

Once you have stepped through, you will find yourself aware of the area of the Astral Plane that corresponds to the symbol you have used. Explore the area carefully, making sure you can find your way back to the symbol doorway. When you have familiarized yourself with it, return through the symbol doorway to normal consciousness. (This method is outlined in greater detail in my book *Astral Doorways*, Thoth Publications, Britain, 1996.)

Your experiments with the tattvas may seem a long way from the Tarot and the I Ching, but they're not. The fact is, you can use both the Tarot Trumps (i.e., the Major Arcana) and the I Ching hexagrams as astral doorways. The techniques are slightly different for each, but if you've practiced with the tattvas you should have little difficulty with either.

The Tarot doorway is the simpler of the two. First separate out the trumps from your Tarot deck and shuffle them. Ask your question, draw one card from your partial deck of trumps, and study its imagery for a moment. Close your eyes and visualize the scene on the card as vividly as you can, then step into the scene and begin your exploration. The experience you undergo will have relevance—and hopefully the answer—to your question.

The I Ching doorway is more difficult, but often even more rewarding. Generate your hexagram or hexagrams using the coin oracle exactly as I showed you above. Sit comfortably, relax, close your eyes then visualize the hexagram you have created as painted on a heavy wooden door. (If you generated two hexagrams because of moving lines, you'll have to repeat this whole process twice.) Stare with your inner eye at this mental image and wait.

You may have to wait quite some time. My first attempt at this technique produced no results at all for twenty minutes. But if you persevere, the door will swing open. It's important that you allow this to happen of its own accord and do not simply visualize the door opening. When it does so, mentally walk through. Here again your experience will be relevant to the question that has been troubling you.

The I Ching doorways seem to produce a much more vivid experience than those of the Tarot. The American travel writer William Seabrook tells the story of how, prior to World War II, he was in an apartment overlooking Times Square in New York as part of a small group that included a career diplomat and a Russian émigré he called Magda. They were experimenting with the I Ching and Magda decided to use a hexagram as a doorway.

The hexagram she drew was *Ko* (figure 16), which carries this interpretation.

The Chinese character for this hexagram means in its original sense an animal's pelt, which is changed in the course of the year by molting. From this the word is carried over to apply to the "moltings" in political life, the great revolutions connected with changes of governments.

The two trigrams making up the hexagram are…the two daughters, Li and Tui…here the younger daughter is above. The influences are in actual conflict and the forces combat each other like fire and water (lake), each trying to destroy the other. Hence the idea of revolution.

(This passage is quoted from the Richard Wilhelm translation of the *I Ching*, rendered into English by Cary F. Baynes, Routledge & Kegan Paul, London, 1969.)

Ko
Revolution (Molting)
Above: TUI The Joyous, Lake   Below: LI The Clinging,

Figure 16

The use of the hexagram as a doorway seems to have enabled Magda to tap into a primitive stratum of her objective imagination, for after a moment she was able to tell her companions that she was lying naked "except for a fur coat" in the snow, then that it was moonlight and she was running through the snow at great speed.

Seabrook recalls that her face took on a feral appearance and she began to show indications of aggression and distress. Oblivious to her surroundings, she howled like a wolf. When the men attempted to wake her, she snarled, snapped, and bit at them fiercely. She was physically a strong woman and it was quite a time before they could overpower her and get her out of trance. She had been temporarily possessed by a spirit wolf (or possibly by the spirit Wolf) exactly like the primitive shamans who followed the wolf totem.

The experience of Seabrook's friend indicates there are certain risks associated with magical work. But I think you may find them well worth taking, especially since now you're almost ready to make the transition from Low Magic to High.

Nine

Magíc anô Mínô

Y ou've learned a lot about Low Magic. Now the
time has come to evaluate. For Low Magic,
despite the light-hearted tone of earlier chapters, is important. Some of its basic principles can lead
you to High Magic, and High Magic can lead you to
levels the person in the street will never dream of.

The one common denominator in every example of
magic is mind. Even if you broaden the scope of your
survey, you will find this holds good. A love potion may
be chemical (or, more usually, biochemical) in compo-
sition, but it is designed to change the mind of the person who takes it. A talisman also must first be charged,
one way or another, by a mental operation.

The simplest method I know for charging a talisman is to activate the Middle Pillar, circulate the force,
then, by an act of visualization, pour it into the chosen
object. The operation requires fairly intense concentration, but provided you avoid synthetics, the object will
hold the charge for quite a time.

Even the ancient tradition of elemental servants falls into this category. Historical records of witchcraft are full of references to "familiars"—creatures often thought to take the shape of small animals that assist the witch in her endeavors. Magician were commonly believed to have supernatural assistants as well. This tradition is reflected by Shakespeare in Prospero's spirit Ariel, and in the Medieval belief that Pope Boniface VIII carried a spirit in his finger ring, and made the house shake when he retired to his room to consult with demons.

While it's certain that the familiars of many witches were nothing more sinister than household pets, elemental servants are far from fictional. They are, in fact, controlled poltergeists and, as psychical research has now discovered, poltergeists are usually conjured not from space, but from a troubled psyche.

(Interestingly, it is not necessarily the psyche of the magician. I was witness several years ago to the attempted healing of a skin disease through the use of an elemental servant. The patient's condition improved dramatically, but she was subsequently bitten and pushed downstairs by the invisible entity. When it was called off, her skin problems returned. The magician who mounted this unfortunate operation told me he had evoked the entity not from his own mind, but from the unconscious mind of the patient.)

As I said in the early stages, all magic works from the inside out. There is another, more familiar, system which works the same way. That system is psychology.

Once you begin to study psychology and magic side by side, some far-reaching parallels emerge.

Psychology postulates dimensions of reality other than the physical. Collectively these dimensions are known as the psyche. The conscious mind forms only a part of the psyche, and a small part at that, but it can make contact with, and is influenced by, other parts. Magic also postulates dimensions of reality other than the physical. Collectively they are known as the Inner Planes. Again the conscious mind may contact them and be influenced by them.

In psychology we learn of certain extra-physical energies. Libido is an example from the Freudian school. The psychiatrist, whose interest lies in healing, stresses the importance of clearing the channels for these energies if the patient is to lead a full and happy life. The magician concurs, with only a slight difference in terminology. He thinks of the energies as spiritual or psychic in the non-psychological sense of the word. For centuries the magician has observed possession, the taking over of a human personality by some non-physical entity. In the unhappiest cases, the entity showed evil characteristics and was consequently considered Satanic or demonic. Unless stopped by exorcism, possession of this type frequently led to the death of the human host. A few years ago, I sat in a courtroom listening to a psychiatrist giving evidence about a patient who was schizophrenic. The patient had felt himself controlled by demons. Eventually the patient's personality disintegrated and he committed suicide.

The magician speaks of spirits. The psychologist formulates theories about "semi-autonomous complexes," constellations of psychic energy that behave as personalities in their own right and exhibit disquieting traits of independence.

The magician deals with gods—superhuman entities whose presence fills him with awe. The psychologist talks of archetypes, dominants of the collective unconscious that exhibit a numinous, awe-inspiring quality. Jung once remarked perceptively that it was pointless denying the reality of the gods when you could better spend your time studying forces in the psyche that behave exactly as the gods were always reputed to behave.

A cardinal rule of magic is "Know thyself." Many psychiatrists and therapists undergo analysis as part of their training.

The magician, particularly the Qabalist, will undertake astral journeys to achieve sufficient balance to allow spiritual forces to flow through him. Jungians use the virtually identical technique of creative imagination in an attempt to integrate the psyche.

Freud's initial experiments involved hypnosis, a very ancient occult technique sometimes known as "Fascination" and sometimes as the "Evil Eye."

The magician forms a very curious, almost telepathic relationship with his apprentice. The psychiatrist seeks rapport with his patients, and is often bemused by apparent instances of telepathy.

This is not designed to be an exhaustive list of parallels, but I think by now I have given enough to support my viewpoint that magic is an archaic system of psychology. Let me now try to show you why I believe it still stands as a valid alternative to the psychology taught in the universities today.

You are now equipped with a workable definition of magic. But like so many definitions of magic, this one has its drawbacks.

Psychology means simply the study of the human mind. Unfortunately most of us tend to think of it as the current study of the human mind, with the unconscious corollary that modern psychology must be correct in its conclusions. This is not so. Modern psychology is neither an exact science nor a complete one. And its only really widespread applications are in the fields of healing (psychiatry) and manipulation (advertising and propaganda).

The fact that there are only two practical applications at the moment does not mean there can be no more. Jung's theory of synchronicity points to a third. So will the current parapsychological experiments, whenever it is realized that parapsychology is a false subdivision and this fascinating field should really form part and parcel of an overall psychology.

The second major drawback is the use of the word "archaic." Although conveying the ancient lineage of magic to perfection, it carries emotional overtones. Anything archaic is usually thought of as outmoded, obsolete, superseded. The danger also arises of thinking of magic as primitive. Nothing could be further from the truth. To underline this, I will now make an interim amendment to my definition: Magic is an alternative system of psychology—and a damn good one!

In building a case for my original definition, it was necessary to stress the parallels between magic and modern psychology. To build a case for the amendment, I have to stress the differences. The heart of these differences lies in how you answer the age-old riddle of the chicken and the egg. In this instance, the chicken is the psyche and the egg, the brain.

Modern psychology pays lip service to the idea that the psyche is real, but makes the tacit assumption that it is somehow less real than the brain. The Behaviorist School, now thankfully in decline, was one of the worst offenders. Every psychic experience could be (at least potentially) explained in terms of brain function. Damage the brain and you damage the mind. Stimulate the brain—through drugs or electrodes—and you stimulate the mind.

Victorian speculation on the subject has left a hangover suffered even by those who would not consider themselves Behaviorists. There is at the back of most psychological theory the woolly notion that the brain gives off mind as a kettle gives off steam, or radium gives off radioactivity. At best, the psychologist admits mind and brain are coexistent and interacting. The idea of a pre-existent mind usually produces a feeling of revulsion.

This attitude has proved immune to the influence of fact. During the latter part of the 1960s, a series of experiments carried out by the distinguished British neurophysiologist, Dr. W. Grey Walter, showed conclusively that far from being a product of the brain, mind is actually its controller.

Dr. Walter's procedure was based on the fact that the human brain generates minute but measurable electrical signals. Electrodes were attached to his subjects' scalps over the area of the frontal cortex. These transmitted any electrical brain activity via an amplifier to a specially constructed machine. Set before the subject was a button which, when pressed, caused what Dr. Walter described as an "interesting scene" to appear on a TV screen.

When you or I decide to take a particular physical action, such as pressing a button, a twenty microvolt electrical surge occurs across a large area of our brain cortex. This is known technically as a readiness wave and both its presence and effect have been familiar to neuro specialists for several years.

What Dr. Walter did was amplify this readiness wave to such a degree that it could directly trigger the TV picture a fraction of a second before the button was actually pressed. He called the process "auto-start."

Subjects usually figured out what was happening fairly quickly and trained themselves to "will" the pictures onto the screen without touching the button at all. Their mental state was all important. For the trick to work, the subject had to duplicate his or her mindset in pressing the button. If attention wandered or the mind locked itself in on focusing on the necessity of concentration, the brain wave potential failed to rise and no picture was delivered. But once the knack was developed, subjects could combine auto-start with auto-stop—they could will pictures onto the screen directly, then dismiss them with the relevant thought when finished.

Once subjects learned they could produce the pictures without pressing the button and began to do so by an act of will, their minds were directly influencing matter—the physical matter of their own brains. A decision of the mind, applied in a particular way, was all it took to change the electrical potential of the frontal cortex. There was no physical aspect to the cause: as the subjects got into their stride, the button was neither pressed nor attempted to be pressed. The totality of cause lay in the mind.

Although a twenty microvolt surge is a small thing, its implications in this case are enormous. It is enough to settle once and for all the bitter controversy about the independent reality of the mind. Dr. Walter's experiment showed clearly the Behaviorists were wrong: It is the mind that controls the brain and not the other way about. Yet decades later, psychologists still cling to the old misconceptions.

These misconceptions grossly limit psychological speculation. Semi-autonomous complexes exhibit personality characteristics. Sometimes one can take over completely from the normal personality. But where does the normal personality go when this happens? To a psychologist, this question is ludicrous. It remains ludicrous even when twin personalities alternate.

The notion that mind is totally dependent on the brain also rules out psychological speculation on the possibility of life after death. Such speculation is left to theologians, who usually make a mess of it. Even Jung, in his commentary on the *Tibetan Book of the Dead*, was careful not to go too far. You can read the commentary from beginning to end without discovering whether Jung actually believed in life after death.

But to the magician, the chicken comes before the egg. The brain is an excellent computer in a fully automated factory. It was built and is operated by the person in charge.

If you hold to this analogy, you will see that it explains observable facts just as well as the Behaviorist conclusions. Remember that the person operating the factory is hidden from you. You can see only the factory and the actions of its machinery.

Damage the computer and the machinery breaks down. You have not, of course, damaged the person who owns it, but you might be tempted to draw that conclusion. If you interfere with the computer's delicate wiring, the production process goes haywire. But this does not mean that the operator has gone insane. Scramble the intercom and the person in charge appears to talk nonsense. But this is the fault of the intercom, not the person.

Regrettably, we can see only the body, never the mind that controls it. We can communicate only through verbal symbols, never directly. We see lunatics and corpses and make assumptions about the mind—or lack of mind—behind them. There is at least a fifty per-cent chance these assumptions are wrong.

While the magician has laid his money squarely on the chicken, the matter does not end there. The magical theory of mind is complex and just as difficult to explain as the psychological.

First, the magician sees a continuity between the psyche and the physical world. one shades into the other with no really clear dividing line. He will go so far as to say that mind and matter are essentially the same thing, or at least different manifestations of the same thing. When someone told the exuberant English critic and author G. K. Chesterton that coal and diamonds were the same thing (because they both consist of carbon) he is reputed to have replied, "Any fool can see they aren't!" Yet the magician's notions are not quite so daft as they seem.

We are accustomed to physicists claiming that the chair we sit on is not solid. Equally, we are accustomed to behaving as if it was. If physics teaches anything at all, it is the fact that experience is worthless for the job of getting to grips with reality.

Common sense tells you that no object can be in two places at once. Physics tells you an electron can. Physics also tells us that mesons can exist only for a millionth of a second—and yet do exist for minutes, sometimes hours. Their energy content seems to distort time.

Since Einstein, physics has been forming a picture of the universe as energy. With each new discovery, this picture grows uncomfortably close to that of the magician.

If you draw a spectrum, shading gradually from white to black, label one end "Mind," the other "Matter," and entitle the whole thing "Energy," you have the magical picture (see figure 17). I fancy that if psychology ever gets together with physics, the scientists will draw a similar diagram.

Mind   **Matter**

Figure 17

Once you accept the magical viewpoint of psychology, a lot of old ideas take on a new lease of life. It is no longer superstition (or science fiction) to consider the possibility of alien dimensions. Nor should you assume these dimensions cannot affect our own.

Magicians have through the ages claimed contact with other, non-physical worlds and claimed such worlds are fountainheads of knowledge, power, and wisdom. Put baldly, it seems fiction. But it is only a very short step beyond the present boundaries of Orthodox depth psychology.

Alien contacts…alien wisdom. It begins to look as if we are embarking on a very romantic adventure, you and I. And so we are. It may also look a little frightening, and so it can be. Before venturing into the realms of High Magic, which is largely concerned with establishing lines of communication with these other worlds and their inhabitants, it might be as well to examine the broad sweep of occult cosmology, which we will do in chapter ten. It could be a comfort to you should things get tough.

Ten

Ground Plan of the Universe

I n the beginning God created the heaven and the earth. The earth was without form and void: and darkness was upon the face of the deep; and the Spirit of God moved upon the face of the waters.

And God said, Let there be light: and there was light. And God saw the light, that it was good: and God divided the light from the darkness.

That's how it all started, according to *Genesis*, the first book of the Bible. At one time you might have taken the words as literal truth. Perhaps you still do, although it has become fashionable these days to dismiss the whole creation story as pure fiction. The magician, an unfashionable figure, doesn't dismiss Genesis as fiction. But he doesn't accept it literally either. Instead, he asks questions. One of the big ones is, What do you mean by God?

For an answer, he turns not to the Old Testament, but to an equally interesting Hebrew source, the Holy

Qabalah. Unlike Genesis, Qabalistic texts do not define a starting point. In the beginning, before the beginning and after the beginning, there is, was, and always will be existence. But there need not necessarily be manifest existence. Immediately we are in deep waters. The Qabalah is not easy to understand. But it definitely repays the effort you must put into it as it provides a structure to which everything known and yet to be known about the universe—visible and invisible, physical and non-physical—can be in some sense related. This is a massive aid to comprehension.

As an arbitrary starting point, you might like to consider the idea of negative existence—or, as the Qabalists refer to it, the Great Unmanifest.

There's very little you can say about the Great Unmanifest. (A fact that hasn't stopped several books being written about it.) Your existence is positive in nature, and so is everything you know. Words like "negative existence" can have no real meaning to you, because they refer to something beyond your experience—and something that, by its nature, must remain beyond our experience. The best you can do is follow the example of the Hindu who describes the Supreme Deity as "Not This. Not That."

Unnoticed by many occultists, physicists have now approached the Great Unmanifest. They've done so by trying to understand the essential nature of matter. In the old days it was easy. Matter was something you could drop on your foot. If you took a lump of matter and cut it into smaller and smaller pieces, you would eventually come down to a bit so small you could not cut it any more. The Greeks named this smallest possible lump of matter the atom.

It was when scientists discovered they could actually crack open atoms that the trouble started. Because what they found inside was no longer matter at all. Worse, it soon turned out to be no longer reasonable. Specifically, they discovered that the entire structure of the physical universe is based on nothing more secure than a statistical probability.

What the Qabalists call the Great Unmanifest is the probability field that underlies the whole of everything we know. The physicists have had no more success in describing it than the Hindus.

But however little else we can say about the Great Unmanifest, we can at least know one thing: Somewhere along the line there was a change. Positive existence came into being. According to Qabalistic tradition, the transition had something to do with the Three Veils of the Unmanifest.

If you take a look at the diagram of Tree of Life (figure 18), you'll notice three dotted halo-like semi-circular bands around the topmost sphere. This is a representation of the Three Veils. In Qabalistic literature they are named as Ain, Ain Soph, and Ain Soph Aur. The terms mean, respectively, Negativity, the Limitless, and Limitless Light.

In a sense, the Veils are another attempt to describe the indescribable. Negativity is the prime characteristic of the Great Unmanifest. It is not this and not that,

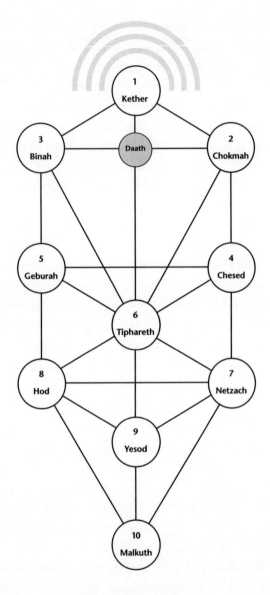

Figure 18: The Tree of Life

because this and that always refer to something positive, something we can see, hear, touch, taste, smell, or at least imagine. Limitless is a speculative term derived from the realization that the Unmanifest underlies everything there is; and since everything there is seems limitless, the Unmanifest must be limitless as well.

But the naming of the third Veil, Limitless Light, is so remarkable you begin to wonder if the ancient Hebrew magicians didn't somehow know as much about physics as the modern physicist—if not even more.

What has light got to do with the transition between the potential of the probability field and the actuality of the known universe?

The phenomenon we know as light is in actuality a stream of sub-atomic particles physicists call photons. The photon stream travels, by definition, at the speed of light—according to Einstein the absolute limit to which anything can be accelerated. But the Theory of Relativity shows that as you move toward the speed of light, time slows down. When you reach the speed of light, time stops altogether.

So the photon stream is traveling outside Time.

If you're finding this brief venture into modern physics difficult, I fear there's worse to come. Einstein's calculations also demonstrated that there's actually no separation between Time and Space. We think of Time as one thing and Space another, but that's really just the fault of our perception. The reality is that there is no separate Space and Time, only a single unity called Spacetime.

So if the photon stream travels outside Time, it must travel outside Space as well.

In other words, light (the photon stream) cannot and does not exist in our universe. It actually lies outside of Space and Time. There is no possible way anything on Earth or elsewhere in the known physical universe could detect the existence of light…yet you could not read these words if you were not equipped to do so. Even more astonishing, if you allow your eyes to adapt to darkness, they can detect the presence of a single photon.

The sheer impossibility of light has passed by the physicists, but it should not pass by you as a magician. For the fact that your eyes can detect light is proof positive of your connection with a reality beyond the physical universe. Light, the Limitless Light of the Ain Soph Aur, is the bridge between the Great Unmanifest and positive existence.

To the Qabalist, positive existence came into being with Kether. Kether isn't a place, or a thing. If anything it's a state. You might call it the first actualization of the infinite possibilities inherent in the Great Unmanifest.

The essential fact of Kether is raw existence. The essence of the sphere is unity. While we could make no speculation about the Great Unmanifest, we can make every speculation about Kether. But each speculation will be equally true and false, because as unity, Kether is beyond all contradiction. Any terms applied to Kether are symbolic. Perhaps the best symbol is the number one.

As one, coupled with zero (the Great Unmanifest) forms the potential of every number, so Kether, contrasted against the backdrop of negative existence, forms the potential of duality. The Qabalist thinks of the situation in terms of pressure. The primordial unity of Kether develops self-awareness—and consequently becomes two. The Chokmah state is born.

Chokmah is the great positive, masculine, yang force of the universe. And since we are now firmly in the realms of duality, its very existence postulates its complementary. Thus Chokmah begets Binah.

It would be a mistake to assume that Kether, Chokmah, and Binah are God, or gods, or even the Trinity. Equally it would be a mistake to assume they are not. Everything depends on your viewpoint. At one level of development, a fact may be experienced as a force. At another level as a god. The fact does not change, only the viewpoint.

From Binah, the Supernal Mother, springs a semblance of stability. The three primordial spheres are balanced...for a time. But manifestation is far from complete. The pressure is still there. The spheres reflect themselves on another level. Chesed, Geburah, and Tiphareth are born.

Chesed is, among other things, the force of growth. Geburah is the force, or rather principle, of destruction. Together they represent progress, the building up and the breaking down, eternally co-existent principles. Tiphareth is the state of balance between them, and a reflection of the higher Kether sphere.

And still the pressure leads to change, bringing into being other states—Netzach, Hod, and Yesod. With the latter, we approach the physical. With the final sphere, Malkuth, we reach it.

★★★★

I don't know how much sense any of this has made to you. Possibly you would prefer the old Gnostic notion of God creating the physical world via a series of emanations. It's not strictly true, but then my talk of spheres and forces isn't strictly true either. All we have to go on are symbols of reality.

The spheres, from Kether down to Malkuth, make up the Tree of Life, a glyph that is the foundation of all Western occult Qabalistic meditational and magical practice. When, in Chapter Five, you learned astrological correspondences in order to perform the $100 bill trick, you were functioning a little like a Qabalist who places correspondence after correspondence on the Tree in order to perform more and more extensive magical operations.

The Tree is the ultimate magical filing cabinet— and one that extends far beyond the traditional doctrines of Qabalah itself. When I trained in Practical Qabalah—the then current euphemism for magic—I quickly discovered that intermixed with the original Jewish mysticism was Gnostic Christianity, Graeco-Roman paganism, Hindu yoga, Chinese esotericism, and a whole host of lesser influences. The Qabalah, it seemed, had become a Hebrew gift to the world. The

Tree can be used, efficiently and effectively, within any occult system—including those with darker aspects.

The reason for this qualifier is that there is an inverse Tree as well as the one I've just described. At one time Qabalists preferred not to talk of it. It was referred to as the Tree of Evil and represented Chaos. Its spheres are the states of existence of the Qlipoth, the Lords of Chaos, the Demons of the Pit.

Today, I notice, there has been a change of emphasis. For some magicians, the old concepts of good and evil have become outmoded. They hold that such ideas are purely subjective, that all you really have is energies working toward given ends. They take the universe as they find it, chaos and all.

It is, of course, quite true to say that the Ultimate Reality lies far beyond both good and evil. It is equally true to say that there are saints and mystics so advanced that they can reconcile the ancient opposites. But I have to tell you I'm not one of them. I believe—with some support from first-hand observation—that the lives of those who tinker with the Qlipoth lack elegance at best and at worst become degenerate, barren, and sometimes desperate. You will find no more about the Tree of Evil in this book other than the heartfelt advice to learn the positive aspects of the Tree thoroughly before you seek to investigate the negative.

Where does humanity figure in the scheme of things represented by the Tree of Life? Our first observable fact is that humanity is a part of the physical universe. Its laws are our laws. Since the states of the Tree are inherent in all matter, they are inherent in humanity. Where humanity differs from most things is that we may become aware of them.

As the innermost core of the universe is Kether, so the innermost core of humanity is the Kether spark. We are, so to speak, chips off the cosmic block.

And God said, Let us make man in our image, after our likeness...

There can be no question of greater or lesser being here. A fire may throw off a spark, but the spark has exactly the same essence as the fire. To produce humanity, billions of divine sparks were thrown off from the central flame. Each one, in the process of manifestation, became overlaid with the microcosmic equivalent of the Tree's spheres. The final overlay was the physical body.

There is, so to speak, a divine plan for humanity. It is embodied in the Tree. But somewhere along the line, something went askew.

Therefore the Lord God sent him forth from the garden of Eden, to till the ground from whence he was taken.

To the Qabalist who understands these things, there is only one real purpose—to correct, so far as he is able, the deviation from the Divine Plan. He begins the job by correcting, again so far as he is able, the deviation in his own Tree. No one pretends the job is easy:

So He drove out the man: and He placed at the east of the garden of Eden Cherubims, and a flaming sword which turned every way, to keep the way of the tree of life.

The Biblical quotations aren't inserted as a subtle appeal to the authority of Holy Writ. I used them in the hope of bringing an air of familiarity into a series of obscure and unfamiliar concepts.

If you have ever taken the trouble to compare the ancient creation myths, Hebrew and otherwise, with modern scientific theories about the origin of the universe, you will have become aware of a very strange thing: the two are just the same. There are, of course, differences in terminology, but the basic ideas are identical. This is not to say, as some people have tried to, that the ancients were equipped with advanced scientific knowledge (although frankly I would not necessarily rule that out). It is to say that the human mind works essentially the same way whether the date is A.D. 2000 or 2000 B.C.

And in order to understand the Qabalah, your mind has to be shifted out of those familiar grooves. The technique necessary to accomplish this is meditation.

Find a good book on the Qabalah. I can recommend Dion Fortune's *The Mystical Qabalah*, Gareth Knight's *Practical Guide to Qabalistic Symbolism*, or Dolores Ashcroft-Nowicki's *The Shining Paths*, along with *Between the Worlds* by Stuart Myers and John Michael Greer's *Paths of Wisdom*.

Read the book of your choice chapter by chapter and meditate regularly on each one as you go. This is, I'm sorry to say, the only way. You will find it a long road but a worthwhile one. As you tread it, you may come to realize something very comforting. Ultimately the angels are on the winning side. This is not because they are good, or because they are strong. It is simply an inevitable aspect of the cosmic situation. Once you realize that, you can safely practice High Magic.

Part Two

High Magic

Eleven

Alien Dimensions

The concept of a parallel universe is inherent in the behavior of sub-atomic particles, although it is only very recently that physicists have faced this fact. A classical experiment in quantum physics produces results so paradoxical that the parallel universe theory is required to resolve them. The experiment, briefly stated, is this:

A beam of sub-atomic particles is directed toward a sensitized surface that will register their impact. A screen is then placed between the source of the particles and the sensitized surface. There are two slits in the screen through which particles can pass—the screen otherwise blocks them. Each of the two slits can be opened and closed independently by the experimenter.

Sub-atomic particles, as their name implies, are thought of as very tiny cannonballs. Common sense— and Newtonian physics—suggests that if both slits are opened, twice as many of these little cannonballs would get through than if you only opened one.

The reality is that more particles get through if only one slit is opened.

When the experiment was first carried out, it presented scientists with a dilemma. To make sense of their findings, they began to postulate that sub-atomic particles were not particles at all, but waveforms. (Nobody knows what the sub-atomic world looks like from direct observation—there are no instruments available that will reveal its mysteries. Physicists create models of this world in relation to the results of their experiments.) Unlike a simple particle, a wave could pass through both slits simultaneously. This meant that you would expect to find no more hits registering on the sensitive surface when two slits were open than when you only opened one. All that would happen was that each wave would split to get through both slits, then reform on the other side. Indeed, since a percentage of these split waves might be expected to collide (thus canceling each other out), fewer waves would actually get through two slits than would get through one—exactly what the experimental findings showed.

Wave theory seemed to solve the mystery, except for one important point. The particles, which behaved like waves while passing through the two slits, promptly turned back into particles immediately afterward. A wave striking the sensitized surface would naturally strike it all at once, like a sea wave breaking on a beach. But the experiment shows this does not happen. The particles strike in specific locations—like little cannonballs.

Physicists started to refer to wave-particle duality (which named the behavior, but did not explain it) and lived for years with the uneasy knowledge that particles behaved like particles in certain circumstances and like waves in others. It is important to appreciate that the wave-particle duality works—that is to say, by considering sub-atomic particles in this way, scientists have been able to predict accurately the behavior of these particles across a whole range of situations. In other words, the duality is real—it just fails to make much sense.

It made so little sense, in fact, that physicists began to wonder if the "wave" existed in the objective world at all. They theorized that it might actually be a mental convenience that enabled them to keep track of what they were seeing: a collection of possibilities that behaved in a wave-like manner. Quantum particles began to be seen increasingly as probability waves.

Physicists are intelligent and often subtle people and this sort of thinking is not particularly easy for non-specialists to follow. But if you apply it to the troublesome double-slit experiment, you can see its attraction. Given the concept of the probability wave, we can return to the comforting picture of particles as little cannonballs. As each little cannonball approaches the two open slits in the screen, the probability wave (which really only exists in the mind of the observer) represents the different possibilities open to each particle—in essence, whether it is more likely to pass through the top slit or the bottom, or to strike the screen and be absorbed or deflected. The probability wave does not predict precisely where the particle would go, only where it is most likely to go.

Probability waves worked just as well to predict results as did the original concept of physical wave form particles. Furthermore, it was very easy to see that the probabilities were bound to change from a situation where one slit was opened, to a situation where you opened two. The theory of probability waves neatly explained particle behavior, but left one nagging problem. If particle waves were actually probability waves and probability waves were actually an organizing function in the mind of the observing scientists, how on earth did you explain the observable fact that probabilities somehow managed to interfere with one another exactly like physical wave forms?

In 1957, a young American physicist named Hugh Everett came up with the answer. In an argument of almost blinding simplicity, he suggested that if two probabilities can interfere with one another, each of them must have an actual existence. But since there is no way both probabilities can exist in our universe, it follows logically that there must be a second, parallel universe to house the second probability.

The implications of the Everett theory are quite bizarre. They involve an ongoing interaction of the two parallel universes, which split and merge continually in relation to specific events. In the famous double slit experiment, the splitting of the two universes produces the wave-like behavior, while the merging gives us back our little cannonball particle.

Since 1957, physicists have postulated many more than two parallel universes. One reading of the math actually indicates there must be an infinity of parallel universes, all but one of which are at least theoretically accessible from our own.

For most people—including the physicists themselves—the concept of parallel universes is something remote from everyday life and personal experience. It is a theory designed to explain the actions of things so small that they can only be detected by their effects, never viewed directly.

But occult theory, which has postulated parallel universes for centuries, insists that the mysterious "second continuum" can be directly sensed by the human mind.

You are in a partitioned room, equipped with a jukebox. The machine is specially set to play a random selection of records, twenty-four hours a day, at maximum volume. You have been told there is another jukebox on the far side of the partition. But since you cannot see through the partition and it resists all attempts at breaking down, you have never examined this second machine. Furthermore, the second machine has been set at minimum volume, so you can't even hear if it is playing because of the noise from your own jukebox.

For a variety of reasons, you decide to investigate the nature of the second jukebox. Your first obvious move is to switch off your own. But once you try, you find that switching off presents such difficulties that you are likely to settle for turning your own machine down to the lowest possible volume.

By doing so, you are in a position to learn something about the music played beyond the partition. Yet with all your efforts, the situation is far from ideal. Until you have attuned your ear through continual practice, you will not be able to tell whether the faint sounds you hear actually originate from the other side of the partition, or come, in fact, from the muted jukebox in your own half of the room.

This situation is very similar to the one you find yourself in when you first try to make contact with the Inner Planes. Occultism teaches that the Inner Planes are alien dimensions lying on the other side of your mind. It is not an easy idea to grasp fully. Can words like "other side" have any meaning in this context? And even if there is an "other side," how can you be sure the Inner Planes lie there and are not simply aspects of the mind itself? You are back in your partitioned room. Is there really another jukebox on the other side of the partition? Is there really an "other side" to the partition at all?

What makes the problem even more troublesome is that you can't reach these alien dimensions directly. The partition can't be broken down any more than fire can mix with water. The best you can hope for is indirect knowledge—the faint strains of music from the second jukebox.

And to make matters worse, even this indirect knowledge must be gained in the most suspect manner possible. For the Occultist insists that the key to the Inner Planes is...pure imagination.

Imagination is one of the most curious functions of the human mind, and one of the least appreciated. When a child daydreams, she's advised sharply to come down to earth. When a man sees a ghost, he's told it's "just imagination" as if this totally negated any value in his experience. Hallucinations are treated with little more than passing reference to their content. The fictional Walter Mitty is a figure of fun, or pity.

Yet side-by-side with this pervasive attitude lies the fact that every worthwhile achievement of the human race springs out of this single curious function. Works of art, from paintings to novels to symphonies, begin in the imagination. So do inventions. So do the technological applications of physical laws. The shape of your house began as a vision in the mind of an architect. The cut of your clothes stemmed from a designer's vision.

Imagination towers like a colossus over the achievements of science. Einstein's Theory of Relativity was, initially, a gigantic leap of the imagination. The mathematical work came later. Darwin used imagination to help him synthesize his observations into an overall concept of evolution. Newton's apple stimulated the same faculty.

If you examine, let's say, a painting from the occult viewpoint, an interesting sequence emerges. The artist starts with nothing other than the tools of his trade—paints, brushes, and an empty canvas. Then he visualizes the picture he wants to paint, calling its various elements before his inner eye. Whether he imagines the picture in its totality before he begins, or builds it up, so to speak, as he goes along, does not matter. In every case, he evokes the picture first as an act of imagination. And this is his only creative act.

What so many people think of as the act of creation—the brushwork on the canvas—is no more than the translation into physical terms of the mental pictures. At this stage what the artist uses is skill, not creativity. The occultist sees this as the earthing of a creative act that took place on another plane.

This sequence is worth stressing, for it is typically magical. Beginning with nothing, we evoke certain stresses on another plane. These are then earthed through skill, training, and knowledge. The result is a change on the physical plane. Virtually every magical operation proceeds in exactly the same way. Small wonder poets and artists take so easily to magic.

Once you begin to examine these facts, the occultist's use of the imagination as a means of contact with the Inner Planes ceases to be quite so ridiculous as it may have appeared at first. But it is still an operation plagued by enormous difficulties.

Following a centuries-old tradition, occultists refer to the realm of the imagination as the Astral Plane, or sometimes the Astral Light. For the purpose of this discussion, you can think of it as a borderland, touching the mind on one side and the Inner Planes on the other (see figure 19).

In itself, this borderland area is formless, but it has the curious property of taking on any form impressed on it; in other words, of giving forces shape. It is essentially a plastic medium.

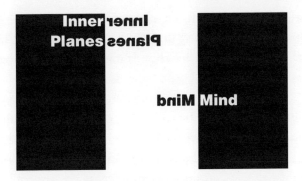

Figure 19: The Astral Light

Before this becomes too obscure, we'd better hark back to the artist. When he first began his act of creativity, there was nothing. His inner eye stared out on the formless billows of the Astral Light. His imagination presented him with a blank screen, matching the blank canvas in his studio. But he desired a picture. He had the will to create one and the inexplicable ability to evoke its form in his imagination. In other words, the forces of his mind created stresses in the Astral Light which, by its nature, translated them into form, the form of the required picture.

Having realized the nature of the Astral Light, you can quickly appreciate the problems of using it as a mirror of the Inner Planes. The forces of the inner Planes may influence it, but so too do the forces of your own mind. Through every waking minute (and most of your sleeping hours) your thoughts, emotions, and desires are impressing forms upon the Astral Light. You are creating continual turbulence. While these circumstances last, contacting the Inner Planes is as difficult as viewing a fish while stirring up a pool. If I may revert to my earlier analogy, your jukebox is making so much noise that it drowns out all other sounds.

So the first step in contact involves getting your "jukebox" under control. Gaining control of your mind is roughly on a par with climbing Mt. Everest—only a very few can manage it. But when you undertake training, it's almost certain you can develop greater control of your mind than you have now. Like everything else, it's a matter of practice.

Fortunately, if you have been playing with Low Magic—particularly the $100 bill trick—you'll already have had practice in the most important essentials: relaxation and visualization.

In Low Magic, relaxation was advocated mainly to break down the tension that blocks free flow of spiritual energies. Now, the same technique is put to use for a slightly different purpose—cutting down distractions.

This approach lies very close to the theory of Hatha Yoga. In the West, Hatha Yoga (usually in a modified form) is presented as a physical fitness program, a sort of pseudo-mystical substitute for a run around the block. But in the East, where the various Yogas were developed, Hatha Yoga has a much more far-reaching purpose. The aspirant has one goal in mind—conscious union with the Godhead. To prepare himself for this ecstatic experience, he must first make sure his body will not distract him. It's realistic to assume nobody thinks divine thoughts with a stomach ache.

Consequently, the yogi uses Hatha techniques to ensure perfect fitness and, even more important, perfect control of the body. Should the whisper of breath disturb his meditations, he can still it. Should the pounding of his heart distract him, he can slow it. These are, of course, extreme results of very lengthy application. But extreme or not, the principle underlying them remains constant.

To put it bluntly, I am not an advocate of Yoga. It is a fine system for the East, but my experience has been that Westerners applying the techniques without adequate supervision (and genuine gurus are as rare in the West as snowballs in Africa) are simply asking for trouble. But this does not deny that the thinking behind the Eastern techniques is sound. From Benares to Birmingham, it makes sense to cut down physical distractions while pursuing the eternal verities.

Fortunately, the remarkable degree of control developed by Hatha Yoga is unnecessary in the West, at least so far as Inner Plane contacts are concerned. Properly applied, relaxation will do the trick just as well. If you refer back to Chapter Four, you'll find the technique given in detail.

While deep relaxation is no cure-all, it will certainly help make a number of complaints more bearable. Furthermore, a relaxed body tends to have an altered pain threshold, with the result that aches and pains become a lot less troublesome.

Almost certainly, your biggest single problem will be maintaining the relaxed state. There is always a tendency for tension to creep in once your attention wanders. The only real answer is continual practice, until relaxation becomes a habit.

In High Magic, maintaining this state is essential. When distractions have been reduced to a minimum and Inner Plane contacts established, there is a strong likelihood of an energy flow along the lines of contact. Should the flow meet a tension barrier, you'll find yourself, to put it mildly, in an uncomfortable position. Worse still, the more successfully you've made contact, the more dangerous it is to erect a tension barrier.

This is not the only danger involved with energy flow, either. This is a point I'll return to shortly when dealing fully with the necessary preparations for contact. Just now, I want to make absolutely sure you appreciate the mechanics of the astral operation involved in such contacts.

First, examine your situation.

I've suggested, in common with many other occult writers, that there's an alien dimension on the other side of your mind. You are interested enough to wish to explore this dimension, but appreciate that by its nature (and your own) you can't simply pull on hiking boots and walk there. You are, to some extent, in the position of a submarine commander who wants to view the surface. Obviously he can't simply stick his head out. Instead, he makes use of an ingenious arrangement of mirrors in a periscope. Through this instrument he can view the outside world usefully, if not directly. The limits of his vision are the limits of his instrument. The clarity of his vision depends entirely on how skillfully the instrument was made.

In viewing the Inner Planes, you're making use of the instrument of imagination. In other words, you hope to see the entities and forces of these alien dimensions reflected on this potent mental screen. Just as the submarine commander can't keep his eye to the periscope if his attention is continually being drawn to trouble in the engine room, you've learned you can't keep your mental eye fixed on the Astral Light if you're continually distracted by the calls of the body. Consequently, you have decided to reduce these distractions to a workable minimum by the practice of relaxation.

But you have still to prepare the instrument, and preparation is far from easy. This is one of the main reasons why so very few occultists master the practice of High Magic, while literally thousands have some command of the system in its lower forms.

From this point on, through the preparation of the "astral periscope" and beyond, there is one vitally important thing to remember. When you make an Inner Plane contact by these methods, the forms you see are astral forms, a translation by your imagination of forces from the Beyond, rather like the magnetic "bottle" used by physicists to contain nuclear energies. The forces are potent, the forms impressive, but it is a fool's game accepting symbol for reality. The only justification for using an astral form of contact is the hope that it will eventually lead you to a direct experience of spiritual reality.

Twelve

Preparation for Contact

E ven if you have read less than a dozen books on the occult, chances are you have already noticed the great stress laid on the "Mysteries," the "Mystery Schools" of antiquity, and their sublime system of initiation.

A number of bodies exist today laying claim to similar techniques and results as the ancient Mystery Schools. Many of these bodies peddle a greater or lesser degree of self-deception. A few of them are outright rackets. A very few have some genuine backing to their claims. But Schools in the final category are hard to find. They seldom advertise. They make no attempts at missionary work. There is a belief among their principals that when a pupil is ready, mysterious forces will lead her to the training she needs.

Even if you are lucky (or evolved) enough to find a genuine Mystery School of the present day, entrance is seldom easy. The barriers are not financial. Any occult School worthy of the name will give tuition free if the occasion warrants it. But no School worth its salt will take on a dilettante. To gain admission, you will work, and work hard, over a period of years. Often, to maintain your membership, you are required to work even harder. The work itself is the most onerous you could imagine, for it is work on your own personality and character.

Aside from these well-hidden organizations, there is only one genuine system of initiation widely available to the European. It was devised by Sigmund Freud, whose interest in the Qabalah is seldom stressed in his biographies, and is called psychoanalysis. Freudian analysis, as originally devised, reflected the sexual preoccupations of its founder and while interesting and useful, they represented a limitation quickly spotted by other workers in the field. Over a period of time, psychoanalysis ceased to be simply Freudian and other schools sprang up with different emphases. One, of particular interest to occultists, was the Jungian, which added both psychic and spiritual dimensions to the human psyche and even drew on certain occult techniques.

But while psychoanalysis is widely available, it is not freely available. Furthermore, it was devised not as a system of initiation, but as a therapy and is still generally used as such, despite impressive evidence of its limitations in this area.

These factors are distinct drawbacks. It is pointless approaching a psychiatrist unless you have a great deal of hard cash to spend. This is no slur on the psychiatrist, merely an indication of the time and effort that must go into a complete analysis. Nor is money everything. Few competent, if, in my view, misguided, doctors will waste their time on a healthy patient. They reserve analysis for the neurotic, who will benefit from it in every way except relief of symptoms.

Fortunately a change seems to be taking place. Non-medical analysts increasingly distinguish between psychotherapy—aimed at the relief of symptoms—and psychoanalysis (of whatever school) aimed at increasing the client's level of self-knowledge. Furthermore, the principles of psychoanalysis are much easier to come by. The founding fathers of modern psychology—Freud, Jung and Adler—left a mass of writings on their systems and these have been enlarged and extended by hundreds of their followers. Nor is this literature always difficult or obscure. Freud himself wrote with the flow of a novelist.

Any of you tempted to embark on the Inner Plane contacts described in later pages, would be well advised to gain a working knowledge of psychiatric literature before you begin. It will give you important insights into the workings of your mind and help you develop self-knowledge. A fund of self-knowledge, the richer the better, is vitally important to any investigation of the Inner Planes. A moment's thought will show you why.

Remember that you will see the Inner Planes reflected in the Astral Light. But that Light also reflects your own hopes, desires, and ambitions. You will, of course, do all you can to still your mind, but until you reach a very advanced stage, you will find total stillness virtually impossible to achieve. In the interim it becomes important to differentiate between an Inner Plane reflection and a projection of your own unconscious. For this, the only tool you have is self-knowledge.

This is an area where, regrettably, many occultists come to grief. Unconscious projections can be both subtle and appealing. The mechanics of wish fulfillment give you, by definition, what you have always wanted.

The explosive results of occult interest without self-knowledge can be seen very clearly in the ease with which so many individuals are prepared to follow cult Messiahs whose nonsensical doctrines are sugar-coated by the suggestion that their followers are somehow chosen, elite, or special.

Even if you do not drift into spectacular psychosis, there are a thousand lesser shades of self-deception. Without self-knowledge, you run the risk of turning an important adventure into a series of illusions.

It is not enough to learn the jargon of psychiatry—you must put it into practice. This is not to say you should become another of the armchair psychologists so prevalent nowadays. It is to suggest that, having read the books, you should attempt to understand the underlying principles and put them to work in evaluating your own impulses and reactions.

Among those underlying principles is the idea that you come equipped with an unconscious mind. The term is in such wide use now that most of us believe we understand it. Yet the reality of the unconscious is almost always surprising and the way it influences our lives is nothing short of terrifying.

In a TV interview, Carl Jung once remarked, "Remember that the unconscious really is unconscious." He had noted that many of his patients believed they could catch a glimpse of their unconscious by careful self-observation, as one might catch a glimpse of movement out of the corner of your eye. But the unconscious does not reveal itself to self-observation alone, only to self-observation and analysis—and even then with considerable difficulty.

One problem with understanding the unconscious is that few of us have ever stopped to examine something far more accessible—our consciousness. Everybody knows about consciousness. It's what returns to you (slowly) when you wake up in the morning. Most people imagine they could not get through their day without it; and in this they are completely—and quite surprisingly—wrong.

Consciousness often plays a part in such activities as perception, judgment, thinking, reasoning, learning, and the assimilation of experience, but it is not actually necessary for any of them.

If, for example, you close your left eye and focus with your right on the left-hand, left-page margin of this book, you will still be fully conscious of the sweep of type across the two open pages.

But if you then place your index finger at the start of any line and move it slowly to the right across the open pages, you will discover there is an area in which the finger vanishes, only to reappear again a little further on.

This conjuring trick is related to the physical structure of the human eye, which has a blind spot in its field of vision. Since we dislike blind spots, we fill it in where it occurs, through a process analogous to a computer filling in a missing part of a picture by deduction from the rest.

Once "filled in" the former blank spot becomes part of our perception. Nor is it illusionary. While the perception does not come about through the usual process of light striking the retina, it is still a valid analogy of what is there on the printed page. Sweep your eye across and you will be able to read it, without having to worry about any blank. (The reason your finger vanishes while the print does not is that the brain finds difficulty in doing the trick with a moving object.)

But while valid, this is a perception in which consciousness plays no part at all. You do not, in other words, notice the blank spot and think to yourself that it is something you must fill in. The process is entirely unconscious. So consciousness is not always necessary for perception.

The notion that judgment is a conscious function was demolished by the psychologist Karl Marbe as long ago as 1901, using an experiment so simple you can carry it out for yourself.

Ask a friend to hand you two small objects, then, carefully examining exactly how you make the judgment, hand him back the lighter of the two. As you undertake this self-examination, you will realize you are aware of a great many things about the two objects:

their feel against your skin, the downward pressure on your hands as they react to gravity, any irregularities in their shape, and so on.

But when it comes to making the judgment, you will find that the answer is simply there, apparently inherent in the objects themselves, but actually handed to you by your central nervous system, which makes the judgment itself at a wholly unconscious level.

It was an attempt by another scientist, H. J. Watt, to punch holes in Marbe's experiment that led to the truly astonishing discovery that thinking—apparently the most obviously conscious of all human activities—is not a conscious process either.

Watt suspected that the whole business of weight judgment was not actually unconscious, but a conscious decision that happened so quickly Marbe's subjects simply forgot what they had done. To try to prove this theory, he set up a series of word-association experiments that allowed the process to be broken down and examined in four constituent parts.

The results of these experiments showed that, provided the subject understood in advance what was required, the thinking process became entirely automatic. It arose of its own accord, once the stimulus word was given. Princetown psychology professor Julian Jaynes has described these experiments as showing that "one does one's thinking before one knows what one is to think about."

Watt's experiments were fairly complicated, but you can check their results quite easily with the aid of figure 20. Look at it now and decide which figure comes next in the series.

Figure 20

It is a childishly simple problem, but that's not the point. The point is that the solution required thought. You had to examine the first square and note that it was followed by the first circle, then by another square and another circle, then by a third square. You had to deduce that the next figure must be a circle.

However, if you paid attention to your mental processes as you solved that little problem, you will have noticed that while thought must have been required, thought did not actually arise. You simply looked at the diagram and knew the final figure must be a circle.

In other words, your thoughts were not conscious. In this instance, consciousness was not necessary for you to think. Nor, as you may have noticed, was it necessary for you to reason. If the square was followed by a circle twice running, then what follows the next square must be another circle. The reasoning was there, but you were not conscious of it. It follows then that consciousness is not a necessity for reasoning.

It is tempting to speculate that while consciousness may not be necessary in so simple a problem, it would certainly be necessary for more complex reasoning. Historical experience shows this is not the case at all.

The celebrated mathematician Poincaré told the Société de Psychologie of Paris how, on a trip, he had solved one of his most difficult problems.

> *The incidents of the journey made me forget my mathematical work. Having reached Coutances, we entered an omnibus....At the moment when I put my foot on the step, the idea came to me, without anything in my former thoughts seeming to have paved the way for it, that the transformation I had used to define the Fuchsian functions were identical with those of non-Euclidean geometry.*

The process by which Poincaré reaches this conclusion did not require consciousness. Nor did the processes by which the structures of the atom and the benzene molecule were discovered. In both instances, the solutions came to scientists in dreams. So, for that matter, did the solution to the problem of how to construct a viable sewing machine, something that had (consciously) baffled engineers for decades.

Learning does not require consciousness either. In fact, in some types of learning the intrusion of consciousness actually blocks learning. This is particularly true of what is called "signal learning," sometimes referred to as conditioning or, less disparagingly, learning by experience.

When you blow a puff of air into someone's eye, they blink—the reflex is involuntary. If you shine a slight into the eye immediately before blowing and continue to repeat the process, you will find that after approximately ten repetitions, the eye begins to blink at the light, before the puff of air. Your subject's body has learned that the stimulus is about to come and anticipates it by blinking.

But there is no consciousness involved in this learning process. So far as your subject is concerned, it simply happens. Furthermore, if the subjects tries to speed up the process by blinking consciously after every flash of the light, the reflex will arise much more slowly, if at all.

You can learn a great deal more than reflex actions without the intervention of consciousness. A charming case-study reported by Lambert Gardiner in *Psychology: A Study of a Search* (Brooks/Cole, California, 1970) tells of students in a psychology class who decided to teach their professor that they preferred him to stand at the right of the lecture hall. Each time he moved to the right, they paid closer attention to what he was saying, and laughed more heartily as his jokes. While he remained totally unconscious of what was happening, he was soon delivering his lectures so far to the right of the hall that he was almost out the door.

Assimilation of experience is often associated with consciousness—indeed there was a time when psychologists defined consciousness as assimilation of experience. That time has long gone.

It is fairly likely that you use a telephone frequently and apply the full light of consciousness to the numbers you dial. But could you say now, without looking, what letters are associated with what figures on the dial?

You brush your teeth each morning. How many teeth are on view in the bathroom mirror as you do so?

Could you list, again without looking, the ornaments on your mantelpiece? A few attempts like these quickly indicate how poor a vehicle consciousness is in assimilating your daily experiences.

The reverse side of this coin arises out of the fact that most people will notice instantly when a clock stops, even though the sound if its tick may not have impinged on their consciousness for years. Not hearing the clock tick until it stops is a familiar cliché, but one which demonstrates clearly that assimilation of experience (the clock stopping) can be carried out very efficiently without consciousness.

This is even more clearly demonstrated by the use of hypnosis in situations like the loss of car keys. In trance, you can often be persuaded to recall where you left them, even though consciously you have no awareness of their location whatsoever. You did not consciously record the experience of leaving down your keys, but it was accurately recorded all the same.

Once you put all this together, it is plain that consciousness is unnecessary to survive even the busiest day. But while unnecessary, it is, for the magician, desirable. For if consciousness is not required for survival, it is certainly required for spiritual evolution. Indeed, increased consciousness and spiritual evolution are so interwoven that one is almost tempted to consider them the same thing.

Unfortunately for evolution, it is observable that consciousness is not only unnecessary in daily life, but also unexpectedly absent from much of it. When you drive a car, for example, you are no longer aware of the various complexities involved. You do not think consciously of applying the brake, changing the gear, or moving the wheel. These things, so far as consciousness is concerned, simply happen—although consciousness can override any one or all of them at will.

The same applies to activities like riding a bicycle, skiing, using a typewriter, or operating machinery. It is as if, during your waking hours, you were accompanied by an invisible robot to whom you could hand over control of those functions with which you did not personally wish to be bothered.

There is strong survival pressure toward handing over as much as possible to the robot, since it can often do the job a great deal better than you can. Cast your mind back to the time when you were learning to drive your car. Every operation had to be carried out consciously, at a substantial investment of memory and attention. You had to remember to depress the clutch before engaging gear. You had to estimate (or read off a dial) the precise engine revs that would allow you comfortably to do so. You had to judge distances and the width of your vehicle accurately and continuously. The whole process was a nightmare; and while it remained conscious, you drove badly.

If you never learned to drive a car, ride a bike, operate a typewriter, or any of the other examples I have used, then watch a baby learning how to walk. It is a pitiful process, full of stumbling and heavy falls. But the interesting thing is that you were like that once, a bipedal animal who could crawl, but not walk. With instinct and encouragement, you learned, but learning—in this, as in so many things—meant turning over control to the robot. When it came to walking, you did this so effectively that, unlike car driving, consciousness no longer has a veto over how it is done. The curious fact is that as an adult, you no longer have the least idea how you walk. You decide where you want to go, of course, and when, but the process that establishes your balance, contracts your muscles, and initiates subtle, continuous feedback controls is as far beyond your reach as the surface of the moon.

Clearly, if there are things like driving a car that the robot can do better than you, there are also things like walking that the robot can do perfectly and you cannot do at all.

This fact—and what may be an inherent laziness in our species—encourages us to hand over more and more tasks to robot control. Sometimes this is done quite consciously. Zen Buddhism, when applied to tasks like archery, is a case in point.

The Zen practitioner is encouraged not to aim at the target, but to "become one with it" and allow the target to attract the arrow. It is a process of giving the bow to the robot, which shoots a great deal more accurately than the archer. More modern sports systems, such as Inner Tennis, aim at substantially the same result. Athletes everywhere readily accept that they reach their peak when they cease to think—and worry—about their game.

So long as we are discussing motor skills, this situation is not so bad. Indeed, it is absolutely necessary, since whatever about functioning without consciousness, we certainly could not function without the robot. But the trouble really arises when the robot starts to do your thinking for you.

Robot thought is quite common. Crass examples abound in politics and religion, where enthusiastic practitioners chant slogans at one another under the comfortable impression that they are having a debate or engaging in argument. They are, of course, doing neither; merely sitting on the sidelines of a robot war.

Other examples are more subtle—and consequently more dangerous. How often have you found yourself parroting an opinion that actually belonged to the newspaper you read this morning? How often have your words reflected a mindless reaction to some stimulus that affected you in ways you do not really begin to comprehend? How often have you passed the time of day with a neighbor, discussing the weather, or even the garden, with no more conscious input than pressing the playback button of a tape recorder? In all these familiar situations, you are listening to your robot speak.

Sad to say, your robot is an eminently helpful little creature, anxious to take more and more of the burden from your conscious shoulders. He will breathe for you, walk for you, drive for you, speak for you, think for you and, unless you are very careful, live your life for you.

There are some people who think he is doing that already. The occult philosopher G. I. Gurdjieff taught that human beings live their lives in a state analogous to sleep; and the only really worthwhile endeavor was trying to wake up.

The contemporary author Colin Wilson, obsessed for decades with the problem of human boredom, has become convinced that it is the robot who saps our vitality, diverting energies to his own ends which we might otherwise have applied to those (conscious) pursuits that really interest us. Essentially stated, the problem is how, in a universe so varied and so wonderful, we could ever manage to get bored.

You may just possibly begin to recognize a little of yourself in all this. Are you able to concentrate as effectively as you would like? Do you have abundant reserves of energy—physical, emotional, and mental—for the things you like to do? Do you find yourself sometimes—perhaps often—bored or listless or depressed?

Lack of energy, boredom, and depression may, of course, be symptoms of a physical condition. But if you are satisfied that your health is all right, then the most likely culprit is your robot.

Since consciousness is such an important function for a magician, you might find it an interesting experience to live a little more consciously than you have done for awhile.

To achieve this, we turn back to Gurdjieff, who created one of the most effective systems ever devised for living consciously. Gurdjieff developed many exercises toward this end. His pupils were, for example, instructed to freeze on a random signal for long periods in whatever position they found themselves. This was easy enough if you happened to be lying down in bed, but became extraordinarily difficult if you were in the act of standing up, making love, kicking a football, or any other of the thousand and one things that place you temporarily in an awkward physical position.

When such temporary positions become prolonged, as they did—and do—at intervals in Gurdjieff schools, your body quickly sets up such a howl of protest that your consciousness is positively forced to pay attention. You have, in short, begun to live a lot more consciously than before. If the exercise is repeated sufficiently often, consciousness becomes something of a habit.

But as some of Gurdjieff's less docile followers eventually discovered, living consciously in a posture of frozen agony is hardly worth living at all. It may be as well to say that I believe Gurdjieff's system, for all its ingenuity and benefits, is too unbalanced to provide the stimulus of consciousness a magician needs. Even as a system for living more consciously, it concentrates on consciousness of the physical world, ignoring the fact that there are other states of consciousness and the possibility that there may even be other worlds. There are, in addition, some indications that the full Gurdjieff training may prove positively destructive for certain personality types.

Despite this, at least one of the more manageable Gurdjieff exercises can be of use to the magician in the preliminary stages of his or her development. This is the exercise of self-remembering.

Gurdjieff maintained that during our day-to-day activities, we have a tendency to perceive the world with one important ingredient missing. That ingredient is ourselves. Since we are in a state of sleep (as Gurdjieff believed) we do not perceive ourselves as having a place in the world, nor do we notice the influence we have upon it. We are, in a very real sense, unconscious of ourselves and consequently unconscious of much that goes on all around us.

The antidote, he suggested, was a regime of self-remembering, the conscious recollection, by a continuing act of will, that we are here, now, doing whatever it is we are doing. Should you begin successfully to self-remember at this very moment, you would become suddenly aware not only of the words on this page, but of the person reading them. It is a step—and not a small step—toward living more consciously.

But it is not an easy step. You have had many years of practice in self-forgetting and you will not overcome the habit overnight. How you go about it is basically a matter of trial and error. You might, for example, try reminding yourself verbally—either aloud or in your mind—who you are, where you are, and what you are doing at a given time. Alternatively, you could concentrate on body sensations, or visualize the scene with yourself in it. Perhaps the most important thing is the effort itself, rather than the direction of the effort. When effort—almost any effort—is applied, results usually follow.

Permanent self-remembering is a lot like yoga enlightenment: it can take years of effort to achieve. At this stage, however, we are looking only for a flavor of more conscious living, so this particular exercise should not become a lifetime endeavor. Approximately two weeks should be devoted to it, with at least one attempt at self-remembering to be made daily.

By its very nature, this exercise should not be attempted at any set time. It is a "catch-exercise" for walking, working, relaxing, chatting, watching a movie, or anything else you may happen to be doing.

Self-remembering is a very curious process and many people find it difficult. Like any attempt to change old habits, it can sometimes be quite uncomfortable. But when you get the hang of it, even for a short time, there are noticeable benefits. Although your attention is directed toward remembering yourself, it is the world around you that will begin to look more vibrant, more meaningful, in an odd way more real.

Your second experiment, to which you can devote the remainder of a four-week month, is also designed to place you more fully in charge of your robot, but in a very different way. Select a job you would like the robot to do for you. This may be something as simple as catching a ball or something as complex as solving a difficult work problem.

If you are seeking robotic help in purely motor skills like playing darts or snooker, then the Zen approach will probably be the most effective. Like many systems that take years to perfect, the essence of Zen is remarkably simple. In two weeks you should achieve enough in the way of measurable results to convince you of its validity.

The trick is to break away from the culturally conditioned response that insists you see most of the world around you as separate and inanimate. Move, at least temporarily, toward the more primitive (and in some ways more valid) form of mentation in which you imagine the physical world and its component parts to be vibrantly alive…with yourself as an integral part of a universal whole.

This viewpoint allows you to feel that the dart may be drawn to the bull's-eye, the snooker ball to the pocket. It allows you to animate your tools in your mind so that you can relax and let them get on with the job, standing to one side in a supervisory capacity only. Mentally picture as happening what you want to happen and note how, in what circumstances, results are better, or easier than you would normally find them.

Robotic assistance in mental tasks is even easier. It involves a technique a great many people use instinctively, without perhaps realizing the exact mechanics of what they are doing. This is the technique of sleeping on your problems.

It is the essence of simplicity. Go to bed. Take a few moments to define your problem clearly in your mind. Then forget it and go to sleep. It is a good idea to keep a notebook and pen beside your bed to jot down any solution that may be present in your mind when you wake up in the morning. Often the technique will work on your very first attempt—your robot really is a very willing little fellow—but if not, repeat it nightly until a breakthrough occurs. You will not usually have to wait long.

Along with psychiatric theory, there are a number of other valuable tools for the development of self-knowledge. Among the foremost is meditation.

For some reason, meditation has become cloaked in mystery. There must be hundreds of books promising to reveal its "secrets." Yet the most difficult thing about meditation is your initial decision to try it.

Admittedly, depth meditation is something of an art, but it is an art you will not learn by reading books. The only way to develop it is to practice it—and the only way to practice it is to sit right down and start. Meditation simply means thinking consistently about a given subject. You follow up the train of thought that arises, turning the subject over and over in your mind, examining it from various angles.

Ideally, you should set aside a given time each day for meditation. Here again, the habit is easily established, and it is a good one. But don't be too ambitious. You should limit yourself to fifteen or twenty minutes, at least in the early stages.

Depth Meditation Exercise

Make sure you won't be disturbed. Lock the door of your room, if necessary. As in many occult exercises, early morning is best, if for no other reason than that you are less likely to be disturbed. And again, relaxation is a necessary preliminary.

Sit in a straight chair and make yourself comfortable with a footstool. (There is always the possibility of falling asleep; hence the straight chair that will ensure you only stay asleep the short time it takes you to fall to the floor.)

Now go through the relaxation process. As I've noted elsewhere, there's a relationship between a relaxed body and a relaxed mind. Without a relaxed mind, you won't get far in meditation.

Start to think about your chosen subject. Since you are seeking self-knowledge, it would be as well to pick something relevant—your emotional reactions for example, or the makeup of your personality.

At first, even with such a fascinating subject as yourself, your mind will wander. Don't let this worry you. It's a perfectly common occurrence. Make a note of any breaks in concentration, then forget them and return to your subject As time goes on and you gain proficiency, you'll find the breaks becoming fewer and fewer.

As you persist, you will soon find ideas and information rising from the deeper strata as you cross the barrier between your conscious and unconscious mind.

Another excellent tool for carving knowledge of your inner self is systematic tabulation. In its simplest form, this simply means making two lists—one taking in your good points, the other your bad points. The trick is to work on the lists until you can't think of another item to put down—then convince yourself you're really only starting.

A more sophisticated and considerably more useful variation on this basic principle is an elemental breakdown. As you probably know, the ancients subdivided matter into four basic elements—Earth, Air, Fire, and

Water—ruled over by a subtle fifth, Aether or Spirit. With the development of chemistry, the elements of matter went out of fashion, but the subdivision holds good when applied to human psychology.

Rule a page into five and head each column with an element name. Then try to fit each of your characteristics into the relevant column. If, for instance, you suffer from outbursts of temper, this should obviously be noted under Fire. Laziness would fit well under Earth. Charitable acts (unless prompted by social pressures or a desire to save income tax) should be listed under Aether, and so on.

The particular benefit of the elemental breakdown is that you can see at a glance where any imbalance lies. If you've made two dozen entries under "Air" and one each under the remaining headlines, then obviously something is wrong with your inner makeup. Not only that, but you know the area of over-emphasis. In these circumstances, you can often do something to correct the balance. (As a matter of passing interest, a number of occultists recommend meditation on each of the elements in strict rotation as a means of achieving inner balance. The idea is excellent, provided you realize that information obtained in meditation must at some stage be translated into action.)

In your search for self-knowledge, it's a useful approach to find out what friends and acquaintances think of you. it may take a certain amount of nerve to ask and a good deal of time to persuade them to tell the truth, but the results are usually worth the effort.

The outsider will make no allowance for your faults, while you will almost certainly fail to notice them at all—or exaggerate them out of all proportion. This single difference is vital to an honest evaluation.

Dream analysis can be another interesting approach. Catch your dreams by keeping a notebook and pencil at your bedside and writing down the details right when you wake up. (Leave it even for a minute and the dream evaporates.) During your analysis of dream content, you can throw away every popular book on the "meaning" of dreams you have purchased. Oddly enough, you can forget most of the tomes on psychological symbolism as well. Your dream is your own. No one can interpret it but yourself.

Certainly your dream will be packed with symbols. But the important thing is what those symbols mean to you. A Freudian may put up convincing arguments that a snake symbolizes the penis. But to you it could symbolize amusement because you once watched a snake eat your grandfather's hat. So look for the personal symbolism in your dreams and evaluate them accordingly.

Armed with self-knowledge and the ability to relax at will, your other great preliminary essential to Inner Plane contact is concentration.

Like the ability to visualize, which you have developed to some degree during your experiments in Low Magic, concentration is a matter of practice. If you have followed the path of meditation in your search for self-knowledge, you will, as a side effect, have developed a fair degree of concentration as well. But there is concentration and then there is concentration. Occultists and psychologists recognize two main types, voluntary and involuntary. Should you be unfortunate enough to find your foot on fire at this moment, it's unlikely you will continue to pay much attention to this book. Your mind will be entirely concentrated on the pain you experience. This is involuntary concentration and there's not a great deal you can do about it.

Involuntary concentration can arise in much more pleasant circumstances. When something interests you, your attention is drawn toward it. Consequently, it is easier for most people to concentrate on a sex scene in a novel than on an article about cybernetics in an encyclopedia. You will appreciate that involuntary concentration needs no development. It simply follows naturally on interest.

Voluntary concentration arises from a different set of circumstances. Here you make a decision to concentrate on something that may run contrary to your natural interests. Your concentration is then held on the subject by an act of will. This is obviously a good deal less easy than involuntary concentration and the chances are you won't do it very well. Once again, the answer is practice, for voluntary concentration will certainly be necessary in most High Magic.

Thirteen

Ritual Workings

There are two broad types of Inner Plane contact—energies and entities. Since the latter can be a bit tricky, I propose to start you off with the former. But before I do, I want to make sure you've got the necessary preparation.

In Chapter One, you learned the Banishing Ritual of the Lesser Pentagram as one of several means of preparing your place of working. Hopefully you've been practicing it since then so that by now it should be fluid and familiar.

In that chapter, I mentioned briefly how the ritual could be used to combat phobias. I'd now like to show you a small, important modification of that technique which I'd like you to use daily for a minimum of two months before moving on to any other ritual practice.

The first step toward the modification—and the most important step—is to recognize what you intend the ritual to do. This you'll achieve by meditation on the following proposition: Your mind is not *in* your body. Rather, your body is *within* your mind. You move, ultimately, in a psychic sea.

While a magical operation (including the Pentagram Ritual) may be designed to influence the outer world, it can only do so by first acting on the inner. If you've discovered that the ritual will, in a manner of speaking, disinfect the environment, you must also accept that it does so by first "disinfecting" your psyche. Continual use of the ritual, with intent, will produce a permanent "cleansing" of the psyche.

Meditation will convince you of the logic of this proposition, thus enabling you to "solidify" your intent on using the ritual. But as you do, there are slight technical modifications to carry out.

In the more usual form of the ritual (as used to prepare your place of working) the pentagrams remain static. That is, they are drawn in place and stay there as cardinal guardians of an enclosed circle. When using the ritual for "inner cleanliness," the pentagrams are visualized as moving, exactly as they were in the technique used to banish phobias. That is, they are drawn close to the body and seen in the mind's eye as swimming outward, clearing a way as they go.

The second, and final, modification is not, strictly speaking, a modification at all, but an addition. If you have done the work advocated in Chapter Twelve, you should be aware of your major faults by now. On using the ritual, visualize these faults in personified form and place them beyond the circle enclosed by the ritual. See them wither and die there for lack of nourishment.

None of this should prove very difficult, except perhaps the personification of faults, which requires a certain creative faculty. If personification does not come easily to you, picture the scene in your life when the particular fault last manifested, and place that scene beyond the circle.

As in almost every other occult exercise, regularity of practice is important. Perform the ritual each day and over the weeks you will begin to feel a benefit. If you have the energy and interest to alternate this with the Fountain Exercise (also given in Chapter One), results will be faster and more noticeable.

There is another useful purification technique you may want to use in preparation for Inner Plane contact. It is called "pore breathing." Once again, the exercise is one of visualization.

Pore breathing is like every other breathing exercise in that it should not be overdone. It's like salt on your stew—just because a little is good doesn't mean a lot will be better. So keep your pore breathing experiments short in the early stages. Start with three minutes a day for the first week, gradually working up to a maximum of fifteen.

Pore Breathing Exercise

Relax systematically and begin a 2/4 breathing sequence. When the rhythm is established, fix your awareness on the fact that air—and energy—are flowing through your nose into your lungs. Realize that your body is taking oxygen and energy from this inflow, replacing it with the waste product of carbon dioxide. Realize too that as you breathe out, this waste product is carried out and away from your body.

Now take the whole thing a step further. Imagine that instead of breathing in only through your nose, you are breathing in a vast sea of light and energy through every single pore in your body.

Properly done (and the exercise is a remarkably easy one), pore breathing produces an unmistakable sensation somewhere between a tingle and an energy surge.

Breathing in "through the pores" is, of course, only the first step of the exercise. As you hold your breath on the two-count, visualize the light as filling your entire body and being absorbed by it. Then, as you breathe out to the count of four, visualize your unwanted psychic qualities flowing out through your pores along with the waste of the body.

(Although irrelevant to Inner Plane contact, it's worth mentioning that pore breathing can sometimes work wonders for physical ailments. The trick is to breathe through a certain area, not always the seat of the pain, thus increasing the supply of psychic energy to that part. The technique doesn't produce quick cures, but it's often very effective in the long term, especially when combined with other therapies.)

Now the bad news. The next ritual, which will let you experience your first powerful Inner Plane energy contact, *can* be worked solo—but it will be much more effective if carried out by a group. It doesn't have to be a large group, but it would obviously make a big difference if the members had some esoteric experience. Failing that, put together a group of interested friends and instruct them in the Pentagram Ritual and the Fountain Exercise. Make sure they use both daily for about a month before you perform your first group ceremonial.

If you simply can't put a group together, you can make the modifications I'll indicate a little later and try the whole thing on your own. You'll find it difficult, but the results may be some compensation.

The ritual contains elements of an extraordinarily interesting system of magic known as Enochian. Since we'll be returning to Enochian before the end of this book, it may be as well to give you a little background.

In 1659 a publisher named Meric Casaubon issued a very curious work entitled A *True & faithful RELATION of what passed for many Yeers Between Dr. JOHN DEE (A Mathematician of Great Fame in Q. Eliz. and King James their Reignes) and SOME SPIRITS*. The Dr. John Dee of the title was Court Astrologer to Queen Elizabeth I, and an Admiralty spy.

Although best known in his day as an astrologer (he predicted Elizabeth's ascension to the throne while she was still in jail, thus earning her lifelong admiration), Dee was greatly interested in communicating with spirits and employed a scoundrel named Edward Kelley as a medium for the sum of £50 a year. The salary was not always paid, but the two stayed together all the same. Their experiments in crystal-gazing, using a shewstone now in the British Museum, began in 1582 and continued, despite various unconnected adventures, until 1587. Their flavor is caught quite neatly in the following extract:

Suddenly there seemed to come out of my Oratory a Spiritu-all creature, like a pretty girle of 7 or 9 yeares of age, attired on her head with her hair rowled up before and hanging down very long behind, with a gown of Sey...changeable green and red, and with a train she seemed to play up and down...like and seemed to go in and out behind my books, lying on heaps, the biggest ... and as she should ever go between them, the books seemed to give place sufficiently, dis...one heap from the other, while she passed between them: and so I considered, and...the diverse reports, which E.K. (Edward Kelley) made unto me of this pretty maiden, and....

DEE: I said...Whose maiden are you?

SHE: Whose man are you?

DEE: I am a servant of God both by my bound duty and also (I hope) by his Adoption.

A VOYCE: You shall be beaten if you tell.

SHE: Am not I a fine Maiden? Give me leave to play in your house, my Mother told me she would come and dwell here.

DEE: She went up and down with most lively gestures of a young girle, playing by her selfe, and diverse times another spake to her from the corner of my study by a great Perspective-glasse, but none was seen beside her self.

SHE: ...Shall I? I will. (Now she seemed to answer one in the foresaid Corner of the Study.)...I pray you let me tarry a little (speaking to one in the foresaid Corner.)

DEE: Tell me who you are.

SHE: ...*I pray you let me play with you a little, and I will tell you who I am.*
DEE: *In the name of Jesus then tell me.*
SHE: ...*I rejoyce in the name of Jesus and I am a poor little Maiden, Madini, I am the last but one of my Mother's children, I have little Baby-children at home.*

And so on. Although not entirely clear from the extract, Dee was communicating with Madini (also given as "Madimi" in Dee's texts) second hand. It was Kelley who spoke for the girl, or allowed the girl to speak through him. By June 1583, the experiments had taken a particularly weird turn. The two men believed themselves to be in contact with a number of entities including an impatient angel called Ave.

Ave dictated a series of "Calls" or evocations to the "Watchtowers of the Universe," which were claimed to make up an entire system of magic known as Enochian. The curious method of dictation—letter by letter and backward—was explained by the fact that the Calls were so powerful even writing them down in the normal way might stir up potent and unwanted magical currents.

The process of transcribing the Calls was bizarre. Dee and Kelley had somehow obtained, or created, more than a hundred large squares, or tablets, measuring forty-nine by forty-nine inches on average, each wholly or partly filled by a grid pattern of letters. During the course of the experiments, Dee would place one or more of these tablets before him on a writing table, while Kelley would sit across the room staring into a crystal shewstone.

When contact was made, Kelley would report sight of the angel in the shewstone, along with the angel's own copies of the tablets. Using a wand, the angel would then point to certain letters on the tablets and Kelley would call out the rank and file of the letter indicated. Dee would then locate the letter in the same position in his tablet and write it down. Thus the Calls were gradually built up.

An example of the sort of message that came through is the following lines:

Micma Goho Mad Zir Comselha Zien Biah Os Londoh Norz Chis Othil Gigipah Vnd-L Chis ta Pu-Im Q Mospleh Teloch...

This translates as, "Behold, saith your God, I am a circle on Whose Hands stand Twelve Kingdoms. Six are the Seats of Living Breath. The rest are as Sharp Sickles or the Horns of Death..." which is only slightly less obscure than the original.

Perusing the *Faithful Relation* and various other accounts of his life, it is tempting to conclude that Dr. Dee, an enormously naive man despite his learning and espionage training, was the victim of a confidence trick when it came to his dealings with spirits. The problem, of course, has always been Edward Kelley.

Before they met, Kelley had had his ears cropped for coining (counterfeiting) and habitually wore a skullcap to hide the evidence of his conviction. He is known to have lived on his wits and was involved —apparently more than once—in extracting money from the credulous on the pretense that he could make alchemical gold. He died in 1597 while trying to escape from jail. This is not the background of a reliable and honest man.

Nor can we suppose that Kelley's affection for Dee—which seems to have been genuine enough—was sufficiently strong to ensure that the good doctor would be excluded from his con games. On one occasion he assured Dee that the spirits had told him that he and Dee should "hold their wives in common,"or all further communication would cease. (Jane Dee was many years younger than her husband and considerably more pretty than Mrs. Kelley.) Dee fell for it, and an Elizabethan *menage á quatre* ensued until the objections of the women forced him to abandon the arrangement.

In face of all this, it is easy to suppose that Kelley made up his talk of angels and spirits to keep his employer happy and ensure the continuation of his yearly payment, along with whatever other opportunities for profit might arise from his relationship with this well-connected man. Kelley was, after all, Dee's only link with the Otherworld: Like many magicians, Dee could not see spirits for himself.

There are two difficulties with this. One is the claim that the Enochian calls are not a code or cipher, but represent an actual language, internally consistent and with its own syntax. I am not qualified to evaluate this claim, but if it is true, it certainly suggests there was more going on during the Dee/Kelley séances than a crude confidence trick.

It is not impossible that Kelley could have invented the Calls, for artificial languages have certainly been created; Esperanto is a modern example. But to do so would have required an enormous investment of time and effort, on top of which, Kelley would then have been obliged to memorize the Calls—there are forty-eight of them in all, forming a substantial body of material—so perfectly that he was able to dictate them backward. Given Kelley's dislike of honest toil, it would be easier to believe he really did talk with angels.

The second problem is that the Calls work. That is to say, they can be used to produce magical results. This fact is attested to by generations of magicians and is something you can experience personally in the ritual that follows.

Talisman Charging Ritual

The ritual itself is designed as a balanced contact with the four great elemental energies under the dominion of Spirit. The energies, once evoked, are then stored for future use. The storage of energy creates a talisman and each participant should have ready, in advance of the operation, some small object for use in this way. This might be a statuette, an item of jewelry, even a coin of medallion. A piece of quartz crystal is ideal. Avoid synthetic materials; they don't hold magical energies very well. Set up your place of working as follows.

Empty a room, or push the furniture to the walls to allow a good sized working space. Set a small table in the center with a white or black cloth on it to serve as an altar. Use a compass to find the cardinal points of the room. If you've made a set of tattva cards as suggested in Chapter

Eight, use them to mark the cardinal points by pinning or otherwise attaching them to the wall. The tattva of Air goes in the east, Fire in the south, Water in the west, and Earth in the north. The indigo egg of Spirit should be placed on the altar along with a single white candle, a lighted stick of incense in a safe holder, and a small bowl or basket suitable for receiving the items to be used as talismans.

Once the physical preparations are complete, have the other members of your group wait outside the room while you prepare the inner place of working with the Banishing Ritual of the Lesser Pentagram (see Chapter One). Follow this by lighting the candle on the altar as symbolic of your desire to have the light of spirit bless your endeavors. Signal to your group when you are ready by knocking on the door three times.

Your group should then enter the room in procession, always moving clockwise around the altar. As they enter, each member should approach the altar and leave the item they want charged in the basket before stepping back and taking his or her place in the room.

Four of the group members should take their places at the quarters to mediate a specific elemental energy. Have them stand in the quarter below the tattva, facing inward. Their job at this point is to attune themselves to the "feel" of the relevant element.

Two comments of relevance here. The first is that if you're working solo you obviously can't have four officers (as they are called in the Lodges) marking the quarters.

In their place you can visualize anonymous officers (not somebody you know, please) facing inward to the alter and robed in the color of their relevant tattva.

The second is that mediating the elemental energies at the quarters is a whole lot easier if the individuals concerned have had some experience of the tattva doorways. To contact the energy of the element, they simply recall the overall "feel" of their experience when they entered the specific tattva.

When everyone has taken their places, a group member carries out the Invocation of Elemental Energies as shown below. (If working solo, you'll obviously have to do this work yourself.) Unlike the Banishing Ritual of the Lesser Pentagram, all the pentagrams used here are invoking—that is to say they call certain energies into manifestation. You can find more information on the subject on pages 281–286 of the 1993 Llewellyn edition of Israel Regardie's *Golden Dawn*.

Invocation of Elemental Energies

Face East. Perform Qabalistic Cross.

Make active Pentagram of Spirit (figure 21), vibrating **Exarp**. Make inner wheel, vibrating **Eheieh.**

Figure 21

Make Pentagram of Air (figure 22), vibrating **Oro Ibah Aozpi.** Make the symbol of the astrological sign Aquarius, vibrating **YHVH.**

Figure 22

Move to south.
Make active Pentagram of Spirit (figure 23), vibrating **Bitom.** Make inner wheel, vibrating **Eheieh.**

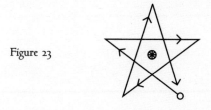

Figure 23

Make Pentagram of Fire (figure 24), vibrating **Oip Teaa Pedoce.** Make the symbol of the astrological sign Leo, vibrating **Elohim.**

Figure 24

Move to west.
Make passive Pentagram of Spirit (figure 25), vibrating
Hcoma. Make inner wheel, vibrating **Agla.**

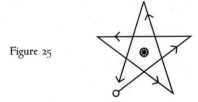

Figure 25

Make Pentagram of Water (figure 26), vibrating **Empeh
Arsel Gaiol.** Make eagle head (the symbol of the astrological sign Scorpio), vibrating **Al.**

Figure 26

Move to north.
Make passive Pentagram of Spirit (figure 27), vibrating
Nanta. Make inner wheel, vibrating **Agla.**

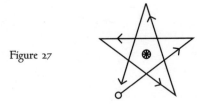

Figure 27

Make Pentagram of Earth (figure 28), vibrating **Emor Dial Hectega**. Make the symbol of the astrological sign Taurus, vibrating **Adonai**.

Figure 28

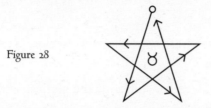

Return to east, and conclude the invocation with the Qabalistic Cross.

With the Invocation of Elemental Energies completed, the group now begins an elemental chant to raise power. Together, vibrate: **Exarp, Hcoma, Nanta, Bitom** (Air, Water, Earth, Fire in Enochian). Continue until the atmosphere in the room changes noticeably, which will take not less than ten minutes and might require as much as twenty.

A group member (or you) then moves to the center to mediate Spirit. He, she, or you should raise the altar light above your head and intone: **I call upon the Powers of Spirit to balance and bless our working.**

Replace the light on the altar.

The quarter mediators now move one at a time to the center, starting with the east and proceeding clockwise. Each circles the altar seven times, then halts, facing the altar, in his or her respective quarter. Each raises the right hand, palm facing the altar and "beams" the relevant elemental energy into talisman basket by visualizing a ray of light in the color of their quarter's tattva emerging from the palm of their hand and playing on the basket:

Air: **I activate thee, spirits of the stones, with the powers of Air.**

Fire: **I activate thee, spirits of the stones, with the powers of Fire.**

Water: **I activate thee, spirits of the stones, with the powers of Water.**

Earth: **I activate thee, spirits of the stones, with the powers of Earth.**

Other members of the group should help by visualizing the radiant beams of energy streaming from the quarters, playing on the basket.

When this is complete, the mediators return to their respective quarters.

(If solo, you can either visualize all this or physically take the place of each quarter officer in turn. Although exhausting work, the latter is more effective until you've become experienced in astral magic.)

A group member mediating Spirit approaches the altar and intones: **I call upon the Powers of Spirit to balance and bless our working.**

Spirit is then invoked by making active and passive Pentagrams of Spirit in succession (figure 29).

The members then approach the altar to take their talismans from the basket. Each moves to the altar and

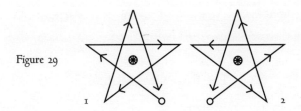

Figure 29

1   2

bows to the four quarters, starting with east and turning clockwise. Each member says:

We thank thee, Powers of Air, for thy help in this working.

We thank thee, Powers of Fire, for thy help in this working.

We thank thee, Powers of Water, for thy help in this working.

We thank thee, Powers of Earth, for thy help in this working.

When every member has his or her talisman, the group raises arms skyward and say in unison: **We thank thee, Power of Spirit, for the balance and blessing thou hast brought to this work.**

The following portion of the ritual between the brackets may be omitted if you're working solo:

[A member steps to center and intones: **The rite is almost ended. May there be peace between us. So mote it be.**

Group: **So mote it be!**

The member returns to his or her place.]

Finally, a group member closes with the Ritual of the Rose Cross, as described below.

The Rose Cross Ritual

Start in the Southeast. Make the sign of the rose cross using a lighted incense stick. Draw the vertical arm first, top to bottom, as in step 1 of figure 30. Step 2 adds the horizontal arm, drawn left to right. Step 3 inscribes the "rose," a circle drawn clockwise from a point on the right hand arm of the cross. As you draw this sign, vibrate **Yeheshuah** (Yay-hay-shoo-ah.)

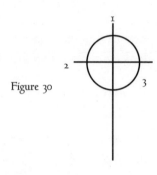

Figure 30

Go to the Southwest and repeat both the sign and the Name. Go to the Northwest and repeat. Go to the Northeast and repeat. Return to the Southeast to complete the circle.

Walk diagonally (toward NW), holding the incense stick above your head, but stop halfway. Make the rose cross and vibrate the Name above your head. Continue to the NW corner, then turn so you're facing SE. Walk to the center again, this time holding the incense stick pointing downward, and make the cross below your feet, vibrating the Name. Continue walking diagonally until you reach the SE.

Walk directly to the SW corner. Now walk the diagonal toward the NE, again holding the incense stick high. When you reach the center, see in your mind's eye the form of the cross you drew earlier above your head. Vibrate the Name again, then continue walking to the NE corner. Turn so you're facing SW. Walk to the center. Visualize the underfoot cross and vibrate the Name then continue walking to the SW corner.

Walk directly to the NW, then NE, then SE, retracing the cross at each point, but making it larger in the SE. At each point, vibrate **Yeheshuah** while drawing lower half of rose, **Yehovashah** while drawing upper half.

Return to the center of the room between the various crosses you have made. Face East. Outstretch your arms in the cruciform position. Vibrate **Yod Nun Resh Yod. The Sign of Osiris Slain.**

Raise your right arm up and stretch your left arm out, head bowed toward your left hand. Vibrate the phrase **L—The Sign of the Mourning of Isis.**

Raise both your arms up to make a "V". Vibrate the phrase **V—The Sign of Typhon and Apophis.**

Cross both your arms across your breast and bow your head forward. Vibrate the phrase **X—The Sign of Osiris Risen.**

Now repeat these positions in sequence (without the phrases) and hold the final position. Now vibrate **L V X. LUX. The Light of the Cross.**

Extend your arms again cruciform, head still bowed. Vibrate **Virgo Isis Mighty Mother. Scorpio Apophis Destroyer. Sol Osiris Slain and Risen.** Raise your arms above your head. Vibrate **Isis Apophis Osiris.** Now raise your head and face upward. Vibrate **I A O. Exarp Hcoma Nanta Bitom.**

Imagine a beam of rose-colored light flowing down over you, head to feet. Vibrate **Let the Divine Light Descend.**

This completes the rite. Members leave the area of working in single file.

The Rose Cross Ritual, which completes the talisman charging, is one of the most pleasing of all the rites used in the Golden Dawn. It functions in a similar way to the Banishing Ritual of the Lesser Pentagram, but much more gently and will leave a warm and pleasant atmosphere in the room. For a fuller explanation of its workings—and, indeed, a complete exposition of the Golden Dawn system, including the basics of Enochian magic, see Israel Regardie's *The Golden Dawn* or Tabatha and Chic Cicero's *Self-Initiation in the Golden Dawn*.

You won't find the full ritual of energy contact in either of these sources since it's my own creation, but you will certainly learn much more about the various elements on which I drew to put it together.

Fourteen

Searching for Miracles

I walked with Helen and Johanna up a seemingly
endless set of narrow wooden stairs in search of the
miraculous. The doorway we entered had been
mean and dingy. The stairs were dirty, so that dust rose
as we walked and caught in our throats. Somewhere
near the top, we heard a perfectly indescribable sound.
We followed it to its source and found ourselves in the
séance room. The sound came from caged birds—perhaps as many as fifty of them—along the walls.

The room was large, but a good third of it had been
filled with junk. Old oil paintings and faded lithographs
were stacked against heavy antique tables, china dogs,
and chamber pots. On one wall was a little darkroom
light. At the other end of the room were a few dozen
"Sunday-go-to-Meeting" chairs set out in rows. A
lectern faced them and on it a huge, open Bible, pon-
derous and dignified as the Book of Life.

Each Saturday evening this room was the site of
contacts with the Dead—or so Johanna told me.

The congregation, when it had finished drifting in, turned out to be small and almost entirely female. Apart from myself, there was only one other man in the place, and he looked distinctly uncomfortable.

When the medium arrived, he shattered all illusions. There was neither power nor personality about him. He was a small man about fifty years old and thin. He looked tired. There was a greyness about him as if dust had collected in the lines of his face. His suit was a non-descript green, unpressed and stained. His fingernails were enormously long, like those of Chinese mandarin.

The weekly séances were his livelihood. He eked out a living from the donations of his regular congregation and the occasional casual caller like myself. But he disliked giving value for money. He was a medium who preferred not to function.

Johanna told me he had been caught cheating at least once. Someone had switched on the light during a trumpet séance and found him on hands and knees waving the instrument about in the air. But she still felt he had a genuine talent.

The proceedings started with the singing of a hymn. It was unaccompanied and gave the whole meeting the feeling of a small town revival. Then our medium read a piece from the Bible, something suitably disturbing about the "Last Days" and suitably spiritualistic about "speaking in tongues." Then the lights went off, except for the little red darkroom light at the far end, and we waited.

We waited not for our little thin medium, who preferred to conserve his energies, but for the developing mediums in the congregation. We didn't have long to wait. A woman with cherries on her hat and bright, compelling eyes, rose to deliver messages in a pleasant, vibrant voice.

"I have a message from Mary," the woman said.

"That's my mother!" someone said excitedly.

"She says she is the mother of someone present here tonight…"

"It's her! It's her!" the person repeated.

It was all perfectly wonderful and perfectly unconvincing. Not, of course, a con game (for con games are really remarkably hard to find in Spiritualism) but something I then considered a mass of deception, mutual and self, as people without much drama in their lives got together in a conspiracy to produce some.

My judgment was far too hasty. In those days I had yet to discover Kenneth Batcheldor.

You'll recall from Chapter Two that Batcheldor's breakthrough theory concerned the importance of "artifacts"—by which he meant natural, but unusual, occurrences that encouraged paranormal phenomena. Batcheldor discovered that the most important thing when it came to getting results was the belief of the group. If you believed table turning or levitation was possible, then table turning and levitation was what you got. If you didn't, the séance produced nothing. Batcheldor's "artifacts" helped switch group belief from negative to positive.

My Spiritualist meeting hall, unimpressive though it seemed at first, positively reeked with conviction. All of the participants (with the possible exception of myself) were true believers. They needed no artifacts to support their faith. They knew, to the depths of their being, that the spirits were waiting to communicate.

In this atmosphere, oddities occurred. The human mind is a curious thing and the group mind is even odder. In the dim light with emotions roused, strange things happened. A stirring subconscious might stretch out telekinetic tendrils to produce a poltergeist or two. A hysterical individual might, quite unconsciously, steal information from another mind.

Such things happen daily among Spiritualists. They don't necessarily point to postmortem communication (although confusion between the two is rife among the faithful) but may someday prove a mine of interest to the parapsychologists.

Very many years later, still searching for the miraculous, I found myself alone in London. It was a quiet end of the city, an avenue with trees where you could actually forget you stood upon a plain of concrete that stretched for miles whichever way you turned.

My taxi driver looked at the houses and opined that the well-to-do lived here. But he was only angling for a bigger tip. Anyone with half an eye could see the district was in decline. Rich residents had obviously lived here once, but not any more. Those who remained were strictly members of the stranded gentry.

I walked through a little garden overgrown with shrubs. The greenery was London green, as if soot had managed to discolor the living plants. I rang the bell.

It was as if I had been swept back through the years. The woman who opened the door would have dropped into that dusty séance room without creating a ripple. She was one of the Faithful. But she was also completely silent, which was out of character for the type.

I went to a little anteroom where I prepared myself with meditation for some fifteen or twenty minutes. Then I was escorted down a flight of stairs to a very different sort of séance.

The room was a Lodge Room, constructed and prepared by ritualists. It was furnished with, among other things, the traditional altar and pillars. Lodge officers, mediating archetypal figures, stood, or sat, at the cardinal points. There was incense and candlelight.

There was also, it occurs to me now, the utter professionalism—no other word can describe it—of people who know what they're doing.

The room had been prepared, almost certainly, by a variation of the Pentagram Ritual given in Chapter One. It had, I presume, been used time and again for evocation. The effect of that room was staggering.

If you have ever walked any distance on a frosty day before pushing open a door into a centrally heated building, you will know what I mean by a wall of air. There was a wall of air at the doorway of the Lodge Room. Its essence was not heat but something else, something that could be sensed perfectly (and, it seemed, at a physical level) by the nerve endings beneath the skin. Houses have "atmosphere," a welcoming feeling or a rejection, an aura of warmth or chill. This was atmosphere solidified, an atmosphere that literally "hits you in the face."

There were no fireworks in the working that followed, no levitations, trances or weird shadows in the incense smoke—just results and an atmosphere pregnant with power.

The essential difference between the group in the Spiritualist meeting hall and the group in the Lodge Room was that the second group had formed a link with the Inner Planes and was drawing power from the other side of the collective mind. The first group had power too, for it produced phenomena. But it was power without control, hence a long way from High Magic.

Inner Plane contacts are most often made within a group setting. The trick is easier that way. But links may also be forged by individuals, if they go about it the right way.

There are, in fact, a number of methods. They produce different kinds of contact, although all originate in essentially the same area. It is as if you had three friends in New York. One owned a fax machine, one a telephone, while the third, impoverished or just sensible, owned neither. You can make contact with all three in different ways. A fax contact is not a telephone contact, which is not a letter contact. Yet your friends all live in New York.

The Qabalist would, for instance, embark on Inner Plane contacts by treading the Paths of the Tree of Life. Unfortunately, to be undertaken properly, this technique requires considerable training in Qabalistic symbolism, which in turn requires a particular type of mind and interest.

It is also true to say that while pathworking—as this form of contact is called—can be a solitary affair, it is always far more successful if undertaken by a group. I have no quarrel with group work when undertaken for a specific purpose, but many groups become a way of life. This to my mind breeds a greater or lesser exclusiveness, a feeling of "us" and "them" that can be the death of spiritual development in its higher aspects.

The technique outlined in this chapter is not a Qabalistic pathworking, but it is effective just the same. The Qabalists have no monopoly on magic and pathworkings are used in many other magical systems. More to the point, once you know the principles, you can construct one of your own, just as you can apply basic principles to construct a ritual. This is not to say pathworkings are inevitably successful, but Inner Plane entities will, as a general principle, "take calls" from those of us who have gone beyond the playing stage.

But I suppose I'd better voice the old familiar warning. This form of contact is not a party game. If it's approached in a party atmosphere, the lines of communication simply break down, leaving you at best with nothing and at worst with an obsessive fascination for the glittering nonsense sometimes produced by toying with the astral.

From time to time when a contact is made, those on the other side will suggest fresh methods and techniques of putting through a call. Sometimes these suggestions involve the reopening of old channels; sometimes the formation of new ones. In the present working, there's a little of both.

By the time you come to begin this exercise, you will, or should, already have established a regular routine of occult exercises. Devote the time taken up by this routine to the establishment of your own Inner Plane contact. From this point until the contact is firmly established, abandon all exercises other than those given.

Your first task is the preparation of the place of working. This simply means the establishment of a suitable astral environment for contact to take place. Remember that the Astral Plane is fluid and you require a place of relative stability—a place to stand, as Archimedes said.

Permanent edifices can be established on the astral only with a lot of hard work and repetition. That's why the reopening of old channels is often suggested: Much of the hard work has already been done.

Your astral place of working falls to some extent into this category. When the original place of contact was formed is a matter for speculation. Those interested in tying the matter down further may conduct their own experiments when contact is made.

What follows is a starting point created specially for readers of this book. There are two broad types of pathworking. One is a wholly scripted inner journey in which you follow instructions from beginning to end. The other is more free-form, allowing you the latitude to wander on the Astral Plane and search out areas of power, information or interest. The exercise you are about to undertake falls into the latter category.

Prepare for your journey by familiarizing yourself thoroughly with the following description, which you might even like to record and play back to yourself.

City of Bridges Exercise

You stand outside the walls of an ancient city. They are high, grey walls, towering up out of a cold and barren landscape. There is a tremendous aura of endurance about these walls, a lasting strength.

Before you are the twin gates of the city. These are wood, inlaid with brass and iron. They are massive gates and on your right, high above you, is a guard, helmeted, armed only with a spear, standing at his post on the walls of the city.

There is a path twisting through the wasteland behind you; and you know that, in a way, you have trodden this path to reach the city.

The gates swing open and you pass through. Immediately, in contrast with the cold and dreary wasteland, you are in bright sunlight. The avenues of the city are broad and clean, the houses high and built in a Medieval style.

Everywhere there are canals, sparkling silver waterways that wander through the city, intermingling with the avenues. On every side, it seems, you are surrounded by bridges.

These bridges are the most striking feature of the city, so that you quickly come to think of it as the City of Bridges.

Quickly, you find your way to the central avenue, a broad, straight thoroughfare boring its way to the very heart of the city. There are a few people about, golden-haired men and women strolling without haste. You pay them no attention, nor they you.

As you walk, you feel, in a curious way, a growing familiarity with this place. You recognize that you know it, and will know it with even deeper insight in the days ahead.

The city, in turn, will recognize you. You will feel its atmosphere welcoming, lifting you a little higher, a little straighter. Your body will feel just a little lighter as you walk within the city walls.

Now you are reaching the end of your journey, for the avenue widens into a vast courtyard. Before you, in the courtyard, is the tallest building you have yet seen. You have reached the Central Temple of the City of Bridges.

Your inner journey is far from finished, but there is a natural break here. Having familiarized yourself with the description, begin to "live it" in the following way.

Sit in your chair and go through the conscious relaxation process, then perform the Fountain of Light exercise see Chapter Four). Both of these are important preliminaries to what follows.

Making sure no tension has crept back in, begin to visualize the journey from the gates of the city to the central temple, as if you were actually undertaking it. Build up the pictures as strongly as you are able, filling in as much detail as possible. The more you can make this picture live, the greater are your chances of successful contact with the Inner Planes.

Perform this exercise daily for at least two weeks, and preferably four, before you move on to its second stage. Record the following description and switch on the audio tape as you reach the Temple in your next journey through the City.

As you watch, you can feel the aura of the temple pulling you toward it. You walk to the broad, white steps and begin to mount them toward a door set between tall, white, marble pillars. Like the gate of the city, this door is wood, inlaid with brass; but it has a newer, lighter appearance. As you mount the steps, it swings open.

You pass through into a vast, domed hall of white marble. Colonnades of slender pillars run on your right and left. High above you, a window in the central dome allows a shaft of golden sunlight to pour through and strike the central altar.

This altar, set as high as your waist on the marble floor, is draped in white, without ornament. Lying diagonally across it, with the handle toward you, is a broadsword.

Behind the sword is a lighted lamp and beside that a dagger and chalice.

Beyond the altar, in the east, are two thick pillars, towering to the roof: one black, the other silver. Between them, inlaid in the marble floor, is a circle with, around its edge, representations of the zodiacal signs.

Nothing more stands in the temple, except a white marble throne in the east, beyond the pillars.

You walk forward, moving to the left of the altar and beyond it, approaching the pillars and eventually taking your stand between them, facing west, your feet in the center of the zodiac circle. You wait.

You are now in the symbolic place of balance. Your body forms the Middle Pillar between those great pillars on either side. It is only from this spot that you may safely handle the cosmic spiritual forces. But the placing is symbolic. Meditate on this.

From this point, there is very little to do except wait. You've done all you can. For anything more to happen, the action must come from the other side: Your friend in New York must decide to pick up the receiver.

On your first attempts, nothing more is likely to happen. But don't get discouraged. Each time you visualize the sequence, you are establishing the environment more and more firmly on the Astral Plane.

You will find, as the weeks, and possibly months, go by, that your vision becomes clearer, more realistic, sharper in detail, fuller in depth. All these things, all this increasing solidity, bring the moment of contact closer.

What happens when contact occurs? In a way I can tell you, and in a way I can't. When you call your friend in New York, I can tell you approximately how you will be holding your phone and describe the dial tone and the ringing sound. But I can't tell you what your friend will say, or what emotions you'll feel at the news, or what action you may feel impelled to take because of it.

When you've built up the place of meeting sufficiently well and the contact on the other side of your mind closes the circuit, you will first feel an energizing sensation as you stand between the pillars. Exactly how you will experience this is difficult to say; but the sensation will be there. Below is one example of the kind of thing you might experience at this point:

As you stand between the pillars, a light ray bathes you from above. You see figures enter the great hall. Like the people of the city, they are golden-haired and handsome, but their dress is different from those who stand outside. They wear monk's robes in white, cowls thrown back to expose their faces. They move silently and serenely, taking their places in orderly rows before the altar.

These figures emerge from a number of entrances dimly seen beyond the colonnades of pillars. As they become evident—which should only happen after you experience the energizing sensation—you move out calmly from between the twin pillars.

You walk again to the left of the altar (your left, that is, so that your movement from the entrance in the west to the pillars and back takes you around the altar in a clockwise direction) and quietly take your place in the midst of the brethren. Soon after, a High Priest or Hierophant enters. After circling the great hall three times in ceremonial procession, he takes his seat on the marble throne in the east.

This is a typical, but not inevitable experience and there may be variation in detail or even in the broad pattern of what happens. Beyond this point, not even a tentative description is valid: Your experiences will be uniquely your own. The description given here was a guide to what you may expect and a safeguard against the—unlikely—possibility of a destructive contact.

Why not visualize the above sequence step for step? Should you not, for instance, intentionally evoke a beam of light as you stand between the pillars?

Again, unfortunately, there is no direct answer. Visualization certainly helps build the forms that the Inner Plane entities activate, and the more the images arise from your own imagination, the more powerful they will be. But always bear in mind that you are like the submarine commander using his periscope. Your visualization is a symbolic representation, and not the real thing. The picture may, with practice, become clear, but it is never direct observation. Everything is seen in the mirror of the Astral Light.

The experiment given in the previous section is not, of course, the only way to establish an Inner Plane contact. It bears the stamp of my Qabalistic training and the flavor of a personal mythology. Other systems have their own points of contact that are just as effective, just as real, as this one.

For greater control and effect, pathworkings from any system may be combined with ritual. Following, for example, are the instructions given to a trained magical group interested in making a specific contact with the spirit of things feminine. It is structured on the Matter of Britain, the Arthurian mythos and quite different in approach from the Qabalistic tradition.

The operation begins as a sort of psychodrama, designed to influence the minds of the participants, some of whom have been assigned parts in advance, as if they were taking part in a play. At a particular point, the psychodrama blends seamlessly into pathworking.

Lady of the Lake Ritual

We begin with four officers present and robed outside ritual room: Arthur in the east, Guinevere in the west, Taliesin in the south, and Morgan la Fey in the north. Additionally, Merlin is in the ritual room, hooded and crouched by altar.

The temple is arranged as such: The altar is central with a lit candle and crystal of spirit, plus a bowl of amulet stones. The quarters marked by the relevant tattvas. The room is lit. Chairs circle the altar, with one chair for each participant, including the quarter officers and Merlin.

The ritual now begins. A drumbeat from within the ritual room signals the start of the ritual. The company processes into the room and forms a circle around the central altar. Each stands behind his or her chair, but doesn't sit down yet. The quarter officers go to their assigned places, and the magus opens the quarters.

Arthur: **Brethren of the Table, is it your will to undertake our task and test?**

Assembly: **It is our will.**

Arthur: **Proclaim the charge.**

Guinevere: **It is charged that on this day we reach out to the feminine within.**

Arthur: **A woman's task?**

Guinevere: **For women and for men. A test of both.**

Arthur: **How shall we know the feminine within?**

Guinevere: **She is the Lady of the Lake.**

Assembly: **We seek the Lady of the Lake.**

Arthur: **Describe the Lady so that we may know her.**

Taliesin: **She is Mistress of Magic.**

Morgan: **She is Queen of occult power.**

Guinevere: **She is Inspiration and Enlightenment.**

Taliesin: **She is Healing.**

Morgan: **She is Wisdom.**

Guinevere: **She is your soul.**

Taliesin: **Your bright soul.**

Morgan: **Your dark soul.**

Arthur: **How shall we find her?**

Taliesin: **By the Power of Poetry.**

Morgan: **And the Magic of Myth.**

Arthur: **Where shall we find her?**

Taliesin: **On a sunlit isle.**

Morgan: **Surrounded by dark waters.**

Arthur: **How shall we greet her?**

Taliesin: **With respect.**

Morgan: **And love.**

Arthur: **How shall she know us?**

Guinevere: **By the talismans we carry.**

Arthur: **Let each brother and each sister take the talisman they need.**

Members of the assembly approach the altar in turn, starting with the member standing nearest Arthur and moving clockwise.

At the altar, each member takes a quartz crystal talisman from the bowl and returns to his or her place.

The quarter officers then take their talismans, starting with Taliesin and proceeding clockwise to end with Arthur. The quarter officers remain at the altar until Arthur has taken his talisman, then all four move back simultaneously to their quarters.

Arthur: **Who shall guide us to the realm wherein the Lady dwells?**

Taliesin: **The realm of mind.**

Morgan: **The realm of mystery.**

Guinevere: **The Merlin shall guide us.**

Arthur: **Is the Merlin not imprisoned?**

Assembly: **We have freed him. We have freed the Merlin.**

Arthur: **(Loudly) Merlin, come forth!**

Merlin rises from crouched position and pushes back hood. He bows to Arthur.

Merlin: **Your command, sire?**

Arthur: **Conduct us, Merlin, to the realm of the mind so that we all may seek the Lady of the Lake.**

Merlin: **So shall it be. Brothers, Sisters, please take your seats.**

Merlin then conducts the group in the following path-working as an introduction and contact point with the feminine archetype.

Merlin: **Close your eyes.**

As you sit in the darkness, utterly relaxed, I want you smell the smoke. This is wood smoke, mixed with the heavier acrid smell of burning turf or even dung. Catch it in your nostrils. Feel it in your throat. It's all around you, stinging your eyes in the darkness. I want you to make every effort to smell that smoke.

As the smoke catches in your throat and in your chest, you will become aware of its source: a mean little fire, nearly out. Just a few dully glowing embers, hardly enough to cast light into this little cottage. As you stare at the glow, waiting for your

eyes to adjust, try to become aware of the other smells masked by the smell of smoke. The smell of old straw. The smell of human sweat and urine. The smell of damp. Animal smells. Earth smells.

It's cold. Not biting chill, but cold. And because it's cold, you become gradually aware of the body heat of your companions. I want you to sense these things, search them out: the smells, the cold, the faint glow of the near-dead fire, the body heat of your companions.

If you look up, you can just make out a smoke-blackened beam above. Not cut wood, just a thick branch from the forest. There is a faint grey light creeping through a crack in the rough wooden shutters over the only window.

Your eyes are beginning slowly to adjust. The floor of the cottage is dried mud with a light scattering of rushes. There is sacking covering the only door in a tattered curtain.

When you are ready, I want you to move as a group to the door and select someone to open it. When he or she does so, I shall tell you what you see...

After Door Opening

Merlin: It is daylight, but overcast, threatening rain with a chill breeze and the fresh clean scent of grass. The cottage behind you is a mean, mud-walled building roofed with stone slabs and sods of turf. You are standing near a well-trodden roadway which winds up a hillside to the towers and turrets of a castle at the top. Even from this distance you can see gaily colored pennants flying above its battlements.

There is a great deal of activity around the castle. Pilgrims, horsemen, even beggars seem to be able to gain admittance.

Behind you, curling behind the cottage and leading away behind the hill, is a rough stony track.

Stony Track

Merlin: Soon you find yourself walking through a wasteland. The little vegetation that remains is stunted, dying. The land has lost its fertility. There is no wildlife. Even the birds are strangely silent. In the distance, outlined against the skyline, is the silhouette of a dark castle, moated and silent...

At this point, the group as a whole begins a free-form description of what is seem by members on the inner levels, encouraged by the Merlin figure. A well-trained group quickly moves toward a consensus on the inner visions and is thus enabled to find its way to the point of contact with the Lady.

A positive Inner Plane contact, as you'll quickly discover, carries a multitude of benefits. It is, for instance, a source of information—or perhaps wisdom might be a better word. Much of the communication will be nonverbal in nature—insights, intuitions, convictions—

which it will be up to you to catch and clothe in words as best you can. Make a habit of taking notes immediately afterward, each time you experiment with contact. Ideas and insights are easily lost unless this is done.

It's important to remember you have *not* been put in touch with some sort of super fortune-telling machine. Any attempt to treat Inner Plane contacts in this light will lead, at best, to their abrupt cessation.

It is even more important to realize that Inner Plane contacts are neither your God nor your boss. One of the most chastening experiences of my life was to witness a large group of intelligent and well-educated occultists making contact with an entity who claimed to be one of the Ancient Egyptian pantheon. Member after member of the group asked the entity variations on one of two questions: How they should live their lives and how they could best serve the entity itself.

To my astonishment, no one asked the contact for its bona fides.

I discussed the incident with an American psychic and occultist some years later, who said "I tell my pupils making an Inner Plane contact is like leaving your house in the middle of the night and shouting down the darkened street, 'Is anybody there?'" she remarked. "If somebody does come out of the shadows, you should make damn sure you know who they are before you invite them into your home."

It's good advice. Never be afraid to ask questions or demand proof of any entity you invoke. If you don't like the answers, cut the contact.

The establishment of positive (and tested!) Inner Plane contacts will usually make a considerable difference to the outcome of any magical experiments you may undertake. Here again, it is impossible to formulate general rules, but there is usually a considerable stimulation in accordance with the individual talents of the magician. If, for instance, you have no flair for prophecy, the contact will not produce one. But if such a flair exists, you will find it coming quickly to the fore, increased in ease of operation and accuracy. The same applies to any active or latent talent you may have.

But as your evolution in the spiritual realities continues, a strange thing will happen. You will find it more and more difficult to perform certain operations of Low Magic. It's a curious paradox. The further you develop in the fascinating realms of magic, the less you can actually do. But there's a reason.

Magic and mysticism both travel, by different tracks, in the same direction. At the end of the road lies a state of contemplation—the reconciliation of the opposites, beyond the possibility of action. Before that state is reached, there is an understanding of cosmic law and an acceptance of the karmic balance. It is as if you reached a stage in magic where further progress can only be purchased by the total acceptance of karma (what you sow, you reap)—and not simply a theoretical acceptance either. The law must become a part of your being. In this state you can no more rock the karmic boat than you can touch your right elbow with your right hand.

This does not, of course, mean you must cease to practice magic altogether, although even that will come about in the final stages when you grow beyond toys of any sort. What it does mean is that you begin to concentrate on a different type of magic.

In the past, as you experimented with Low Magic, you used the forces to change your environment—to bring you a $100 bill, for instance, or discover a well so you could take a drink. But now the forces will be used increasingly in another direction. For as you grow in spiritual stature, you will realize that much more important than changing your environment is changing yourself.

Fifteen

Godforms

E very dramatist must be something of a wizard, just as every actor must be something of a medium. When a great play is written, its characters take on a life of their own. They become as real, for instance, as any celebrities or political figures you have never met, and often stick in the memory a great deal longer.

Of all dramatists, Shakespeare had the greatest talent for creating living characters. Hamlet and Prospero are personalities lacking only bodies to make them people. Falstaff was so imbued with vigor that he actually ran away from his creator.

A great actor does not, as many people imagine, interpret his part; he lets the part interpret him. By careful study and something akin to meditation, he forms a link with the ethereal character, then, medium-like, invites it to take him over. Such men as Sir Laurence Olivier are not so much great actors as great puppets. They provide temporary bodies for Hamlet or

Falstaff and these immortal creatures from another plane reach out to pull the strings.

The stage, more than any other art form, is magical in essence. The fact may be widely recognized at an unconscious level, else why should we bother with theaters when we have the greater scope and technical perfection of the cinema? When a dramatist creates, he does something suspiciously like the magician's evocation of "spirits from the vasty deep." When an actor steps into a role, he does something suspiciously like the magician's assumption of a godform.

The assumption of a godform is, in a way, one of the most appealing operations in High Magic. Given the usual prerequisite of visualization ability, it requires no knack but work. And the bulk of the work, unlike so much of the grinding repetition of magical training, is interesting in itself.

There are a variety of reasons why you might wish to undertake the godform operation. You may, for instance, want to balance some aspect of your character. You may wish to investigate, at first hand as it were, the characteristics of the god concerned. Or you may wish to mediate the godforce for some specific purpose. Whatever your motive, the mechanics remain the same.

The use of the godform (or, to be modern and scientific, the assumption of an archetype) is associated with Ancient Egypt, where it appears to have played a fairly major part in the magical life of the initiate priesthood. Among other references in the *Book of the Dead*, for instance, is one which reads, "I have made myself a counterpart of Isis and her spirit hath made me strong."

Because of this link. the forms assumed, even to the present day, are often Egyptian. Fortunately the pantheon is a self-contained and comprehensive system of magical images in its own right, which will amply repay the study necessary to use it nowadays.

The assumption of a godform is a potent method of invocation, the calling up of force to inward manifestation, as opposed to evocation, which requires the force to manifest objectively.

To begin the operation, you must first choose your god or goddess. There is no reason why an archetypal godform from any pantheon may not be used, but the beginner would be well advised to stick to the Egyptian source. The use of Egyptian forms is traditional in magic, so the operation is easier to perform as the relevant channels are already half formed in the Astral Light. (Remember morphic resonance!)

Obviously, your final choice of godform will depend on the result you want. For the sake of illustration, let me assume you've chosen the Egyptian Sun God, Ra.

Before attempting any magical operation, you must find out all you can about Ra. Egyptology has produced a prolific literature. Use it. Read the characteristics of Ra, the mythology of Ra, the descriptions of Ra. Never begrudge the time spent in this type of study: it is laying the foundations of a successful operation. Become an expert on Ra, so expert you could hold your own with any academic.

Pay particular attention to the god's appearance. That is, the appearance typically ascribed to him by artists. Take note of the characteristic poses in which he is depicted. It is particularly important to know how the god was traditionally painted by the artists of Ancient Egypt. These people were, by definition, closer to the source you are seeking.

A local library will almost certainly have books that will throw light on the subject. If not, ask your librarian to order some. Especially useful are the works of Wallis Budge, especially his *Gods of the Egyptians*.

When you study the traditional poses of the god, pay particular attention to gesture. These are seldom random and can be duplicated in your magical experiment with considerable benefit to the outcome.

Note too the implements traditionally associated with the god. Ra, for instance, traditionally carries an ibis wand in the left hand and an ankh (the Egyptian looped cross) in the right.

Only when you have steeped yourself in this knowledge to a degree that it springs instantly to memory when needed should you begin your actual experiments.

Magical exercises are best done in the morning; magical operations in the evening. Experience shows you get better results that way. So pick an evening for the assumption of the Ra godform. Or rather, pick your evenings, for you are unlikely to succeed at first.

Begin by putting your accumulated knowledge to use. Once again, you will be image-building, or, as the occultists say, creating stresses in the Astral Light.

Seat yourself in a comfortable position close to the traditional posture of the god. Then go through the relaxation process, combined with the 2/4 breathing sequence. If you can relax in the identical posture associated with the god, so much the better; although this is not always possible. (Should the god's traditional posture be a standing one, as is the case of Hathor, for instance, perform the relaxation, breathing, and initial visualization exercises in your usual meditation posture, then assume the stance of the god at the moment of assuming the godform.)

When you are fully relaxed, begin building up the vision. Again using the example of Ra, you should see the Sun God as a gigantic form standing before you, radiating light and heat. His form will be that with which you have already familiarized yourself through your studies.

Attempt to insert clarity and color into your vision. Try to see the golden hue of the skin, the glowing nimbus around the head. Bring your other imaginary senses into play, so that you seem to feel the heat, seem to hear the lordly voice.

When you invoke a godform, you stand in the same relationship to the force behind it as a worshipper to his god. This is a point worth remembering, for the assumption of a godform can't be a cold, scientific business. It involves deep emotions and a degree of commitment. Indeed, one of the most certain signs that your visualization has been successful is its ability to produce in you a feeling of awe.

The theory of the operation is straightforward enough. Ra as a person does not exist, and possibly never did. But the idea behind Ra is real enough. That's to say, the constellation of powers and characteristics which the Egyptians personified as Ra are real enough on another level of existence. (We are, in fact, back to the Inner Planes, but that's not important at the moment.)

The traditional pictures, postures, and gestures of Ra are the forms—discovered through trial and error—by means of which the Ra-force can most easily manifest. These forms, through the activities of Ra's priesthood and devotees, gradually took on a semi-permanent existence in the Astral Light. In Ancient Egypt, results followed quickly and easily on any magical operation evoking or invoking Ra. But as the Egyptian civilization degenerated, the astral forms faded.

There is a connection here with the occult theory of the artificial elemental. When a number of people concentrate with emotion on a single object, an artificial elemental is formed on the Astral Plane. The elemental persists only so long as it is fed by the emotion of the individuals. Without worshippers, the gods can no longer exist on astral levels. But this does not mean the gods cease to exist altogether: The worshipper produces only the *form* of the god and not the essence. And even diminished, the old Egyptian forms are still best for manifestation.

Once you appreciate this, you will readily appreciate what you are doing in building up the vivid Ra image.

You are, by an act of devoted concentration, producing a form through which the forces of Ra can manifest.

Provided you have built the form accurately, there will be little trouble in animation. Indeed, animation is something over which you have no control. Your job— at least your main job—is finished with the building of the form. The rest is up to Ra.

When the form has been established in the Astral Light to the greatest degree your talent allows, assume physically the traditional posture and gestures of the god. Then, by an act of imagination, have the astral godform coincide with your body. What you are in fact doing here is blending it with your own astral body, providing points of contact for the godforce to flow into you. As the form coincides (something which may take a little practice) invoke the god verbally.

Most authorities suggest you create your own invocation. The theory seems to be that this is nearer your true nature and consequently more likely to produce successful results. My own experience has been that traditional invocations work equally well, provided you choose one that appeals to you and don't use it simply because you feel you must. Certainly, you shouldn't use one that you have a negative reaction to.

A good (i.e., workable) invocation is like good poetry—it must affect the emotions. If you find an invocation that inflames your imagination, use it. If you can't find one, create one that does.

It may be of help to point out that there are two forms of workable invocation. The first, frequently used by beginners, salutes the god as an external force and goes on to invite him to animate the prepared form. Thus:

Hail to Thee, Ra. Eye of the Morning…

The second form identifies the practitioner with the god, as if animation of the assumed godform had already taken place. Thus:

I have united myself with the divine Apes who sing at dawn and I am a divine Being among them…

(These two fragments are from the Budge's *Egyptian Book of the Dead*.) Whichever choice you make is largely a matter of taste, although identification does seem to have marginal advantages for a majority of operators.

Results of assuming a godform become evident the instant the operation is properly performed The prime result is a staggering inflow of sheer energy, but as the practice continues, there is a gradual change in your own personality as it takes on more and more of the god's characteristics.

A danger here, seldom stressed, is that of one-sided development. Few of the old gods were fully rounded, balanced personalities. But I assume that by the time you come to High Magical experiments of this type, your development will be sufficient to ensure you realize dangers of this sort for yourself.

Since the assumption of a godform is a type of Inner Plane contact, the cleansing preparations outlined previously are relevant here. If you have already undergone the exercises in preparation for the Central Temple visions, there is no need to repeat them. But if not, do them before attempting the godform operation.

Complete the operation by separating the godform from your body by projecting it before you and gradually allowing it to fade away through an act of imagination. It's a good idea to complete proceedings with a ritual gesture, giving a clear demarcation line between your magical experiments and your life in the mundane world.

Sixteen

Conjuration

R ay leaned across and whispered, "Have you fallen into trance?" I wasn't in a trance, but I had certainly sunk into reverie. We were at Mass and the sacrifice had been performed by one of the very few priests who seemed to know what he was doing. A Catholic, I assume, becomes accustomed to the Mass and thus, to a degree, hardened to it. For a Qabalist like myself, unfamiliarity made the ritual that much more striking

The Roman Catholic Mass is, of course, an excellent example of High Magic ceremonial, although often it goes unrecognized as such and outside the Liberal Catholic Church is all too frequently worked without power. (The Liberal Catholic Church is one of the more esoteric of Christian churches, founded by Bishop C . W. Leadbeater, a follower of Madame Blavatsky.)

Like all magical operations, the Mass has an inner and outer aspect. Unfortunately Rome has either forgotten, or come to ignore, the inner aspect, with the result that too many priests gabble their way through the ritual.

But what a difference when the priest is a member of a contemplative order, or has experienced the reality behind such visualization exercises as those of Saint Ignatius Loyola. In the hands of these men, the Mass comes to life and the congregation staggers off afterward, emotionally uplifted, spiritually exalted and, one suspects, wondering what hit them.

The Mass is an evocation of spirit, a drawing down of power by the priest for the benefit of the congregation. But another type of evocation is far more closely associated with the world of magic—evocation to visible appearance.

Evocation to visible appearance is something that has caught the public imagination. It is the operation fiction writers most often feature in occult romances. In fiction, the entities evoked are usually Satanic. How far this reflects the real-life situation I cannot say. I can only say I've never seen an infernal evocation. To be honest, I only know a handful of individuals with the talent to evoke entities at all.

The basic pattern of an evocation is easily described. The magician and his helpers crowd into a protective circle. From this fortress, the magician performs a rite designed to raise a spirit entity. If the rite is successful, the entity manifests within the confines of a triangle placed beyond the circle. Unless himself psychic, the magician typically works with a clairvoyant. It's a pattern that's remained unchanged since the days

of Dr. Dee and Edward Kelley. The magician questions
the spirit through the clairvoyant.

Since this arrangement produces all the results you
need, the more difficult evocation to visible appearance
has been largely abandoned today. It was not always so.
The Order of the Golden Dawn used it as a Grade test
(the evoked spirit had to attain the consistency of
steam before the candidate passed) and there are many
records of the operation in the annals of the occult.

One of the most detailed accounts—and its
results—is contained in the private papers of Benvenuto Cellini, Italy's Renaissance master painter.

In 1533 or 1534 (the exact date is uncertain),
Cellini met with a Sicilian priest versed in the art of ritual magic. In the course of their conversation, Cellini
remarked that he had always wanted to see a magical
operation. After voicing a few dire warnings about the
dangers, the priest agreed to show him.

The site chosen for their experiment was the impos-
ing ruins of the Roman Coliseum. With Cellini came his
friend Vincentio Romoli, while the priest was accompanied by a second magician from Pistoia. The equipment
laid out included ceremonial robes, a wand, several grimoires, a pentacle (a disc, made from wood or metal,
inscribed on both sides and used for the control of spirits), incense, kindling, and a supply of asafoetida grass.

While the others watched, the Sicilian drew circles on the Coliseum floor and fortified them by means
of some impressive ceremonial. One of the circles was
left incomplete. The magician led his companions

through the gap before closing it and concluding his ritual preparations.

Cellini and Romoli were given the job of lighting a fire. When they got it going, they were instructed to burn quantities of incense. While the man from Pistoia held the pentacle, the priest began a lengthy ritual of evocation. An hour and a half later it bore fruit. According to Cellini's own account, the Coliseum was filled with "several legions," presumably of spirits.

Never one to miss an opportunity, Cellini promptly asked that these entities should bring him a young woman he fancied named Angelica. The spirits ignored him. Despite his disappointment, Cellini expressed himself well enough satisfied with the demonstration. But the Sicilian seems to have been something of a perfectionist, for he undertook to perform the ceremony again in the hope of obtaining more spectacular results. To this end, he made a fresh stipulation: he wanted a virgin boy to attend. Cellini brought a young servant with him, a twelve-year-old named Cenci.

Romoli returned to the Coliseum for the second operation, but the magician from Pistoia didn't. His place was taken by another of Cellini's friends, Agnolino Gaddi. Once again the circles were drawn and consecrated, the fire lit and the incense burned. Cellini himself held the pentacle this time as the Sicilian priest began the evocation.

It's plain from Cellini's account that the conjuration was directed toward those demons who controlled legions of infernal spirits. It was spoken in a mixture of

Hebrew, Greek, and Latin not uncommon in the grimoires and seems to have been a remarkable success. Much sooner than before, the Coliseum was packed tight with entities whom Cellini again asked for the miraculous transportation of his lady-love. The spirits replied through the mouth of the magician that Cellini and the woman would be together within a month.

Although all seemed well at this point, the operation quickly began to go wrong. The magician himself was the first to notice. There were, he said, too many spirits present—possibly as many as a thousand times more than he had called up. Worse, they had begun to misbehave. Twelve-year-old Cenci screamed that they were all being menaced by a million of the fiercest "men" he had ever seen. Four giants, fully armed, were trying to enter the fortified circle.

The priest launched into a formula of dismissal. The little boy began to moan and buried his head between his knees, convinced they were all as good as dead. Cellini tried to reassure him but failed, possibly because he himself was shaking like a leaf. The child cried out that the Coliseum was on fire and that flames were rolling toward them. He covered his eyes with his hands in a paroxysm of terror.

The magician broke off his chanted license to depart in favor of stronger means. He instructed Cellini to have his assistants pile asafoetida on the fire. Cellini's assistants were by now too paralyzed with terror to comply, so Cellini lost his temper and shouted at them. This had the desired effect, and soon the foul-smelling grass was burning merrily. The spirits began to depart "in great fury."

None of the experimenters felt like leaving the protection of their magic circle. They stayed huddled together until morning when only a few spirits remained "and these at a distance." With the sound of Matins bells ringing in their ears, the sorry group left the circle and headed home, with little Cenci clinging desperately to Cellini and the Sicilian. Two spirits accompanied them, racing over the rooftops and along the road.

Despite the detail of Benvenuto Cellini's diaries, it's not absolutely certain his experience was an evocation to visible appearance—although there's a clear likelihood that it was. There is, however, no doubt at all about the nature of the magical evocation carried out by Victor Neuburg and Aleister Crowley in North Africa in 1909.

Crowley's name is well known in esoteric circles to this day. He was a Golden Dawn initiate who became one of the most notorious magicians of his day. Neuburg is today perhaps better known as a poet. In 1909, he was an initiate in a magical Order called the *Astrum Argentinum* and Crowley's homosexual lover.

On November 17, 1909, the two arrived at Algiers. They took a tram to Arba, then walked south. By November 21, they were in Aumale where Crowley bought Neuburg some notebooks. Crowley wanted Neuburg to use the notebooks to record the results of an operation in Enochian magic.

Crowley carried in his rucksack a copy of the Enochian Calls he'd made from Dee's manuscripts in the British Museum. He had already experimented with two of the Calls and wanted to find out what would happen if he used the rest. Over a period of days and nights Crowley and Neuburg worked their way through the Calls until, by December 6, they reached what was technically known as the Tenth Aethyr, an area of magical reality inhabited, according to Kelley, by the "mighty devil" Choronzon, Lord of the Powers of Chaos.

On a more mundane level, Crowley and Neuburg were stopping at Bou Saada. In the early afternoon they walked a considerable distance from the town to reach a valley of fine sand. There, in the desert, they traced a magic circle of protection, sealed with words of power, and the equilateral triangle of the art fortified with divine names. Crowley sacrificed three pigeons so that the released energy would give Choronzon something with which to manifest.

Neuburg moved into the circle. Crowley, acting on an impulse experienced magicians must find bizarre, entered the triangle.

(It's possible that Crowley, as eccentric in his magical practice as he was in most other aspects of his life, wanted to find out what it felt like to be possessed by a demon. Jean Overton Fuller, who wrote *The Magical Dilemma of Victor Neuburg* [W. H. Allen, London, 1965], the biography of Neuburg from which the account of this magical operation has been drawn, considered Crowley had "ceased to be completely sane" by this stage, having assumed the initiate grade of Master of the Temple, following a homosexual act with Neuburg on an altar set up on the summit of Dal'leh Addin mountain.)

Neuburg began the ceremony by chanting a magical oath then performing the Banishing Ritual of the Lesser Pentagram. With the place prepared, Crowley, wearing a black magician's robe, made the relevant Enochian Call (quoted in translation from Regardie's *The Golden Dawn*) in his high-pitched, rather nasal voice:

The thunders of judgment and wrath are numbered and are harbored in the North in the likeness of an oak whose branches are nests of lamentation and weeping, laid up for the Earth which burn night and day: and vomit out the heads of scorpions and live sulfur, mingled with poison. These be the thunders that 5678 Times (in ye 24th part) of a moment roar with an hundred mighty earthquakes and a thousand times as many surges which rest not neither know any echoing time herein. One rock bringeth forth a thousand even as the heart of man does his thoughts. Woe! Woe! Woe! Woe! Woe! Woe! Yea Woe! Be on the Earth, for her iniquity is, was And shall be great. Come away! But not your mighty sounds.

It's difficult to see why such obscurities, even in the original tongue, would attract the attention of a demon, but something certainly happened. Neuburg heard Crowley's voice call out "Zazas, Zazas, Nasatanda Zazas" followed by a string of blasphemies. Neuburg glanced toward the triangle and there discovered a beautiful woman, somewhat similar in appearance to a prostitute he had known in Paris. She began to call softly to him and make seductive gestures. Neuburg stolidly ignored her.

The woman then apologized for trying to seduce him and offered instead to lay her head beneath his feet as a token of her willingness to serve him. Neuburg ignored this too.

The demon—for so Neuburg considered the women to be—promptly changed into an old man, then a snake which, in Crowley's voice, asked for water. Unmoved, Neuburg demanded "in the name of the Most High" that the demon reveal its true nature. The thing replied that it was Master of the Triangle and its name was 333. (This is a reference to Gematria, a Qabalistic sub-system whereby numbers are substituted for letters in an individual name, then totaled to provide a final code. The best-known example of Gematria appears in the Biblical Book of Revelation where the Anti-Christ is numbered as "six hundred, three score and six"—double the number of Neuburg's demon.)

A curious argument developed between Neuburg and the creature. Neuburg called on his own and Crowley's Holy Guardian Angels. The demon claimed it knew them both and had power over them. Neuburg firmly demanded that it reveal its nature and the demon finally admitted that its name was Dispersion and, as a consequence, it could not be bested in rational argument.

Equipped with the exercise book Crowley had given him, Neuburg was trying to write all this down when the demon cunningly swept sand over the boundary of the circle and leaped upon him in the form of a naked man.

An amazing scene ensued. The two, now locked together, rolled over and over on the sand, Neuburg trying desperately to stab the demon with his magic dagger. The creature in turn attempted to bite him in the back of the neck. Eventually Neuburg got the upper hand and drove the demon back to its triangle. He then retraced the part of the circle that had been obliterated with sand.

After remarking that the tenth Aethyr was a "world of adjectives" without substance, the demon asked permission to leave the triangle to get its clothes. Neuburg refused and threatened it with the dagger. After some further rather childish argument, the demon finally disappeared and the black-robed Crowley took its place. They lit a fire to purify the place, then obliterated both circle and triangle. The total ceremony had lasted two hours and exhausted them both.

From the Cellini and Crowley accounts, it's easy to see why magicians fight shy of evocation to visible appearance today. Besides which, unless some artificial adjunct is used, visible evocation can only be performed by a magician with certain physical characteristics. His bodily makeup must be such that he can manufacture that curious half physical, half ethereal substance called ectoplasm. Ectoplasm is produced in some mysterious way from the gastric juices, and you can either spin it or you can't. The ability to produce it makes the materialization mediums of Spiritualism.

Without ectoplasm, the psychic entity must be presented with some other material suitable for molding into a temporary body. This was the rationale behind Crowley's slaughter of the pigeons. Blood is believed to give off a subtle evaporation that the spirit can use. The idea is very old and underlies the religio-magical blood sacrifices of Voodoo and Santeria.

But there are magicians—myself among them—who were taught that blood sacrifice is both cruel and unnecessary. Consequently flowers—again believed to have a subtle evaporation—are often used. More frequently still quantities of incense are burned.

Once the entity is called into the triangle, it uses particles of incense smoke to build a body of sorts. The body is not very useful, but at least it's visible. Some racial memory of the process is embodied in the *Arabian Nights* stories of the djinn that manifest in the smoke of a lamp.

I cannot evoke to visible appearance. My stomach has enough problems without asking it to produce ectoplasm and it seems to me much easier to use a good clairvoyant when information from spirit entities is required. But none of this stopped me making the attempt during a week-long conclave of highly trained magicians in England's Malvern Hills a few years ago.

The techniques used were fundamentally those of the Medieval magicians. A circle was drawn on the floor and beyond it, in the east, an equilateral triangle was marked out. Both were "fortified" by divine and angelic names. Candles were lit and incense burned.

There were, however, departures from tradition. The grimoires specify that the operator and all others present should remain within the circle. The triangle is set to contain the manifesting spirit.

In this instance there were only two people within the circle. I was one of them. The other was an old friend and colleague who has forgotten more about magic than I'll ever know. But it wasn't her skills as a magician that put her in this privileged position. It was the fact that she was also a channeler. The whole experiment was aimed at evoking to visible appearance the entity she channeled.

Three others of those present were stationed just outside the triangle at its points. Five more—including my wife—stood in a bow formation to the south, outside the circle. The remainder were ranged in two groups to the north and south, again outside the circle.

There were reasons for each of these departures from tradition and safeguards were built in to reassure the more conservative elements present.

The theory of the operation was that the three magicians at the points of the triangle should build up by an act of imagination an "astral vehicle" within the triangle suitable for the entity to inhabit. (Everyone present—some thirty-five trained minds—was required to aid in the building of the astral vehicle, but the main task remained the prime responsibility of the three at the triangle.)

There was an altar in the center of the magic circle on which, in accordance with instructions from an

Inner Plane source, had been placed an astral bow and astral arrow. The duty of the five people stationed just outside the circle was to "stabilize" these astral items again by acts of visual imagination.

The remainder of those present were to act as a sort of energy battery from which the entity could draw in his attempt to manifest. There was an incense burner within the circle that was producing copious clouds of smoke.

The ceremony began with some twenty minutes of rhythmic chanting in an environment that was close to darkness. When the timing was judged correct, I was to shoot an astral arrow into the point in the channeler's spine at which the entity normally made contact. We had been advised that this action would catapult the entity out of the circle and into the astral vehicle within the triangle. Our theory was that at the point of occupying the astral vehicle, the entity would become at least briefly visible.

In this, the experiment was a failure. If anyone present saw the entity materialize, even briefly, they did not report it. But that's not to say it lacked results.

The astral arrow had a profound effect on the channeler. As it struck, her head fell forward and she passed into trance. At precisely the same instant, the officer at the easternmost point of the triangle—a Bishop of the Liberal Catholic Church who stood well over six feet in height—was lifted some eighteen inches off the floor and slammed against the wall behind him. He slid slowly downward, uttering guttural sounds deep in his throat.

The channeler was even more profoundly—if less spectacularly—affected. Her trance state resisted all attempts to break it for more than an hour. While it lasted, she was fully possessed by the entity we had been trying to evoke who conducted an impromptu ceremonial aimed at bringing errant energies under control.

After the working was closed down, I had the opportunity of speaking with our levitated Bishop who told me he had seen the entity catapulted from the circle as planned, but instead of entering the prepared astral vehicle, it had struck him instead—an experience he described as ecstatic.

The reason given for these unexpected effects was that too much "power" had been generated.

Seventeen

Ceremonial Magic

I t is easy for the spiritually-minded to forget mundane considerations. But forgotten or not, mundane considerations have a habit of making themselves felt, regardless. One of the most mundane considerations about magical ceremonial is that it costs money.

Books take time to appear in print and prices seem to rise a little every day. So any detailed costing I might give now would certainly to be out of date by the time you read it. Consequently I'll content myself with listing a few of the items needed for ceremonial and allowing you to make up your own price list.

Robes are fun to wear in magical ceremonies. They make you feel like something out of an occult movie. But they really do have a serious purpose. When you put on your robe, you cut yourself off from the considerations of your day-to-day life. You look different so you feel different. With this change comes a change of attitude. Rituals work better when participants are robed because the fact of wearing robes creates a new and different mindset—one conducive to magical results.

With the renewed interest in esoteric pursuits that has followed the New Age movement, magical robes are easily available. You can even have a choice of various styles—Egyptian, Greek, Celtic, and so on—many of them elaborate and ornamental in the extreme.

I hate to be a killjoy, but while a robe flashing with gold thread and embroidered with mystic sigils is very impressive to the uninitiated, it's not strictly necessary for working magic. A plain white or plain black robe is more than adequate, belted at the waist with a simple (white) cord. If your New Age store has nothing quite this simple, you can buy from a church supplier.

Before moving on to the rest of the equipment you will need, the following table may prove useful to you. It shows the traditional associations between some of the equipment we'll be discussing and other aspects of your ceremonial practice.

Table of Elemental Correspondences						
Element	Color	Direction	Archangel	Weapon	Tattva	Creature
Earth	Black	North	Auriel	Pentacle	Yellow square	Gnome
Air	Yellow	East	Raphael	Dagger	Blue circle	Sylph
Fire	Red	South	Michael	Wand	Red triangle	Salamander
Water	Blue	West	Gabriel	Cup	Silver crescent	Undine

Associated color and direction are self-explanatory and you've already met with the four archangels in the Banishing Ritual of the Lesser Pentagram where, you will note, they stood at the cardinal points allocated to them in the table above. The associated creatures are probably familiar to you as well, if only through fairy tale and myth, but they have an astral reality as you'll discover with experience.

The real purpose of the table, however, is to help you use and understand the basic tools of the magician's trade, the elemental weapons. Traditionally you should make them yourself. In the old days this meant forging the steel for blades and blowing the glass for cups, but for some time now occultists have believed that adaptation of existing artifacts is fine for dagger and cup.

It is important, though, to work personally on your weapons rather than buying them ready-made from an occult supplier. There's an old belief that personal work will imbue the weapon with your own energy and magnetism. Whether or not this is true, it is a matter of experience that making your own weapons changes their emotional charge for you, hence their value.

Magical weapons should be consecrated to magical work, used for nothing else, and wrapped in silk when not in use.

Earth Pentacle

The pentacle is a wooden disc about four and a half inches in diameter and anywhere between one half inch to one inch thick. Each side should be painted as follows.

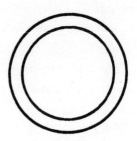

Figure 31

First, paint a circular white border around each face of the disc, as in figure 31.

Next, paint two straight lines within the circle, which will give you four equal subdivisions inside the inner circle, as in figure 32.

Figure 32

The four subdivisions should then be colored (in clockwise order) citrine, olive, russet, and black. With the black subdivision to the bottom, you should paint a white hexagram within the circle, as in figure 33.

Your finished design should appear on both sides of the disc.

Figure 33

Air Dagger

Buy a short dagger or knife with a straight blade and cross-piece pommel (see figure 34). Sports shops will usually have something suitable. Paint the hilt and pommel a bright clear yellow.

Figure 34

Fire Wand

Take a length of bamboo between ten and eighteen inches long showing three natural lengths (which when cut will give you four knots in the wood). Insert a magnetized steel rod through the length of the bamboo—you may have to drill through the knots in order to do so—allowing it to project one sixteenth of an inch at each end.

Attach a cone of wood (which may be turned from a wooden spool) to the

Figure 35

end of the wand marked by the south pole of the magnet. (This is the end that will attract the north pole of a compass.) Paint the body of the wand scarlet and the knots yellow, to form four bands. Paint the cone red with three wavy yellow flames (see figure 35).

Water Cup

Use any plain chalice-shaped glass that tapers slightly toward the rim. Paint eight flower petals in blue, then rim them with bright orange. Hobby shops will often have paint suitable for use on glass, but if you find this approach daunting, you can make the petals by pasting colored paper onto the glass (see figure 36).

Figure 36

The objects mentioned above are the magical basics, and I've worked many an effective ceremonial with nothing more. All the same, you may like to go further and equip yourself with some, or all, of the following.

Magical Ring

The ring works in a way very similar to the robe. When you put it on, you affirm a change in your consciousness, for you put on at the same time your magical personality, the part of you that isn't seen outside the place of working. Buy a ring if you must. Make one for preference—something that requires materials and a few lessons in the art of the silversmith.

Magical Sword

This spectacular weapon is the ultimate in entity control since it manifests spirit in the place of working. Unless you have an iron lode in your back garden, search the antique shops. You're looking for a straight, double-bladed weapon—the type they used to call a broadsword. If you're anything like me, you'll be tempted to buy the largest you can find, but please do bear in mind that swords are heavy and this one isn't going to decorate your wall. In other words, select a sword of a weight and balance you can comfortably use. Congratulate yourself when you find one suitable. Wince when you hear the price.

Paint the hilt and pommel of your sword a bright, clear red.

Incense

The sort of incense you'll need will vary depending on the type of ceremonial you attempt. Since even the most specialized incenses are relatively easy to obtain nowadays, it makes sense to lay down a small store. Start by buying one each of the twelve zodiacal incenses, one each of the four elemental incenses, plus one solar and one lunar incense. Frankincense, the most spiritual of the incenses, should be in your cupboard as well.

Since incense needs to be burned, you'll want charcoal and a burner. If money is running short by now, it's worth knowing that a clay pot (of the type used by gardeners) half filled with sand is a safe, economical incense burner. If money is no object, get yourself something wonderful in metal and buy a brass censer while you're at it.

For full-scale ceremonial, you'll need a place to work. Unless you have the space available at home, rent a room. But before you decide you don't have space at home, think about the following.

The most important working space for ritual is on the Astral Plane. The energies do need earthing, but that doesn't mean you have to build a magical cathedral. Oddly—and irritatingly—spectacular physical surroundings are more important for the beginner than for the experienced magician. But even as a beginner, if you're prepared to concentrate on improving your visualization, you can work—literally—in a cupboard with a model of the magical temple.

When laying out your ceremonial space, large or small, you normally will need an altar. To begin with, this need only be a small table, ideally standing waist high to you, with a plain cloth covering. The cloth should be either white or black.

★★★★

In the final chapter of this book, you'll find instructions for a magical operation almost as spectacular as, but considerably safer than, evocation to visible appearance.

It's a frivolity and I've included it purely to satisfy an artist's promptings to conclude his work with a grand climax. The operation is ceremonial in construction, so you'd better know something about the mechanics.

All magic, as you're now aware, works from the inside out. Magic is a psychological science and the physical operations, spectacular though they may be, are nothing more than stimulants to mental processes.

The greatest single tool your mind uses is the symbol. You speak and think in verbal symbols, which are pictorial symbols of reality. So are pictures in a book, even the stylized diagrams in this one. You understand them because your mind is attuned to the use of symbols.

If your mind uses symbols, it might almost be true to say that certain symbols can use your mind. Some configurations have an appeal that amounts to fascination and cannot be explained by logic. The cross, for instance, is one of them. It was used as a religious symbol for centuries before Christ. Why? Because the cross, as a symbol, has some deep-rooted, largely automatic effect on the human mind. Which is another way of saying nobody quite knows why.

Symbols can be visual, verbal, olfactory, tactile, graphic, simple, or complex. One of the most complex is a well-constructed occult ceremonial.

To witness or, better still, take part in a magical ceremonial is to have the senses assaulted from all directions. Many traditional rituals embody an archetypal drama (death and rebirth is a favorite for initiation rites), which can have a striking effect on the unconscious mind.

The circumstances enhance this effect. Even the most agnostic has some residue of tension about taking part in a magical ceremony. The lights are low, the candles flicker eerily. The mind is receptive—as the compilers of the ritual intended it should be.

All this is, of course, the ritual working from the outside inward. But the reverse process is also under way.

Part of the inner working of many rituals is the process discussed in the last chapter—the assumption of godforms. Participants mediate the spiritual forces and potent energies arising from the old gods, the angels and archangels and, in some cases, the elemental rulers. These energies, pouring through the participants, form, so to speak, a pool of power that is then directed by the ritual itself to further the work in hand.

No workable ritual can be constructed without considerable psychological knowledge. The great rituals of antiquity are, in the main, archetypally based, with the result that they can scarcely fail to produce some effect.

But there are other rituals, almost equally potent, that require a certain psychological training for their results. If the ancient rituals would please a Jungian psychologist, these latter appear to have been constructed expressly to delight behaviorists. The mechanics of behaviorism (association, conditioning, auto-hypnosis) are harnessed to the ceremonial cart, with results striking in proportion to the effort expended in the preparation.

My personal familiarity with this form of ritual is largely based on my Qabalistic work. An example drawn from this source will illustrate the mechanics. Through working on the Tree of Life, a Qabalist learns to associate many apparently diverse items. He would, for instance, associate the Moon, the color purple, the mandrake plant, the perfume jasmine, the number nine, and the Egyptian god Shu. All these associations, and many, many more, fall within the sphere of Yesod.

Assume for a moment that a Qabalist wished to construct a ritual that would put him in touch with the lunar (Yesod) forces. He would begin by establishing an environment in which as many items as possible drew his mind back to the central Yesod theme.

He might, for instance, drape his entire temple in curtains of purple. He could place nine mandrakes on the altar. His incense would, of course, be jasmine. He could begin his ceremony with a reading of the relevant Yetziratic Text: "The Ninth Path is called the Pure Intelligence because it purifies the Emanations. It proves and corrects the designing of their representations, and disposes the unity with which they are designed, without diminution or division…"

All this turns the Qabalist's mind in the direction of the sphere of Yesod. And here the result of months, years, or even dozens of years of meditation becomes evident. The Qabalist's continual meditations carve unconscious channels for the Yesod forces, and these are stimulated into activity by the ritual. Elaborate and impressive though the ceremonial may be, the channel is always the same—the mind (and on occasion the body) of the operator.

There is a similar psychological dynamic in the world of art where originals are held to be far more valuable than copies or reproductions, however technically perfect the latter may be.

Eighteen

Ritual Invisibility

Most things reflect light. You and I sense these reflected rays in the process we call seeing. When there is no light source present, we see nothing. This we experience as a sort of three-dimensional blackness.

Under certain lighting conditions, glass is invisible. Instead of reflecting, light rays pass completely through it. And under certain lighting conditions, mirrors are invisible. This is because a mirror reflects light too well. Our attention is caught by the image. Our eyes are dazzled by the reflection. We see something, but not the mirror itself.

You'll note the experience of looking at something invisible, such as properly positioned glass, is different from not being able to see it while the light is out.

From the point of view of physics, invisibility occurs in practice only when light rays pass through an object. But it can occur in theory when light rays are bent around an object and straightened out on the far side.

This remains theoretical. As far as I know, light rays can't be bent and straightened in this way. Invisibility does not occur when all light is absorbed by an object. You may not be able to see the object itself, but you'll certainly be able to see something is there.

All this is basic optics. It's worth mentioning because most people think of invisibility, when they think of it at all, in terms of light rays. But there's a second form of invisibility that has nothing to do with light rays. Once it's explained, people usually find it a lot easier to accept than the pseudo-explanations of Wellsian science fiction.

If you walked into a room where the President of the United States was chatting to the Queen of England, you might be forgiven if you failed to notice me sitting in a corner. There are people who seem fated not to be noticed whether the celebrities are present or not. Their personalities, or lack of them, ensure that they are over-looked. They are nature's nonentities, the colorless people who make little impression. You'll have met them—although you may find it difficult to recall their faces. As your eye slides over them at a party, they are, for all practical purposes, invisible to you. Their presence does not register. They blend with the background. They have the invisibility, not of glass, but of the chameleon.

Any competent hypnotist can show you this psychological trait pushed to extremes. A subject in deep trance can be told there's no one in the part of the room where you're sitting. When he looks, he will not see you. Should he try to sit in your chair, he'll land on your knee with total bewilderment. When the spell is broken, he'll apologize profusely, explaining that he didn't notice you.

Here, perhaps, is a secret of invisibility worth examining. What makes one person notice another? Movement, for one thing. A moving object is easier to distinguish than a static one. Certain animals know this instinctively and freeze in moments of danger. A variety of predators know it too and impose a type of movement on the scene by bobbing their heads while hunting.

If you wish to be overlooked, try sitting still. Positioning plays a part. Put crudely, you are less likely to be seen in a corner than in the middle of the room. More subtly, the lighting and decor of a room tend to produce a focus of attention. Move out of this area and you are less likely to be seen.

These, and such obvious factors as whether or not you chatter are physical aspects of the problem of why you're noticed. But they do not seem to be all the aspects. One person sitting still in a corner will draw attention like a magnet. Another will be virtually invisible. The difference between the two appears to lie on the psychological level.

Some things are so commonplace that we never think about them. Yet it's really a remarkable thing that my attention will be instantly drawn toward another human being in a room even though he or she is (apparently) doing absolutely nothing to attract it.

Occultists, who generally accept the reality of telepathy, assume the reason this happens is contact between minds. Not, of course, anything specific. But even if you cannot read thoughts, you may be aware of a stream of consciousness. Something inside our heads keeps up an incessant chatter. If I may use an exploded analogy, the transmitter is broadcasting garble but while your receiver picks up no detail, you're aware of the direction of the signal.

This sort of theory leads to a very interesting approach to the whole question of invisibility. Suppose you were able to shut off the chatter inside your head, would this produce a situation in which you were less likely to be noticed? The answer is yes, but the chatter is difficult to switch off.

If I make myself known to you in a darkened room by talking, my most obvious way to hide is to stop talking. But if I'm cursed with an irresistible compulsion to keep talking, my next best move is to surround myself with a soundproof screen. It's this form of thinking that lies at the root of the invisibility ritual given here.

The sequence is an abridged and modified version of a ceremonial used in the Golden Dawn. The full ritual is a massive affair and, from a practical viewpoint, probably reflects a Masonic love of ceremonial for its own sake. Those interested, however, should refer to Israel Regardie's major work *The Golden Dawn*; it's available in most book shops.

Invisibility Ritual

First, prepare your place of working. You need space for ceremonial and the more you skimp, the more difficult the working will be. Pick a reasonably sized room and clear it out completely. It goes without saying you should make sure you will not be disturbed.

Set up your altar in the center of the room. A small table draped with a black cloth will do. The top of the altar is a working surface. Arrange to have it at a height that suits you.

To the east of the altar there should be the physical analog of the twin pillars you saw in the temple of the City of Bridges—the black pillar on your left as you face east, the white, or silver pillar on your right. You may be able to make these pillars, but if not, they should still be represented. You might, for instance, use two boxes, or even two discs painted the relevant colors. But be sure to visualize the pillars strongly; and always behave as if they were whole and entire. (If you have contacts in a carpet warehouse, ask for two of the spools around which carpets are wrapped. Painted, they make excellent pillars.)

For the surface of the altar, you will need a Calvary Cross and an equilateral triangle. Both may be cut from cardboard, and both should be painted red.

You will also need a goblet of water and a lamp. The lamp should be small enough to carry and of the type fueled by oil or something similar.

Place the cross to the east on the altar, with the triangle to the west. The lamp stands in the south, the cup below the triangle in the west.

Although not strictly necessary for the performance of the ritual, it's good to balance these elemental symbols by placing a rose (symbol of Air) to the east and bread and salt (symbol of Earth and the fruits thereof) to the north. Alternatively, you can use the relevant elemental weapons.

When you are ready to begin, perform the Banishing Ritual of the Lesser Pentagram. Make sure it has worked (there's a curious but unmistakable sensation of emptiness when the astral atmosphere is cleansed) before continuing with the main ritual. If in doubt, start again.

Now, while standing at the altar facing east, recite the following invocation.

Ol Sonuf Vaorsag Goho Iad Balt, Lonsh Calz Vonpho. Sobra Z-ol Ror I Ta Nazps, od Graa Ta Malprg. Ds Hol-q Qaa Nothoa Zimz, Od Commah Ta Nobloh Zien. Soba Thil Gnonp Prge Aldi. Ds Vrbs Oboleh G Rsam. Casarm Ohorela Taba Pir Ds Zonrensg Cab Erm ladnah. Pilah Farsm Znrza Adna Gono Iadpil. Ds Hom Od Toli. Soba lpam Lu lparnis. Ds Loholo Vep Zonid Poamal Od Bogpa Aal Ta Piape Piaomel Od Vaoan. Zacare Eca Od Zamran Odo Cicle Qaa. Zorge Lap Zirdo Noco Mad. Hoath Iaida.

Adgt Vpaah Zong Om Faaip Said, Vi-i-vl, Sobam lalprg lzazaz Pi Adph, Casarma Abramg Ta Talho Paracleda, Q Ta Larslq Turbs Ooge Baltoh. Givi Chis Lusdi Orri, Od Micalp Chis Bia Ozongon. Lap Noan Trof Cors Ta Ge 0 Q Manin Iaidon. Torzu

Gohe L. Zacar Eca Ca Noquod. Zamran Micalzo Od Ozazm Vrelp. Lap Zir lo-liad.

This Enochian text of the First and Second Keys and the translation a little later in the chapter are quoted from Israel Regardie's *The Golden Dawn*.

Despite appearances, these paragraphs are far from gibberish. They're a further example of the Enochian language you've met earlier and form an invocation comprised of the first two Enochian Calls. Since the original revelation was dictated letter by letter rather than spoken, there is no "authorized" pronunciation guide, but pronunciation obviously present difficulties, especially in those words where consonant follows consonant without vowel intervention.

Fortunately, we have the help of research by Golden Dawn members on this point. From their findings, it seems the best practical spoken form of the language is developed by taking each letter separately in those words where lack of vowels makes this necessary.

Most of the consonants are pronounced as they are in English with the following exceptions:

Z becomes Zod, with a long o.

A becomes Ah, rather than Ay.

P becomes Peh, rather than Pee.

B becomes Beh.

D becomes Deh.

T becomes Teh.

V becomes Veh.

In sounding vowels, I is pronounced as ee, while E is invariably short, that is, renounced Eh, as in "bed."

As an example, a difficult word such as "Znrza" in the Call, would be pronounced "Zod-en-ar-zod-ah." "Ds" is pronounced "Deh-ess"; "Eca" is pronounced "Eh-ka." "Vpaah" is pronounced "Veh-peh-ah-ah-heh."

Once these principles are grasped and, more important, once the "swing" and rhythm of the invocation is picked up, pronunciation difficulties fade quite quickly.

(There's a great deal of further information on the Enochian language and magical system now available, including Gerald and Betty Schueler's *Enochian Magic* and *Enochian Workbook*; David Allen Hulse's *Key of It All Book 2: The Western Mysteries*; Bill Whitcomb's *The Magician's Companion*; and Geoffrey James' *Enochian Magick of Dr. John Dee*.)

The invocation may also be performed in English, although the effect will not be so pronounced. A translation is given below. Even if you intend to employ the original Enochian, study of the English is recommended: it's as well, in a magical operation, to understand what you are saying—even though that isn't always possible.

The translation follows.

I reign over you saith the God of Justice, in power exalted above the Firmament of Wrath: in Whose hands the Sun is as a sword and the Moon as a thorough-thrusting fire: Who measureth your garments in the midst of my vestures and trussed you together

as the palms of my hands: Whose seat I garnished with the fire of gathering: Who beautified your garments with admiration: to Whom I made a law to govern the Holy Ones: Who delivered you a rod with the Ark of Knowledge. Moreover ye lifted up your voices and sware obedience and faith to Him that liveth and triumpheth: Whose beginning is not nor end cannot be: Which shineth as a flame in the midst of your palace and reigneth amongst you as the balance of righteousness and truth. Move therefore and show yourselves: open the mysteries of your Creation. Be friendly unto me for I am the servant of the same your God, the true worshipper of the Highest.

Can the wings of the winds understand your voices of wonder, O You the Second of the First, Whom the burning flames have framed within the depth of my jaws: whom I have prepared as for a wedding or as the flowers in their beauty for the chamber of the righteous. Stronger are your feet than the barren stone and mightier are your voices than the manifold winds. For ye are become a building such as is not save in the Mind of the All-Powerful. Arise, saith the First. Move therefore unto thy servants. Show yourselves in power and make me a strong seer of things, for I am of Him that liveth forever.

When you have completed the invocation, hold still a moment and experience the force flow it controls. Then, continue with:

In the name of Yeheshuah, Yehovashah, I invoke the power of the Recording Angel. I adjure thee, 0 Light invisible, intangible, wherein all thoughts and deeds of all men are written. I adjure thee by Thoth, Lord of Wisdom and Magic who is thy Lord and God. By all the symbols and words of power; by the light of my Godhead in thy midst. By Harpocrates, Lord of Silence and of Strength, the God of this mine Operation, that thou leave thine abodes and habitations, to concentrate about me, invisible, intangible, as a shroud of darkness, a formula of defence; that I may become invisible, so that seeing me they see not, nor understand the thing that they behold.

Go to the east, kneel and meditate on the Sephirah Binah on the Tree of Life. (Should your Qabalistic training be limited, it is as well to read as much as possible about the sphere in advance. Some such work as Dion Fortune's *The Mystical Qabalah* is recommended.)

Return to the altar and, visualizing Binah as the Supernal Mother, address her.

Lady of Darkness who dwellest in the Night to which no man can approach, wherein is Mystery and Depth unthinkable and awful silence. I beseech Thee in thy name Shekinah and Aimah Elohim, to grant thine aid unto the highest aspirations of my Soul, and clothe me about with thine ineffable mystery. I implore Thee to grant onto me the presence of Thy Archangel Tzaphqiel (pronounced Zaf-key-el) the great Prince of spiritual initiation through suffering and of spiritual strife against evil, to formulate about me a shroud of concealment. O ye strong and mighty ones of the sphere of Shabbathai, ye Aralim, I conjure ye by the mighty name of YHVH Elohim (Yod-heh-vav-heh El-o-eem) the divine ruler of Binah and by the name of Tzaphqiel, your Archangel. Aid me with your power, in your office to place a veil between me and all things belonging to the outer and material world. Clothe me with a veil woven from that silent darkness which surrounds your abode of eternal rest in the sphere of Shabbathai.

Now comes what is essentially a stilling of the mind through an invocation of Hoor-po-krat-ist, Lord of the Silence. The name should be vibrated in the Kether position, then circulated through the aura by means of the Middle Pillar exercise. Then:

Hoor-po-krat-ist, Thou Lord of the Silence. Hoor-po-krat-ist, Lord of the Sacred Lotus. O Thou Hoor-po-krat-ist, Thou that standest in victory on the heads of the infernal dwellers of the waters wherefrom all things are created. Thee, thee I invoke, by the name of Eheieh (Eh-heh-yeh) and the power of AGLA. (Ag-el-ah.)

Meditate for a moment on the incoming force represented by the God, then, visualizing Hoor-po-krat-ist strongly, continue:

Therefore I say unto Thee, bring me unto thine abode in the Silence Unutterable, all-wisdom, all-light, all-power. Bring me to thee, that I may be defended in this work of art. Bring me to thine abode of everlasting silence, that I may awake to the glory of my godhead, that I may go invisible, so that every spirit created, and every soul of man and beast and everything of sight and sense and every spell and scourge of God, may see me not, nor understand.

And now, in the name of Elohim, let there be unto the void a restriction. Be ye opened, ye everlasting doors, that the King of Glory and of Silence and of Night may come in.

Thus do I formulate a barrier without mine astral form that it may be unto me a wall and as a fortress and as a sure defence. And I now declare that it is so formulated, to be a basis and receptacle for the Shroud of Darkness, the Egg of Blue with which I shall presently gird myself.

Now comes a second, shorter Enochian invocation:

Ol Sonuf va-Orsagi. Goho Iada Balata. Elexarpeh Comananu Tabitom. Zodakara. Eka Zodakare Od Zodameranu. Odo Kikle Qaa Piape Piaimoel Od Vaoan.

Then:

And unto ye, O ye forces of the Spirit of Life whose dwelling is in the invisible, do I now address my will. In the great names of your ruling Angels Elexarph,

Comananu, Tabitom, and by all the names and letters of the Holy Tablet of Union, by the mighty names of God, Eheieh, Agla, YHVH Elohim, and by the great Lord of Silence, Hoor-po-krat-ist, by your deep purple darkness and the brilliant light of the Crown above my head do I conjure thee. Collect yourselves about me, and clothe this my astral form with an egg of blue, a shroud of darkness. Gather yourselves, ye flakes of Astral Light, and shroud my form in your substantial night. Clothe me and hide me, but at my control. Darken men's eyes that they see me not. Gather at my word divine, for ye are the watchers and my soul is the shrine.

Perform the Qabalistic Cross, then visualize vividly the blue-black egg materializing around you. On no account rush this portion of the operation, for it is possibly the most important for results. Your entire attention should now be taken up with the idea of becoming invisible. Say:

Let the Shroud of Concealment encircle me at a distance of eighteen inches from the physical body.

Let the Egg be consecrated with fire and water...

Do not proceed to consecration (which tends to stabilize the astral form) until you are completely satisfied with your formulation of the Egg. For the consecration place the lamp on your right and the water on your left and repeat:

O Auramo-oth and Thaum-Aesh-Neith, ye Goddesses of the Scales of the Balance, I invoke and beseech you that the vapours of the magical water and this consecrating fire be as a basis on the material plane for the formation of the Shroud of Art.

Again visualize the Egg as strongly as possible. Go to the east of the altar, facing initially west, turn three times on your own axis, then say:

In the name of the Lord of the Universe and by the power of my Augoeides and by the aspiration of thine own higher soul. O shroud of darkness and of mystery, I conjure Thee that thou encirclest me, so that I may become invisible. So that seeing me, men may see me not, neither understand. But that they may not see the thing that they see, and comprehend not the thing that they behold. So more it be!

Circle the temple, clockwise, once, then go to the south and facing the altar, visualize twin pillars of fire and cloud. Visualize the shroud hanging between them. Move to the west and say,

Invisible, I cannot pass by the Gate of the Invisible, save by virtue of the Name of Darkness.

Visualize the Egg enveloping you again and affirm:

Darkness is my Name, and Concealment. I am the Great One Invisible of the Paths of the Shades. I am without fear, though veiled in darkness, for within me, though unseen, is the magic of the Light Divine.

Go to the north and perform the same visualization you did in the south. Say:

Invisible, I cannot pass by the Gate of the Invisible, save by virtue of the Name of Light.

Visualize the Egg clearly. Then:

I am Light shrouded in Darkness. I am the wielder of the forces of the Balance.

In your imagination, see the darkness of the Egg growing even more intense. Return to your former position to the west of the altar and say:

O thou divine Egg of the creative darkness of spirit, formulate thou about me. I command thee by the name of Yeheshuah. Come onto me, Shroud of Darkness and of night. I conjure ye, O particles of spiritual darkness that ye enfold me as an unseen guard and as a shroud of utter silence and of mystery. Egg of divine darkness, shroud of concealment, long hast thou dwelt Concealed. Quit the Light, that thou mayest conceal me before men.

Again see the shroud formulating around you.

I receive thee as a covering and a guard. Khabs Am Pekht. Konx Om Pax. Light in Extension. Before all magical manifestation cometh the knowledge of the hidden light.

Stand between the pillars of the temple, facing west and allow the Egg to formulate around you, gradually causing your physical form to fade from sight. Walk three times around the temple clockwise, then say from the east:

Thus have I formulated unto myself this shroud of Darkness and Mystery as a concealment and a guard. Supernal Splendour which shinest in the sphere of Binah, YHVH Elohim, Aimah Shekinah, Lady of Darkness and of Mystery, Thou High Priestess of the Concealed Silver Star, Divine Light that rulest in thine own deep darkness, come unto me and dwell within my heart, that I also may have power and control, even I, over this shroud of darkness and of Mystery. And now I conjure thee, O shroud of Darkness and of Mystery, that thou conceal me from the eyes of all men, from all things of sight and sense, in this my present purpose, which is to remain Invisible for the space of ( ) hour(s) and to receive therein the holy mysteries of the Lord of Silence enthroned upon his Lotus, Hoor-po-krat-ist.

And so the ceremonial—a modification of a much longer ritual used in the Golden Dawn—concludes. What results may you expect from it? At best, exactly what it promises—a period of invisibility during which you may move about unnoticed by those around you. But during one group working of an invisibility ritual based on elements similar to those above, a very different result arose.

Although experienced in ceremonial, almost all members of the group found the working disturbing. Many believed at first this was due to the inclusion of Enochian, a language and system with which few of them were familiar. They talked about a distortion of the energies in the place of working.

It took one of the more skilled practitioners to suggest what had actually happened. He believed that the ritual—and the full Golden Dawn ceremonial on which, like this one, it was based—was actually designed to hide not the physical body, but the astral. It was, in fact, an act of camouflage for use in preparation for an astral projection into dangerous territory.

But whether the invisibility is physical or astral, you may be glad of the reversal ceremony that follows:

Return to your temple and perform the Qabalistic Cross, visualizing vividly. Then say:

In the name of YHVH Elohim, I invoke thee who art clothed with the sun, who standest upon the moon, and art crowned with the crown of twelve stars. Aim Elohim Shekinah, who art Darkness illuminated by the Light divine, send me thine Archangel Tzaphkiel and thy legions of Aralim, the mighty Angels of the sphere of Shabbathall that I may disintegrate and scatter this shroud of darkness and of mystery for its work is ended for the hour.

I conjure thee, O shroud of darkness and of mystery which has well served my purpose that thou now depart unto thine ancient ways. But be ye, whether

by a word or will, or by this great invocation of thy powers, ready to come quickly and forcibly to my behest, again to shroud me from the eyes of men. And now I say unto ye, Depart ye in peace, with the blessing of God the vast and shrouded one, and be ye very ready to come when ye are called.

Visualize the shroud disintegrating, then close the operation with the Banishing Ritual of the Lesser Pentagram forcefully performed.

Bibliography

Ashcroft-Nowicki, Dolores. *The Shining Paths*. Dallas, TX: Aquarian Press, 1984.

Baynes, C. F. and Wilhelm, R. *I Ching or Book of Changes*. London: Princeton University Press, 1967.

Blatavsky, Helen Petrovka. *The Secret Doctrine*. Wheaton, IL: Theosophical Publishing House, 1980.

Budge, E. Wallis. *Book of the Dead*. NY: Dover Publications, 1967.

Burgess, Jaquie. *Healing With Crystals*. Dublin, Ireland: Gill and Mcmillan, 1997.

Cicero, Chic and Sandra Tabatha. *Self-Initiation into the Golden Dawn*. St. Paul, MN: Llewellyn Publications, 1995.

Crowley, Aleister. *777 and Other Qabalistic Writing of Aleister Crowley*. NY: Samuel Weiser, Inc.

Fortune, Dion. *The Mystical Qabalah*. NY: Samuel Weiser, Inc., 1984.

Fuller, Jean Overton. *The Magical Dilemna of Victor Neuberg*. London: W. H. Allen, 1965.

Gardiner, Lambert. *Psychology: A Study of a Search*. CA: Brooks/Cole, 1970.

Greer, John Michael. *Paths of Wisdom*. St. Paul, MN: Llewellyn Publications, 1997.

Hulse, David Allen. *The Key of It All*. St. Paul, MN: Llewellyn Publications, 1993.

James, Geoffrey. *The Enochian Magick of Dr. James Dee*. St. Paul, MN: Llewellyn Publications, 1994.

Knight, Gareth. *Practical Guide to Qabalistic Symbolism*. NY: Samuel Weiser, Inc., 1978

Mumford, Dr. Jonn. *A Chakra and Kundalini Workbook*. St. Paul, MN: Llewellyn Publications, 1994.

Myers, Stuart. *Between the Worlds*. St. Paul, MN: Llewellyn Publications, 1995.

Regardie, Israel. *The Golden Dawn*. St. Paul, MN: Llewellyn Publications, 1989.

————. *The Middle Pillar*. St. Paul, MN: Llewellyn Publications, 1995.

Scheuler, Gerald and Betty. *The Enochian Workbook*. St. Paul, MN: Llewellyn Publications, 1993.

————. *Enochian Magick*. St. Paul, MN: Llewellyn Publications, 1984.

Sutro, Alfred. *Celebrities and Simple Souls*. NY: French and European Publications, 1933.

Whitcomb, Bill. *The Magician's Companion*. St. Paul, MN: Llewellyn Publications, 1993.

Index

$100 bill, 45, 47, 49-50, 85-87, 89, 91-93, 95-99, 101, 166, 182, 253

A

acupuncture meridians, 5, 69, 73

Ajna chakra, 75

amethyst, 8

Anahata chakra, 73

archangelic figures, 21, 23

archetypes, 112, 150

Ark of the Covenant, 15

artifacts, 37

asafoetida grass, 7, 267

astral body, 60, 68-70, 72-73, 75, 261

astral energy, 10, 46

astral leeches, 101

astral plane, 4-6, 8, 16, 141-142, 180, 238-239, 242, 260, 286

astro-mental system, 61

astrology, 53-54, 89-90

Atlantis, 135

Aurum Solis, 82

auto-suggestion, 79

automatic writing, 38-40

B

Banishing Ritual of the Lesser Pentagram, 11, 17-20, 211, 221-222, 230, 272, 280, 296, 308

Batcheldor, Kenneth, 34-38, 40, 47, 233

Belfast, 25, 31

Belfast College of Art, 31

belief, 33, 45-48, 52-53, 99, 148, 187, 233, 281

bio-electrical energies, 5

Birmingham, England, 40, 183

Blavatsky, Madame Helena Petrovna, 4, 265

Boniface VIII, Pope, 148

Book of Changes, 137

breathing exercises, 65

Burgess, Jacquie, 9

C

cardinal points, 23, 220-221, 235, 280

Cellini, Benvenuto, 267-270, 274

chakras, 21, 60-61, 68-69, 73-75

Circe, 13

circle, 12-14, 19, 21-23, 26, 108, 115, 128-130, 133, 194, 212-213, 218, 228, 242, 245-246, 266, 269-271, 274-278, 280, 282, 304

City of Bridges, 239-240, 295

College of Psychic Studies, 86

correspondences, 48, 166, 280

Coventina, 30

Cromwell, Oliver, 28

cross, 12-13, 17, 19-22, 124-126, 207, 222, 225, 228-230, 258, 287, 295, 303, 307

Crowley, Aleister, 43, 89, 115, 270-275

Crusaders, 15

crystals, 7-11

cup, 18, 44, 280-281, 284

D

dagger, 242, 274, 280-281, 283

Dee, Dr. John, 215-219, 267, 271, 298

demons, 7, 148, 167, 268

depth psychology, 4, 157

diabetes, 40

Diddington Manor, 28

divination, 4, 136-137

divine king, 13

dowsing, 123, 125, 130, 133

dreams, 8, 59, 91, 195, 209

E

ectoplasm, 274-275

Einstein, Albert, 54, 156, 163, 179

elemental intrusions, 24

elemental magic, 4

elemental servant, 148

elementals, 101

energy body, 60

energy matrix, 58, 60

Enochian Calls, 219, 271, 297

Enochian language, 297-298

etheric body, 60, 68-69, 73

evil eye, 150

exorcism, 16, 24, 149

F

familiars, 148

Firmicus Maternus, 14

flying pencil, 39

Fortune, Dion, 9, 35, 44, 137, 169, 300

Fountain Exercise, 101, 213, 215

frankincense, 7, 285

Frazer, Sir James, 48

G

Gawain, 14

gematria, 273

ghost, 28, 37, 111, 118-119, 131-132, 179

glass-moving, 30

God-names, 21, 82

Goddess, 13-14, 257

godform, 256-259, 261-263

Golden Bough, 48

Golden Dawn, 12, 82, 92, 141, 222, 230, 267, 270, 272, 294, 297, 306-307

Great Unmanifest, 58, 160-161, 164-165

Great White Brotherhood, 135-136

Great Work, 75

Great Yantra, 15

grimoires, 46, 78, 267, 276

guardian angel, 33

Gurdjieff, G. I., 59, 200-203

H

hallucination, 107

Hatha Yoga, 69, 112, 182-183

healing, 25, 81, 101, 148-149, 151, 246

Henry, Jim & Julie, 108-111

Hermetica, 4

hexagram, 12, 14-16, 20-22, 139-140, 143-145, 282

Hexagrams, 137-138, 140-141, 143

Hitler, Adolf, 57

Homer, 13

Houston, Jean, 70

hypnosis, 4, 150, 197

I

I Ching, 137-139, 141, 143-144

imagination, 5, 8, 44, 49, 62, 68, 78-79, 81, 90-91, 131, 142, 145, 150, 178-181, 185, 244, 261, 263, 266, 276-277, 305 imagination of matter, 8

India, 115-116

inner aura, 85-86

Inner Planes, 149, 178, 180-182, 185, 236, 241, 260

Ireland, 88, 107-108, 131

Ishtar, 14

Isis, 14, 229-230, 257

J

Jesus Christ, 57

Judaism, 14

Jung, C. G., 50-54, 150-151, 155, 189, 191

K

Kelley, Edward, 215-220, 267, 271

kinaesthetic body, 70

King, Stephen, 13, 27, 92, 215, 302

Kirlian photography, 69

Know Thyself, 150

Kore, 13

L

Leek, Sibyl, 132

leprechaun, 104-107, 125

Leslie, Desmond, 132

Levi, 8

levitation, 35, 233

Liber 777, 89

Liberal Catholic Church, 265, 277

Little People, 105-108

London, 8, 31, 48, 86-88, 130, 144, 234, 271

lucid dreaming, 59

M

magic circle, 270-271, 276

Major Arcana, 136, 143

malevolent entities, 100

Malkuth, 17, 81, 83, 166

Manipura chakra, 73

mantra, 112-116

Mass, 88, 189, 233, 265-266

meditation, 4, 16, 50, 112, 142, 169, 206-209, 211-212, 235, 255, 259, 289

Megan David, 11

meridians, 5, 69, 73

Merlin, 245, 247-250

Middle Pillar, 75-76, 82-83, 86, 89, 94-95, 99, 147, 242, 301

miracles, 36, 43, 97, 231, 233, 235, 237, 239, 241, 243, 245, 247, 249, 251

Morgan, Hilda, 103-104, 106

Morgan la Fey, 245

morphic resonance, 87-90, 257

Muladhara chakra, 73

myrrh, 7

Mystery Schools, 82, 187

N

Neuburg, Victor, 270-274

New Age, 7, 135, 280

New York, 101, 144, 236, 242-243

O

obesity, 40

occult anatomy, 55, 57, 59-61, 63, 65, 67, 69, 71, 73, 75, 79, 81, 83

occult hygiene, 100

Ogden, Roy, 133

Olivier, Sir Laurence, 255

Omphale of Lydia, 12

Opening of the Channels, 97

ouija, 26-27, 32

outer aura, 86

Owen, Dr. George & Mrs. Iris, 28

P

Paracelsus, 101

Pauli, 54

Pavlov, 67

Peek, 123

pendulum, 126, 128-129, 131-133

Penry-Evans, Violet, 44

pentacle, 267-268, 280, 282

pentagram, 11-14, 16-21, 23, 211-212, 215, 221-225, 230, 272, 280, 296, 308

Philip, 28-30

phobias, 22, 24, 211-212

physical phenomena, 27, 34

physics, 54-56, 58, 68, 156-157, 163, 173, 291

Pliny, 13

poltergeist, 30, 40, 234

possession, 24, 96, 149

prayer, 46, 107

Primal Androgyne, 15

psi tracking, 131

psychic channels, 68, 112-113

psychic healers, 40

psychical research, 28, 34-35, 130, 148

Q

Qabalah, 49, 82, 89, 160, 166, 169, 188, 300

Qabalism, 15

Qabalistic Cross, 17, 20-22, 222, 225, 303, 307

Quantum physics, 56, 68, 173

quartz, 7-9, 220, 247

R

Regardie, Dr. Israel, 75, 81-82, 222, 230, 272, 294

reincarnation, 15

relaxation, 63-65, 67, 75, 94-95, 182-185, 206-207, 240, 259

rose cross, 228, 230

rose quartz, 8

S

sacred space, 6-11, 16, 22, 26

sage, 6-7

Sahasrara-padma chakra, 75, 113

Santeria, 275

Scotland, 88

Seabrook, William, 144-145

Seal of Solomon, 11, 14

séance, 26-27, 29, 32-33, 35-36

second body, 60

Secret Doctrine, 4

Servants of the Light, 82

Shakespeare, 148, 255

Shakmah Winddrum, 47

shamanism, 7, 48

Shekina, 15

Sheldrake, Dr. Rupert, 87-89

Shield of David, 11, 14

sidhe, 108

smudging, 6-7

Society for Psychical Research, 28, 34-35, 130

Society of the Inner Light, 82

Spain, 15

spirit world, 39

spirits, 6, 14, 25, 27, 29, 31, 33, 35, 37-41, 97, 101, 109, 112, 150, 215, 218-219, 226, 234, 256, 267-270

Spiritualism, 34, 233, 274

sub-atomic particles, 56, 58, 163, 173-175

subtle energies, 5

suggestion, 125-126, 190

Summerland, 25

Sutro, Alfred, 117-120

Svadhisthana chakra, 73

Sweden, 130-131

synchronicity, 51, 53-54, 99, 151

T

table tapping, 4

table turning, 35, 47, 233

talisman, 97, 147, 220, 225, 227, 230, 247

Tantric Hinduism, 15

tarot, 135-137, 141, 143-144

tattvas, 141, 143, 245

telepathy, 31, 150, 293

telesmatic figures, 12, 22

Tiphareth, 49, 80, 165

Toronto Society for Psychical Research, 28

trance, 38, 44, 108, 139, 145, 197, 265, 277-278, 292

Tree of Life, 49-50, 75, 77, 92, 113, 161-162, 166-167, 169, 236, 288, 300

U

unclean spirits, 41

unconscious mind, 12, 63, 89, 114, 126, 129, 148, 190, 207, 287

universe, 3, 5, 15, 47-49, 55-58, 60-62, 113, 156, 159-161, 163-165, 167-169, 173, 176, 201, 217, 304

University of Aston, 40

V

vibration, 17, 78-79, 94, 113

Visuddha chakra, 73

Voodoo, 275

W

Walter, Dr. W. Grey, 153-154, 179

wand, 43, 218, 258, 267, 280, 283

water divining, 123

wave-particle duality, 56, 175

Western Esoteric Tradition, 120

witchcraft, 28, 148

wood nymph, 103-104, 107

words of power, 78, 94, 101, 112, 115, 271, 300

X, Y, Z

Yesod, 80, 166, 288-289

yoga, 5, 21, 61, 65, 69, 112, 114, 166, 182-183, 203

REACH FOR THE MOON

Llewellyn publishes hundreds of books on your favorite subjects! To get these exciting books, including the ones on the following pages, check your local bookstore or order them directly from Llewellyn.

Order by Phone
- Call toll-free within the U.S. and Canada, 1-877-NEW-WRLD
- In Minnesota, call (651) 291-1970
- We accept VISA, MasterCard, and American Express

Order by Mail
- Send the full price of your order (MN residents add 7% sales tax) in U.S. funds, plus postage & handling to:

    Llewellyn Worldwide
    P.O. Box 64383, Dept.1-56718-086-8
    St. Paul, MN 55164–0383, U.S.A.

Postage & Handling
- **Standard** (U.S., Mexico, & Canada)

If your order is:

    $20.00 or under, add $5.00
    $20.01–$100.00, add $6.00
    Over $100, shipping is free

(Continental U.S. orders ship UPS. AK, HI, PR, & P.O. Boxes ship USPS 1st class. Mex. & Can. ship PMB.)

- **Second Day Air** (Continental U.S. only): $10.00 for one book + $1.00 per each additional book
- **Express** (AK, HI, & PR only) [Not available for P.O. Box delivery. For street address delivery only.]: $15.00 for one book + $1.00 per each additional book
- **International Surface Mail:** Add $1.00 per item
- **International Airmail:** Books—Add the retail price of each item; Non-book items—Add $5.00 per item

Please allow 4–6 weeks for delivery on all orders.
Postage and handling rates subject to change.

Discounts
We offer a 20% discount to group leaders or agents. You must order a minimum of 5 copies of the same book to get our special quantity price.

Free Catalog
Get a free copy of our color catalog, *New Worlds of Mind and Spirit*. Subscribe for just $10.00 in the United States and Canada ($30.00 overseas, airmail). Call 1-877-NEW-WRLD today!

Visit our website at www.llewellyn.com for more information.

The Magical I Ching

J.H. BRENNAN

It's the oldest book in the world . . . yet scholars disagree about its age
It has been consulted by millions in the Orient . . . yet no more than a
handful have ever read it all. It is revered for its wisdom . . . yet it is used
to tell fortunes.

Using coins, yarrow stalks, or even a computer, you can cast for
tunes using six-lined figures known as hexagrams. This wholly new
translation of the ancient Chinese I Ching helps you interpret the hexa
grams, whose meanings continue to be useful throughout the ages, pro
viding profound and strikingly accurate divinations.

More than a divination tool, the I Ching also has links with th
Astral Plane and the Spirit World. Use it in ritual and pathworking, a
an astral doorway or a spirit guide. Although there are many versions o
the I Ching on the market, this is the first to delve into the magica
techniques that underlie the oracle.

1-56718-087-6
264 pp., 7 ½ x 9 ⅛ $14.9

To order call 1-877-NEW WRLD
Prices subject to change without notice.

Occult Tibet
Secret Practices of Himalayan Magic

J.H. BRENNAN

Use little-known secrets of Tibetan mysticism in your magical practice . . .

A great esoteric tradition developed in the Himalayan vastnesses of the Tibetan plateau. Over centuries of isolation, this unique culture investigated the mysteries of mind and magic to a degree never before attempted. Today, as Tibetan spirituality spreads across the world, the practices of Tibetan magic have scarcely been investigated by Western occultists. *Occult Tibet* presents this body of techniques, based partly on Buddhist practice and partly on shamanic Bön (the aboriginal religion of Tibet). With many of its aspects linking seamlessly with Tibetan mysticism, Tibetan magic has a great deal to teach the esoteric community of the West.

0-7387-0067-3 $12.95
6 x 9, 240 pp., bibliog., glossary, index

To order call 1-877-NEW WRLD
Prices subject to change without notice.

Time Travel
A New Perspective
J. H. Brennan

Scattered throughout the world are the skeletal remains of men and women from long before humanity appeared on the planet, and a human footprint contemporary with the dinosaurs. Where did they come from? Are these anomalies the litter left by time travelers from our own distant future?

Time Travel is an extraordinary trip through some of the most fascinating discoveries of archaeology and physics, indicating that not only is time travel theoretically possible, but that future generations may actually be engaged in it. In fact, the latest findings of physicists show that time travel, at a subatomic level, is already taking place.

Unique to this book is the program—based on esoteric technique and the findings of parapsychology and quantum physics—which enables you to structure your own group investigation into a form of vivid mental time travel.

1-56718-085-X, 6 x 9, 224 pp., photos, softcover $12.9

To order call 1-800-THE MOON
Prices subject to change without notice.